LAVENDER BLUE
MURDER

This Large Print Book carries the
Seal of Approval of N.A.V.H.

LAVENDER BLUE MURDER

LAURA CHILDS

WHEELER PUBLISHING

A part of Gale, a Cengage Company

GALE

A Cengage Company

GALE
A Cengage Company

LIBRARY OF CONGRESS CIP DATA ON FILE.
CATALOGUING IN PUBLICATION FOR THIS BOOK
IS AVAILABLE FROM THE LIBRARY OF CONGRESS

ISBN-13: 978-1-4328-7627-2 (hardcover alk. paper)

Published in 2020 by arrangement with Berkley, an imprint of Penguin Publishing Group, a division of Penguin Random House, LLC

Printed in Mexico
Print Number: 01   Print Year: 2020

Thank you so much, and I promise you many more Tea Shop Mysteries!

ACKNOWLEDGMENTS

A special thank-you to Sam, Tom, Grace, Tara, Jessica, Elisha, Fareeda, M.J., Bob, Jennie, Dan, and all the amazing people at Berkley Prime Crime and Penguin Random House who handle editing, design, publicity, copywriting, social media, bookstore sales, gift sales, production, and shipping. Heartfelt thanks as well to all the tea lovers, tea shop owners, book clubs, bookshop folks, librarians, reviewers, magazine editors and writers, websites, broadcasters, and bloggers who have enjoyed the Tea Shop Mysteries and helped spread the word. You are all so kind, and you help make this possible!

And I am forever (forever and a day!) filled with gratitude for you, my very special readers, who have embraced Theodosia, Drayton, Haley, Earl Grey, and the rest of the tea shop gang as friends and family.

Thank you so much, and I promise you many more Tea Shop Mysteries!

1

Summer no longer held sway in the low country of South Carolina. Golds and russets had replaced vivid greens, while a cerulean blue sky offered the promise of cooler weather.

Then, suddenly . . . BANG! BANG! And another BANG! BANG! A series of gunshots exploded like a riff of Black Cat firecrackers, the retorts echoing off sweeping vistas of yarrow and pine forests.

"Got one!" a woman's voice called out, triumphant.

"You seriously got one?" a male voice responded, surprise mixed with admiration.

Theodosia Browning lowered her shotgun and nodded. This wasn't her first shooting party. She'd hunted game birds before, especially quail and grouse. Spending childhood summers at nearby Cane Ridge Plantation, she'd also once shot a wild turkey, along with a few varmints that had over-

7

stepped their bounds and tried to make a tasty meal out of her aunt Libby's exotic French Crèvecoeur chickens.

"Well done," Drayton said. "Obviously, you have a much keener eye and steadier aim than I do. I haven't managed to hit a single thing."

"It helps if you actually pick up the gun," Theodosia said. An amused smile danced across her face.

"Well." Drayton fingered his bow tie nervously. "I'm not sure I really want to do that."

It was a fine Sunday afternoon, and tea shop owner Theodosia and her tea sommelier Drayton Conneley were tromping through the vast fields of Creekmore Plantation at the kind invitation of Drayton's good friend, Reginald Doyle. Doyle had previously served on the board of Charleston's Heritage Society with Drayton and was CEO of Celantis Pharmaceuticals as well as part owner of Trollope's Restaurant.

Doyle and his wife, Meredith, were also rabid Anglophiles. Thus, this entire day had been styled in the precise manner of a traditional English shooting party. Which meant elevenses (in this case glasses of bourbon and gin fizzes), gun loaders, five fine-looking bird dogs, and shooting costumes of tweed, herringbone, and suede. All teams had drawn "pegs" to determine which area they'd be hunting in.

"You very much look the part today," Theodosia said to Drayton. "As if you just stepped out of an episode of *Downton Abbey.*"

"I *feel* like I just did," he said.

Drayton was sixty-something with a kind face, a slightly arched nose, and a patrician bearing. He was kitted out today in a tweed jacket, wool slacks, and English Wellington boots. Drayton had added his trademark gentleman's bow tie to the outfit, and at the last minute, Theodosia had presented him with a shooting vest from Huntley's Ltd. in Charleston. A traditional Balmoral cap completed his outfit.

Theodosia, on the other hand, was wearing a tailored suede jacket, white shirt, tweed slacks, and low walking boots. Being outdoors today, reveling in the abundant sunshine and cool breezes, seemed to impart an extra sparkle to her crystalline blue eyes and an excited flush to her peaches and cream complexion. Theodosia once mused that her abundant halo of auburn hair might have come compliments of ginger-bearded Vikings who'd long ago arrived on English shores and found themselves smitten by her distant English relatives of the female persuasion.

"So how should I be carrying this thing?" Drayton asked. He was referring to the shotgun that Reginald Doyle had loaned him and that he held gingerly, as if it were a plague-infested rat.

"Always break your gun while walking and keep the barrels pointed down," Theodosia said. "That way there's no chance of an accidental discharge."

Drayton grimaced. "Heaven forbid."

"Beautiful out here, isn't it?" Theodosia said. A line of poplars stretched off to their left, silvered leaves fluttering in the wind. To their right was an undulating hillside of tall golden grasses. Beyond that, a line of purple stretched to the sky.

"Lavender," Theodosia murmured. "I believe that's a field of lavender."

"Beg pardon?" Drayton said. Then, suddenly, his face lit up, and he let loose a hearty wave and a loud, "Hello!"

"Hey ho!" Reginald Doyle hailed back as he emerged from the trees along with Jack Grimes, his caretaker. "You two having any luck?"

"Theo got a bird," Drayton said as the two men joined them.

"A grouse," Theodosia said.

"Excellent. Well done," Doyle said. He was ruddy faced and breathing hard, an older gent who'd made his fortune in pharmaceuticals and enjoyed his role as lord of the manor. Grinning, Doyle pulled out a silver flask and offered it to them. "Have a celebratory nip, then?"

"No, thank you," Theodosia said. She didn't think it was particularly wise to drink and shoot, even though she was guilty of sipping a single gin fizz at elevenses.

"None for me, either," Drayton said, holding up a hand.

"Then I shall help myself," Doyle said. He unscrewed the top of his flask, raised it in a kind of salute, and tipped it back.

Grimes, a weathered, outdoorsy-looking man dressed in a barn jacket, khakis, and mud-streaked leather boots, looked on with faint disapproval.

"Sir," Grimes finally said. "We need to move on. Check on Mr. Jacoby and Mr. Thorne."

"Right you are," Doyle said in a jovial tone. He capped his flask and said, "And we need to let our friends here get back to their shooting."

"Yes, sir," Grimes said.

When the two of them were alone again, Drayton glanced about nervously.

11

"I hope no one sends a wayward shot in our direction."

"This is a big, sprawling plantation," Theodosia said. "So I doubt that's going to happen. Besides, we all drew pegs to determine our own particular area."

They traipsed along a faint trail for a half mile or so but didn't flush any birds. As they stopped to mull things over, a few faint shots sounded ahead of them, but still far off in the distance. Then, as if in response, two chocolate brown Boykin Spaniels suddenly flew past them, amber eyes gleaming, feathered ears streaming out behind.

"Someone must be having a good day," Theodosia said.

"If your aunt Libby knew we were out shooting birds she'd have a royal conniption," Drayton said.

Theodosia had to agree with him. Her aunt Libby, who lived nearby, was a bird lover of the first magnitude, always putting out suet, seed, and her ubiquitous cracklins. Yes, this part of the county teemed with all manner of birds. They fluttered, flew, nested in the grasses, perched in the trees. In fact . . .

"There!" Theodosia shouted as a pair of grouse flew up directly in front of them. "Drayton, take a shot!"

12

The grouse continued on their flight path, not a feather touched.

"You have to aim," Theodosia said.

Drayton looked uncomfortable. "I did aim."

"I meant at the birds."

"Well . . ."

"I get it, Drayton. You're not a natural-born hunter."

"Sweet Fanny Adams, no, I am not," Drayton declared.

"That's okay. We'll just . . ."

Pop.

Theodosia's words trailed off with a sharp intake of breath. That was a single shot off to her right that she'd just heard. Not the loud boom of a shotgun, but a faint pop, like the distinctive retort of a handgun. And how strange that it sounded so near to them in an area where not many game birds had been flushed. An area they were supposed to have all to themselves.

Drayton's head jerked toward Theodosia. "Was that a shot?" He glanced around again, looking even more skittish.

"I *think* so," Theodosia said. "But I don't believe anyone in our hunting party is over this way. Much less shooting with a . . ." Her voice trailed off again as she lowered her shotgun. That *had* been a handgun she'd heard. But who could have fired it?

Could it be a distress signal? she wondered. *Was someone injured? A twisted leg or something worse?*

After a few moments' hesitation, Theodosia said, "Give me a minute. You stay here while I check this out." She struck off in the direction of the gunshot.

"Where are you going?" Drayton called after her.

Theodosia waved a hand without turning around. "I want to investigate that shot."

"Please don't."

"I'll be back in two minutes, tops."

"Be careful!"

Theodosia tromped through long grasses for sixty, then seventy yards. She was out of sight of Drayton now, but it was slow going. The ground had turned hilly and uneven, and she was forced to traverse around a miniature forest of shrubs and small trees. Another five minutes of bushwhacking, and she was almost at the lavender field.

But that isn't part of Reginald Doyle's property.

Still, she'd heard that gunshot.

I can't believe anyone was hunting over here. And yet . . .

Topping a small rise, Theodosia came to a stop and peered around carefully. And

14

saw . . . nothing. A few insects buzzed nearby; off in the distance a hawk circled lazily in a robin's-egg-blue sky. Perhaps she hadn't heard a pistol shot at all, but rather a . . .

A sudden chill trickled down Theodosia's spine as she was overcome by a weird, preternatural warning.

Did something happen? Is something about to happen?

Theodosia bent her head forward cautiously, walked another ten feet, and abruptly dropped her gaze. That's when she saw him. A man. Lying in the grass some twenty feet in front of her.

He was half-hidden by the sway of gold, looking crumpled and broken, like a bird that had fallen from its nest.

As Theodosia rushed toward the man, she heard him let loose a terrible moan.

Oh no! He's been shot . . . and it's . . .

Reginald Doyle was lying there as if he'd been steamrollered. He was on his back, eyes half-open and dark with pain as they floated, practically unseeing, back and forth in his head. His mouth was pulled into a horrible scowl, and his pale lips trembled uncontrollably. The poor man seemed unable to frame any actual, meaningful words, so only a low, continuous moan seeped out.

One hand, twisted into a claw, clutched at his shotgun as if he still hoped to defend himself from whatever had happened.

"Mr. Doyle!" Theodosia cried.

Theodosia wondered if he'd collapsed from a sudden heart attack — because he certainly wasn't a young man anymore. Or maybe he'd experienced a brain-jangling dizzy spell. Or worse, a brain aneurism.

Then Theodosia saw a faint spot of red dotting the front of Doyle's shooting jacket. And watched with morbid fascination as the blob grew bigger, brighter, and even more intense. That's when it all clicked into focus and she knew it had to be a gunshot wound. Retreating a few steps, Theodosia shouted, "Drayton, Drayton, Mr. Doyle's been shot! Round up anybody you can! We need help!"

Theodosia turned back to Doyle and threw herself down on her hands and knees, trying to figure out just how serious his injury might be. But as she stared down at him, red patches continued to bloom like errant poppies across his herringbone jacket.

Grasping his lapels, Theodosia ripped Doyle's jacket wide open, sending a row of brass buttons flying. And stared in awe at a gaping, gushing chest wound.

Center of mass. He's been shot directly in his heart.

16

And just as the human heart was biologically engineered to do, it continued to pump like crazy. With every beat of Doyle's failing, fluttering heart, red blood flowed copiously out of him. Theodosia wondered how long it would take before Doyle was in mortal danger. Soon. Too soon. She knew she had to act fast.

Ripping the white silk scarf from around her neck, Theodosia crumpled it into a tight ball and pressed it hard against Doyle's chest. If she could somehow stanch the flow of blood . . . then maybe . . .

"Help!" she cried again even as she fumbled for her cell phone. But she couldn't keep pressure on Doyle's chest wound and dial at the same time.

It seemed like an interminable wait, but it was probably only a few minutes before Theodosia heard loud shouts as well as footsteps pounding in her direction. Drayton had managed to alert some of the nearby shooters, thank goodness, and they were rushing to help!

"What happened?" Someone flung himself down beside her. She glanced over. It was Jack Grimes, the caretaker.

"He's been shot!" Theodosia cried. "A chest wound." She was dismayed that precious seconds continued to slip by. This

17

man needed a trauma team, not just a few concerned friends.

"But I was just with him!" Grimes shouted back. He looked genuinely shattered at seeing his employer lying on the ground and practically bleeding to death.

"Oh my heavens!" came another voice, shrill and frantic with worry.

Then a pale face came into view, and Theodosia recognized Reginald's son, Alex, whom she'd been introduced to earlier in the day.

"Pop! Oh no, something's happened to Pop!" Alex stood there, frozen in place like a human statue, his face blanched white as if he were about to faint.

"What can I do?" Grimes asked as another half-dozen members of the shooting party suddenly rushed in to form a tight circle around a failing Reginald Doyle.

"Keep pressure on his wound while I call an ambulance," Theodosia said as she finally managed to punch 911 into her phone. "We have to get him to a hospital as soon as possible."

Seconds later, the dispatcher was on the line, listening to Theodosia's frantic plea for help. But even as the dispatcher assured her that an ambulance would be sent immediately, that she would radio the sheriff, Theo-

18

dosia worried that it might be too late.

Through a jumble of shouted directions, and the dispatcher's urgent voice telling Theodosia to remain on the line, she focused her gaze on Doyle.

His face was ashen gray, and he lay almost motionless now. His eyes were wide open, but something had changed dramatically. His pupils appeared fixed, and there were none of the faint gurgling or breath sounds she'd heard moments earlier.

Jack Grimes grasped Doyle's hand and pleaded for him to hang on.

But it seemed there was little hope.

Theodosia let out a faint sigh even as the wind whooshed and whispered through nearby poplars. It looked to her that Reginald Doyle was clearly and unequivocally dead.

2

And then, of course, Doyle's poor wife came running up.

Meredith Doyle was one of those women who was high-strung bordering on a nervous wreck. With her doe eyes, pale complexion, sleek blond hair, and angular, almost anorexic, physique, she looked like she might have been one of those heroin-chic runway models that were popular some thirty years ago.

Meredith was also verging on full-blown hysterics. Horror animated her face as she watched Drayton kneel down, touch a hand to her husband's pulse, then put an ear to Doyle's chest and listen for breath sounds. When Drayton shook his head, indicating that Doyle was no more, she let loose a shrill, piercing cry that sounded like the death knell of a dying animal.

"He can't be dead!" Meredith wailed. "He *can't* be."

"No, no, no," Alex shouted, as if he could change the outcome through sheer force of will. "Pop *can't* be dead."

"I'm so sorry," Theodosia said. "I tried to stop the bleeding, but his wound was just too grievous."

"His wound?" Meredith shouted. Her eyes narrowed into suspicious slits. "What? How . . . ?"

"He either shot himself by accident or someone else did," Theodosia said.

Meredith's mouth opened and closed soundlessly for a few moments, then she said in a low hiss, "Reginald would *never* be so careless. I can hardly believe this."

With an angry, puzzled look on his face, Alex turned his gaze on the small gathering that was clustered around Doyle. "Who would do this?" he demanded. "Who would be so clumsy and stupid?"

Feet shuffled in dry grass, throats were cleared, watchful eyes bounced from one person to another. Nobody stepped forward to admit that it was their misfortune to accidentally shoot their gracious host.

Alex gritted his teeth together and clenched his hands into tight fists as he confronted the group. "I said *who*? I demand an answer!" His complexion had turned a blotchy purple, and his blood pres-

21

sure must have been sky-high off the charts.

Nobody wanted to meet his gaze.

From far off in the distance, a plaintive whine pierced the air.

Drayton glanced down the hillside. "Ambulance," he said.

"Maybe it's not too late," Meredith suddenly shouted. She threw herself onto the ground alongside her husband and picked up one of his limp hands. "Maybe the EMTs can give him some plasma or blood or some sort of shot . . . adrenaline, maybe . . . to restart his heart."

"Can they do that?" Drayton whispered to Theodosia.

"I don't think so," Theodosia whispered back. She was certainly no medic or EMT, but she knew dead when she saw it. And, for all intents and purposes, Reginald Doyle appeared to be clinically dead.

One of the shooting guests, a man with a square jaw, hazel eyes, and curly red hair, moved closer to peer at Doyle's body.

"I think we should carry him back to the house," the red-haired man said.

Two other men in the group hastily agreed. A paunchy guy in a khaki-colored Carhartt jacket produced a red-and-black plaid blanket and set it down next to Doyle. The three men knelt on the grass and prepared to roll Doyle's body onto it. Drayton reached out to help.

"You can't do that," Theodosia said, her sharp tone cutting through their low grunts and murmurs.

Standing directly next to her, Alex immediately stiffened. "Why not?"

"We have to wait until the sheriff arrives," Theodosia said.

"Nonsense, we can carry him just fine," the red-haired man said. He seemed angry and ready to override anyone who tried to oppose him.

"Please, someone has to do *something*!" Meredith begged. She started to moan and hiccup at the same time. Then, looking as if she would pass out, she dug a white hankie out of her pocket and pressed it to her mouth.

"This is beyond hideous — letting Pop lie here in the middle of nowhere," Alex said in an angry, tremulous voice.

Theodosia paused for a few moments, acutely aware of the soft rustle of nearby lavender plants, as well as the dry *chi-chi-chi* sound of late-season cicadas. Finally, she said, "This isn't the middle of nowhere. It's a crime scene."

"Dear me," Drayton said as he dropped

one corner of the blanket. "Theodosia's right."

They were still arguing and snarling at one another when Sheriff Clay Burney arrived some five minutes later, along with two deputies, an ambulance, and a pair of EMTs. One of the EMTs immediately slipped a breathing tube down Doyle's throat. With his other hand he rhythmically squeezed a ventilator bag. His partner touched a stethoscope to Doyle's chest, listened, and grimaced. He hastily dug into his mobile kit and pulled out a large syringe.

"Epinephrine," Sheriff Burney said. "Gonna try to reboot his heart."

Tall and lean with short silvered hair and a craggy face, Sheriff Burney had been county sheriff for more than twenty-five years and had seen his share of accidents, killings, and death. He watched as the EMTs worked quickly and professionally on Doyle, but the disheartened look on their faces said it all. There was no hope.

When the EMT who'd administered the epinephrine finally shook his head, Burney bent down next to Doyle and carefully studied the body. He touched his hand to the end of Reginald Doyle's gun barrel, then looked around at the group and asked —

"Could this have been suicide?"

"Absolutely not!" Meredith protested.

"How dare you suggest such an awful thing!" Alex shouted.

Sheriff Burney raised his hands, palms facing out. "I had to ask." He wasn't apologetic; he was just doing his job.

"Isn't it obvious he was killed by someone in our shooting party?" Alex asked. He looked around angrily. "Maybe someone right here."

"Is everyone from the shooting party present and accounted for?" Sheriff Burney asked the group.

Meredith shook her head. "A few people are still out and about." She dabbed at her eyes. "Still hunting, I suppose. Or maybe they've heard the sirens and have wandered back to the house by now."

Sheriff Burney cocked an eye at one of his deputies. "Seth, you go back to the house and round everybody up. Don't let anyone leave."

"Got it," Seth said.

Burney looked at his other deputy. "Bobby, you collect all the guns here while I check the perimeter and take photos."

"Excuse me," Theodosia said in a brook-no-nonsense tone.

Everyone paused to stare at her.

25

"I believe I heard a *pistol* shot."

Sheriff Burney pushed his Smokey Bear hat up on his forehead. "You heard what?"

"Right before I discovered Mr. Doyle lying here, I was pretty sure I heard a pistol shot."

Sheriff Burney's sharp gaze traveled around the group. "Anybody here carrying a pistol?"

No one responded.

"Best to speak up now."

No one spoke up.

"Huh," he said.

Sheriff Burney and his deputy worked quietly and efficiently for a good thirty minutes. They took photos, dusted Doyle's gun for prints, moved everyone back, and searched the area thoroughly. It wasn't quite the way they did it in the big city, but it was competent and methodical.

Finally, Sheriff Burney signaled for the EMTs to put Reginald Doyle in a black plastic body bag.

With Meredith weeping and everyone else looking somber and a little scared, they watched as Doyle's body was gently rolled into the bag. Then the bag was zipped and a backboard slipped beneath it.

Everyone trooped back to the main house

in a silent caravan, and once they arrived there, the questioning began. Deputies checked IDs and wrote down names and addresses. The sheriff interviewed everyone separately. One hour passed, then another.

Finally, Sheriff Burney turned his attention to Theodosia. "You were the one who heard the shot and discovered him?" he asked.

Theodosia nodded. "Yes, unfortunately."

"It was a single shot?"

"That's right."

"And you can tell the difference between a pistol shot and a rifle shot?" Burney asked.

"I know the difference. And what I heard sounded most like a pistol shot." Theodosia paused and lowered her voice. "Sheriff, you saw the victim's chest wound, plus you have a good working knowledge of guns. What type of gun do *you* think made that entrance wound?"

"Pistol," Burney said. "Although I'm going to let my ballistics guy and the coroner render the final judgment." He looked around. "Okay then, I'd appreciate it, ma'am, if you'd drive back out there with me so I can take another look around. Show me exactly where you were standing when you heard that shot. Can you do that? You're not too upset to go back, are you?"

Theodosia stared at him, all business. "Let's do it."

Ten minutes later, Theodosia and Sheriff Burney were back in the now-darkening woods. Theodosia showed him where she'd been standing when she first heard the shot, then led him to the spot where she'd found the body.

Burney asked a few more questions and fell silent, thinking. A few minutes went by, and then, almost as if he were talking to himself, he said, "Shot at close range."

"That means Doyle knew his killer," Theodosia responded.

Burney aimed an inquiring gaze at Theodosia. "Interesting you picked up on that," he said. "Most ordinary citizens wouldn't."

"I'm dating a Charleston detective."

Burney glanced sharply at her. "One of Tidwell's boys?"

"That's right."

He nodded and looked around. "And you're fairly sure no one else was stalking birds in this particular area?"

"I didn't think anyone was nearby. Mr. Doyle — the victim — made us all draw pegs, so we were assigned different areas of the fields and woods. That way we wouldn't risk shooting each other."

"But someone shot *him,*" Burney said. "So after Doyle and his man Grimes stopped by to talk to you and your friend . . . Drayton, is it? You say they took off?"

"That's right."

"So why did Doyle end up back here?" Burney slipped off his hat and ran a hand over his sparse gray hair.

"I don't know. Good question. Maybe Doyle was circling back to check on Drayton and me?"

"Maybe." But Burney didn't sound convinced. He gazed at a nearby hill bathed in purple-blue that seemed to melt seamlessly into a sky that was darkening to indigo. "What is that up there? Some kind of crop?"

"Lavender plants," Theodosia said.

Burney put his hat back on, knelt down, and ran a hand over the area where Doyle's body had been. When he stood up again, his knees cracked like walnuts.

"Getting too old for this," he said.

"How long have you been sheriff?" Theodosia asked. She liked that he was older; it meant that he had experience.

"Maybe too long." Burney looked around at the scene again, his eyes keen with interest. "Or maybe not."

3

Back at Creekmore Plantation, a dozen or so folks still milled about on the front lawn. Most looked apprehensive; a few looked perfectly at ease.

When Drayton saw Theodosia heading in his direction, his first words were, "Meredith wants us to stay."

Theodosia frowned. "What are you talking about?"

"She's invited us to spend the night."

"You've got to be kidding." An overnight at Creekmore Plantation was the absolute last thing Theodosia wanted to do. She was tired and not in the mood to hang around and rehash this afternoon's disaster.

Drayton pressed on. "As you can imagine, Meredith is extremely upset."

"Everybody's on edge," Theodosia said.

"What I mean to say is Meredith is bouncing-off-the-walls crazy."

"Give me a moment." Theodosia held up

a finger. She'd just spotted Jack Grimes and was eager to ask him a question.

Grimes saw her coming, turned a shoulder, and tried to slip away. Theodosia cornered him anyway near the buffet table.

"I have a question for you, Mr. Grimes," she said.

Grimes looked apprehensive. "What's that?"

"I was wondering how you and Mr. Doyle got separated?"

"What do you mean?" Grimes asked.

"I mean exactly that. As far as I could see, you were accompanying Mr. Doyle all day long. Reloading his gun, carrying his pack, and everything. So what I'm wondering is, why did you end up over near the pond while Doyle ended up near the lavender field?"

Grimes's face darkened. "Because he asked me to go check on Mr. Thorne."

"Yes, but why exactly did Mr. Doyle turn back? What was *his* reason?"

"I don't know." Grimes's face pulled into an unhappy mask. "But it sure sounds like you're accusing me of something."

"Really, I'm just asking a simple question," Theodosia said.

"Well, I don't care to answer. I'll talk to the sheriff, sure enough, but not to you."

31

Grimes took off in a huff, heading for a nearby barn.

"Why were you talking to Grimes?" Drayton asked when Theodosia rejoined him.

"Just trying to satisfy my curiosity."

"Grimes seems like a tough character, so you might want to tread cautiously." Then Drayton nodded toward Meredith and her family. "This is beyond heartbreaking. Just look at them."

Meredith's son, Alex, had his arms around his mother, trying desperately to soothe her. At the same time, Alex's young wife, Fawn, was huddled next to them, looking shocked, barely uttering a single word. Two men they'd encountered earlier, the one wearing a khaki Carhartt jacket and the red-haired man, were also attempting to comfort Meredith.

When the two men moved away, Drayton said, "We should go . . . talk to her."

"Drayton," Meredith said tearfully as he came up to her and gave her a chaste embrace. "Can you believe my dear Reginald is dead?"

"It's inconceivable," Drayton said.

"I'm so sorry for your loss," Theodosia said to Meredith. They'd been introduced earlier but hadn't really had much chance to talk.

Meredith grasped Theodosia's hand. "You were the one who found him. You were with him when he died!"

"I'm afraid so."

Meredith looked almost fearful to ask her next question. "Did Reginald have any last words?"

Theodosia thought about the terrible grunts and groans she'd heard coming from the dying man, but she wisely said, "I'm afraid not."

Meredith wrung her hands. "This is just so unbelievable. I can barely . . . process . . . what happened today."

Alex's hand was visibly shaking as he drank from his glass of bourbon. "It's so bizarre. I mean, everybody *loved* Pop," he said.

Theodosia gazed at Alex. Clearly, someone had *not* loved Pop. Or else Pop wouldn't be riding back to the Charleston medical examiner's office tucked neatly into a black plastic body bag.

"How many, um, guests were here today?" Theodosia asked. Some folks had left soon after being questioned by Sheriff Burney; the rest still milled about on the lawn, talking in soft voices, drinking, making frequent forays to the buffet table to pick at barbequed pork, fried chicken, candied yams, fried okra, and corn bread. The bar with its liveried bartender also seemed to be doing a brisk business.

"I don't know. I guess around fifteen," Alex said. He took another large gulp of his drink and gave a helpless shrug.

"There were exactly twenty guests," Meredith said. "But I can't believe any one of them would . . ." Her voice trailed off with a sorrowful note.

"It *had* to be one of the guests," Alex said. "Who else . . . ?" His voice cracked, then faltered mid-sentence.

"Perhaps it was someone who wandered onto the property unnoticed and set up some kind of shooter's nest," Theodosia said.

"There was a shooter's nest?" Meredith took a step backward, visibly shaken by Theodosia's suggestion.

"A member of the shooting party could have snuck off, too," Alex said in a huffy voice. "It's not like we had everyone under strict surveillance."

"Speaking of which, are there any cameras on the property?" Theodosia asked. "Security cameras or cameras for tracking game?"

Both Meredith and Alex shook their heads.

"I suppose it could have been a neighbor,"

34

Meredith said slowly. She glanced at Alex and gave him a meaningful look.

"You've had problems with one of your neighbors?" Drayton asked.

"Carl Clewis has been absolutely horrible," Alex blurted out. "He dammed up Axson Creek without getting the proper county and state authorization. Pop was furious with him. Even filed an injunction order against him."

"So they'd had words," Drayton said.

"More than words, terrible arguments," Alex said.

"Did you tell Sheriff Burney about this?" Theodosia asked.

"Of course I did," Alex said. He thought for a few moments, then said, "And there's the Lavender Lady."

"Not the Lavender Lady," Meredith said.

"Who's the Lavender Lady?" Theodosia asked. She'd noticed the nearby field of lavender and was more than a little curious.

"Her name is Susan Monday," Meredith said. "You know, like the day of the week? Anyway, her Blue Moon Lavender Farm is some sixty acres, all of it these big sweeping fields of lavender."

"I noticed the edge of her field, and I have heard of Susan Monday," Theodosia said. "I believe my friend Delaine carries her

35

dried lavender sachets at Cotton Duck Boutique. So, Miss Monday had a dispute with your husband?"

"About a strip of land," Meredith said.

"The county calls it an 'orphan strip,'" Alex said. "Apparently, the dispute goes all the way back to the early eighteen hundreds."

Theodosia knew that in South Carolina land disputes could stretch on for decades. There were issues concerning Native American land, boundaries that had been arbitrarily moved after the Civil War, and meandering creeks and rivers that shifted course over time.

"Can you think of some overriding issue that might have been the straw that broke the camel's back? That set someone on a collision course against Reginald?" Theodosia asked.

"What do you mean?" Meredith asked.

"Political ideology? Religious ideology?" Theodosia said.

Meredith looked confused. "Oh. Well. Reginald was a Republican, if that's what you're talking about. But he had friends who were Democrats as well." She fluttered her hands, a little unsure of where she was going with this. "And he was brought up a Methodist . . . Why, Reverend Potter and his wife were even our guests today."

"Is there anyone your husband was having a dispute with? Anyone in a business context?" Theodosia asked.

"I can't think of anyone," Meredith said. "Reginald was a smart businessman, an absolute *genius* when it came to making money."

A hard look stole across Alex's face. Theodosia couldn't help but catch it.

"What?" Theodosia asked him.

Alex shook his head. "I don't know. I really can't think of anyone else."

"For a minute there, it looked like you had someone in mind."

Alex pursed his lips and blew out a glut of air. "No, I have to say I'm at a complete loss." He reached for his wife's hand and squeezed it. Fawn gazed back at him, a sorrowful look on her face.

They all stood there for a few moments, and then Theodosia said, "I'm afraid we have to be going. Again, I'm so sorry for —"

"No!" Meredith cried, her eyes wide with alarm. "You have to stay."

"We couldn't possibly impose on you," Drayton said.

"Please," Meredith begged. "You must. The guest rooms are all made up with fresh flowers and linens. Truly, you'd make me so happy if you'd stay and partake of our hospitality. You've both been so kind. Really . . . I insist."

Against their better judgment, Theodosia and Drayton stayed. They fixed themselves a plate of food and sat in wicker chairs on the expansive veranda. Finally, when the sun had dropped below the horizon and the evening turned chilly, Drayton said, "What we need now is a cup of tea. Something tasty and soothing."

"Let's explore," Theodosia said. "Go find the kitchen."

They wandered into the plantation house and noticed a foursome, two men and two women, sitting in a parlor and talking quietly. They kept going, passed a handsome library with floor-to-ceiling shelves lined with hardbound books, and eventually found their way into a large kitchen completely updated in white marble and pale green tile that looked like sea glass.

Drayton discovered a tin of Earl Grey tea in the pantry.

"This will have to do," he said. "It's a pity I didn't bring some . . . Well, I didn't."

They brewed a pot of tea, found teacups and saucers, and carried everything into a second parlor. This one was even grander in size and scale with Oriental carpets, damask-covered chairs and sofas, and European tapestries hung on the walls.

"I do believe that's a Bakshaish Persian," Drayton said, gazing at the large carpet spread out at his feet. "All handloomed silk."

"This is a gorgeous house. And the decor is impeccable," Theodosia said.

"What you see here is Reginald's taste," Drayton said. "Meredith's preference runs to contemporary and mid-century modern. You know she owns Divine Design over on Royal Street?"

"I've heard of it. Supposed to be incredible. A furniture shop and a design studio?"

"That's right. Meredith even showcases some of the great modern designers such as Charles Eames, Isamu Noguchi, and Edward Wormley."

They talked for another three hours. About the shooting, possible suspects, the Doyle family. Eventually, they got on to other subjects, too. What was happening at the Heritage Society, where Drayton served as a board member, what were their upcoming plans for the Indigo Tea Shop? Would they expand or remain small and cozy? All the while, they heard people ghost past them in the hallway, were aware of whispered voices. Still, they continued to drink tea and talk.

Finally, when a large grandfather clock bonged out eleven chimes, they made their way to the grand staircase and tiptoed upstairs.

"According to Meredith, I'm down here to the left," Drayton said. "Your room is the second on the right, and I daresay it's probably —"

He stopped mid-sentence.

Somewhere on the second floor — or maybe it was up on the third floor — two people were having a hellacious argument. Voices were raised in fury, then just as quickly fell with cold conviction. There was hissing and derision back and forth, but all slightly muted.

"What's going on?" Theodosia whispered. It was difficult to make out actual words. Or tell who they were coming from.

Drayton shook his head. "No idea," he whispered back.

They stood at the top of the stairs, feeling somewhat guilty but still straining to hear. In a matter of a few moments, the voices died out.

"Good night," Drayton said, stifling a yawn as he drifted off to the left.

"Good night," Theodosia said, still burning with curiosity about what had sounded like an appalling and dreadful war of words.

Theodosia was dreaming. Somewhere in her sleep-fogged mind she was in a desert, the sun looking like a fried egg in the sky and burning down unmercifully. It was horribly hot, and she was overdressed. And now a strong wind had come up, a sirocco, and it felt as if an enormous hair dryer had been turned on to heat and crisp everything.

Theodosia came awake, coughing. It was warm and hazy in her small guest bedroom, and she felt as if her strange, nightmarish dream had somehow morphed into reality — was affecting her so vividly that she was having trouble breathing.

Two seconds after that, Theodosia realized the house was on fire! There was heat, intense heat. And an ominous crackling sound.

And, oh dear Lord, there's smoke seeping into my room!

Pulling on her slacks and jacket, Theodosia dashed from her room, frantic to spread the alarm. She started knocking on doors up and down the hallway, shouting for everyone to wake up and evacuate the burning house.

41

Her cries worked. People came streaming out of their rooms, half-dressed and in a full-blown panic.

Spotting Drayton, Theodosia gripped his arm tightly as they galloped down the stairs together.

Outside, some ten feet from the burning building, Theodosia looked around, found a frantic Meredith, and asked, "How many? How many people were staying here tonight?"

"Nine!" Meredith cried. Her eyes were round as saucers, and she was wheezing hard, struggling to catch her breath.

Theodosia counted heads. Eight. They were missing someone!

"Alex!" Fawn was suddenly spinning around in a blind panic and screaming, "Where's Alex?"

Theodosia's heart dropped like a stone. Alex was missing? Oh no. Against her better judgment, she clambered back up the few steps that led to the veranda.

"Alex!" she cried out. "Where are you? Come this way, follow my voice!"

Theodosia felt waves of heat pulsing against her face, practically singeing her hair. She stood there for ten seconds, then twenty. Would Alex find his way out? She prayed he would.

Suddenly, a shadow wavered in front of her. Alex was hunched over, battling his way through a wall of smoke, trying desperately to escape the flames inside.

Thank goodness, Theodosia thought as she took a step back and watched Alex hurtle toward her. He was coughing and staggering so badly he was almost on his knees. But he was all right!

Fawn dashed up to Alex and threw her arms around him as the two of them tumbled to the ground.

By the time the first fire truck arrived, the house was a fiery inferno.

They watched as flames swirled upward in a twisting volcano of red and orange. Firefighters quickly hooked up their hoses and shot gluts of water into the burning building. Windows cracked and popped, flaming timbers fell into what had been the sunroom. A sinuous line of flames crawled across the roof.

"How can two horrific events occur on the very same day?" Drayton asked in a strangled voice. "A second terrible accident."

"Maybe accidentally on purpose?" Theodosia said.

Drayton gasped, a look of utter shock on

43

his face. "What are you talking about, Theo? Why would anyone want to torch this lovely old plantation home?"

Theodosia's eyes never moved from the burning building as she said, "Maybe to destroy evidence?"

Drayton reared back, wild-eyed with his hair sticking up, and stared at her. "What evidence?"

Theodosia shook her head slowly. "I don't know yet."

4

Theodosia and Drayton were calm and collected at the Indigo Tea Shop this Monday morning. Haley was not. As the three of them sat at a table, sipping cups of English breakfast tea, their youthful chef and baker stared at them. Wide-eyed with amazement, Haley's shoulder-length blond hair swished nervously about her shoulders.

You see, Theodosia and Drayton were telling Haley all about the shooting of Reginald Doyle and the subsequent fire that had engulfed his plantation home.

"Holy crap, you guys were lucky to escape from that place alive. One of you could have been popped instead of Mr. Doyle. Or you could have been flambéed in that awful fire," Haley said.

"Don't we know it," Drayton said. "What started as a lovely and fashionable afternoon turned into a veritable madhouse. And in our bumbled escape last night, I happened

45

to leave my favorite leather valise behind. Now I'm positive it's been burned to a crisp."

Haley stared at him. "A valise, Drayton? Not a suitcase?" She didn't always understand Drayton's formality.

"It was vintage."

"Okay, so what happened then?" Haley asked. She'd been somewhat shaken by their vivid descriptions but intrigued as well. "I mean after the shooting and the big fire, which, by the way, sound like multiple plot devices in a Lifetime Movie."

"Obviously, Sheriff Burney had to drag himself back out to Creekmore Plantation a second time. To inspect the premises and interview everyone who survived the fire," Theodosia said.

"Thank goodness, we *all* managed to survive," Drayton said.

"Did the sheriff have any ideas about how the fire might have started?" Haley asked.

"Nobody has any ideas," Drayton said. "The only people in the house last night were Meredith, Alex, Fawn, Reverend Potter and his wife, and an elderly couple named Lincoln." He looked at Theodosia. "And the two of us."

"Do you think the fire was electrical? Like caused by faulty wiring?" Haley asked. "Or was some yahoo smoking in bed and got super careless?"

"I imagine Sheriff Burney will bring in a fire investigator to do a careful analysis," Theodosia said. "Locate the point of origin, determine if any accelerants were used."

"Theodosia thinks the fire may have been set by someone," Drayton said in a quiet voice.

"You do, really?" Haley practically squealed with surprise.

"I said it was *possible*," Theodosia said. "Considering that Reginald Doyle had been murdered in cold blood a few hours earlier."

"So you're pretty sure his death wasn't an accident, either?" Haley asked.

"It didn't look like it to me," Theodosia said.

Haley leaned back in her chair. "Wow." Then, "Are there any suspects? For either crime?"

"Not really," Drayton said.

Theodosia held up a finger. "That's not quite true. Alex seemed to be highly suspicious of one of the neighbors, a man by the name of Carl Clewis. And I have the feeling he didn't much like the Lavender Lady, either."

"Who's the Lavender Lady?" Haley asked.

"A woman named Susan —"

47

"Oh, wait, I think I know who she is," Haley cut in. "Because Delaine carries those —"

"Lavender sachets," Theodosia said, nodding. Her eyes drifted to the cup of tea she held in her hands, and then she looked up and said, "I was thinking . . . if we got in touch with this Lavender Lady, it might be fun to incorporate her into the Lavender Tea we're having on Saturday."

"What are you talking about?" Drayton asked. "You mean invite the *actual* Lavender Lady to our tea?" He seemed unsettled by the idea.

"Why not?" Theodosia said. "After all, she's an expert."

"Then we should call it the Lavender *Lady* Tea," Haley said. "I mean, we're already serving lavender cream scones and decorating the tables with lavender candles and sachets. And Drayton's probably going to create a special house-blended tea that incorporates lavender culinary buds."

Drayton nodded. "That was my plan."

"Works for me," Theodosia said. "And what if we also asked this Susan Monday to give a short talk about lavender? You know, about how the Victorians adored lavender and all its special properties."

"I thought Drayton was going to do that,"

Haley said. "He usually gives the talks about tea lore and historical facts."

"I can easily cede that responsibility," Drayton said. He leaned back in his chair and fixed his gaze on Theodosia. "But isn't there an off chance this Miss Monday might be a suspect?"

"A very *off* off chance," Theodosia said. "But in the meantime, if we discover evidence against her, then she's out."

Haley looked from one to the other. "So, what's the final verdict?"

"I'll talk to Susan Monday," Theodosia said. "Find out if she's even interested."

They got busy then, readying the shop for morning tea. Haley scooted back to her kitchen, where scones and muffins were still baking in the oven. Theodosia lit a fire in the small stone fireplace, then set the tables. She put out antique blue linen place mats she'd picked up at a tag sale in Moncks Corner, small tea lights, cream and sugar, and silverware. Then she opened one of her antique wooden cabinets and gazed at the various sets of dishes she'd collected over the years. Some plates and teacups were mismatched (perfect for an event such as a Patchwork Tea), but she also had wonderfully complete sets of Haviland Princess,

Belleek Country Trellis, and Staffordshire Blue Willow, as well as several more.

"The Coalport blue and white, I think," Theodosia said aloud. "The basket weave and garland trim feel perfect for today."

"Hmm?" Drayton said. He was behind the front counter, juggling chirping teakettles and brewing pots of tea.

"Just making an executive decision."

"Hmm," Drayton said again.

Theodosia gazed with approval at her cozy tea shop with its beamed ceiling, wood-pegged floors, and leaded windows. She grabbed two new grapevine wreaths that she'd brought in, hung them on the far brick wall, then replenished her retail cupboard with jars of DuBose Bees Honey, tins full of tea, paisley cosmetic bags, and a few tea strainers. The T-Bath products came next. These were tea-infused proprietary products that she'd created herself and included two brand-new items — Green Tea Glow Facial Moisturizer and Chamomile Lotion Bars.

At nine o'clock, customers began to trickle in. First by twos, then suddenly groups of four and five started arriving, a virtual torrent.

Drayton handled the front counter with great efficiency, brewing more tea and readying take-out orders of tea and scones.

"We're certainly scrambling for a Monday morning," Theodosia said, a little breathlessly, as she grabbed a Brown Betty teapot of Formosan oolong for one of her tables.

"Either you run the day or the day runs you," Drayton said.

"Aren't you the one with the silver tongue and clever quips," Haley said. She'd suddenly appeared with a glass cake saver filled to the brim with poppy seed muffins and apple pie scones.

"What perfect timing," Theodosia said. "My ladies at table six were just asking about scones."

"These babies are steamin' hot from the oven," Haley said. "And don't you just love the heavenly aroma of Sri Lankan cinnamon?" She gave a quick wave, then disappeared as quickly as she'd appeared.

Theodosia got busy with her tea shop ballet, dipping and swaying as she took and filled orders. Then, she gracefully twirled about, grabbing fresh pots of tea and refilling cup after cup for her guests.

When it looked as if they couldn't squeeze one more person into the Indigo Tea Shop, the front door flew open and whapped hard against the wall, as if an ill wind had suddenly blown into town.

Theodosia's brows puckered at hearing this nasty disturbance, and she glanced up, wondering who or what had caused such an awful racket. Then her eyes fell upon Meredith Doyle. Framed in the doorway, Meredith stood there unmoving, eyes hard as marbles, wearing a severely tailored black jacket and slacks. With her fine hair slicked tightly against her skull, she looked like a religious zealot who'd arrived to pass out tracts and preach about the fires of hell.

Only Meredith's sad, downturned mouth said otherwise. Because her expression wasn't just intense; this was a woman who looked completely devastated.

"Meredith!" Theodosia exclaimed. Without hesitation, she flew to the front door, wrapped her arms around Meredith's small form, and pulled her into a gentle embrace. Theodosia didn't know Meredith all that well, but the poor woman had just endured the tragic loss of her husband as well as the fiery demise of her home. So, kindhearted Theodosia understood that Meredith deserved as much care and sympathy as she could give.

"May I come in?" Meredith asked in a small voice once Theodosia had released her from her grasp. "Or are you frantically busy?"

"Please do come in," Theodosia urged. "In fact, we happen to have a cozy little table just for you. Right next to the fireplace."

Thank goodness Mrs. Hawley and her sister just left!

"You are too kind," Meredith said. She allowed Theodosia to lead her to the table, then sank gratefully into a cushioned captain's chair that was parked there.

"And I'll have Drayton bring you a pot of tea as well."

Meredith reached out and grasped Theodosia's wrist. "Just so you know, I came here to ask for your help."

"Oh, Meredith." Now Theodosia wasn't sure what to say. Instead, she glanced at the front counter, where Drayton gave a quick, knowing nod. He understood that these circumstances called for a pot of strong, bracing tea.

"Please," Meredith said. "Can you spare a few minutes?"

Theodosia did a quick check of the tea shop. Everyone was sipping tea and enjoying their scones and Devonshire cream. So yes, she did have a couple of minutes.

"You want my help . . . with what exactly?" Theodosia asked.

Meredith furrowed her brow as she fought

53

to gather her words. "After everything that's happened in the last twenty-four hours, I feel like I'm in way over my head. As if I'm drowning. Unable to . . ." She hesitated, struggling to organize her thoughts, then said, "Losing my beloved Reginald . . . and then that horrible fire last night."

"Awful," Theodosia murmured. "I'm sure you must be heartsick."

"I am. The only thing, the single thing, that's sustained me is that Creekmore Plantation is still standing. It wasn't a case of total devastation. In fact, I've got a meeting with my insurance agent this very afternoon to talk about major repairs that need to be done."

"So at least you have a . . . home base." Theodosia was practically at a loss for words herself.

"Actually, Creekmore is a disaster zone. Windows smashed, the sunroom incinerated, a chimney partially crumbled. Of course there's extensive smoke and water damage everywhere." Meredith touched a hand to her cheek. "And my woodwork . . . all my beautiful Carolina pine! Do you know some of that wood was logged over a hundred years ago?"

"It sounds as if Creekmore Plantation will

require considerable restoration," Theodosia said.

"Yes, and thank goodness Alex has stepped in to spearhead that," Meredith said. "In the meantime, I've taken a suite at the Lady Goodwood Inn so I can catch my breath and get a much-needed respite from all this . . . tragedy."

"That's probably a smart idea," Theodosia said.

"I also have a funeral to plan." Now a tear dribbled down Meredith's pale cheek. "Then, afterward, I intend to spend more time at Divine Design. Getting back to work, designing interiors for some new clients, will help take my mind off . . . well, you know."

"Dear lady," Drayton said, suddenly appearing at Meredith's table with a carefully arranged tea tray. "I've prepared a pot of Darjeeling tea for you. A flavorful tea with some serious body and briskness."

"Thank you," Meredith murmured, as Drayton poured a stream of amber tea into her teacup.

"And an apple pie scone," Drayton said.

"Meredith was just telling me that she'll be staying in town at the Lady Goodwood Inn," Theodosia said.

"That sounds like a fine idea. And what

about Alex and his wife, Fawn? Where will they be staying?" Drayton asked.

"They own a home just a few blocks from here. A small cottage on Tradd Street."

"Such a lovely area," Drayton said. "Smack-dab in the middle of the Historic District." Drayton lived in that same part of town himself. So did Theodosia.

Meredith took a quick sip of tea. "Delicious." Then her eyes sought out Theodosia's. "So. Will you help me?" Then, before Theodosia could manage an answer, Meredith said, "You realize, your aunt Libby is forever telling everyone what a complete *genius* you are when it comes to unraveling problems and ferreting out clues and . . ." She hesitated. "And dealing with unusual murders."

Theodosia waved a hand in the air as if trying to dispel Meredith's words.

"Oh no. Not really."

"Libby Bertrand doesn't lie," Meredith said. Her words were sharp and clipped. Just this side of being a pronouncement.

"Theodosia *is* rather skilled at crime solving," Drayton offered. "You could say she's Charleston's very own Nancy Drew."

Theodosia's eyelids dropped a notch. She didn't need Drayton lobbying her as well. "I believe, Drayton, that you have a cus-

56

tomer waiting at the front counter?"

"Oh my," he said, rushing off.

"You asked so many good questions yesterday," Meredith said. "But I can see I've sprung my request on you way too fast . . . and I apologize." She favored Theodosia with a self-deprecating smile. "But I have a wonderful idea. Why don't you and Drayton join me for dinner tonight at Trollope's?"

"The restaurant your husband owns."

"My *late* husband." Meredith looked like she was about to cry again. "Oh, how I despise that term." She blinked rapidly and managed to recover some of her poise. "If the two of you would come for dinner, maybe we could discuss some of these, um, issues. Perhaps bring Guy into the conversation as well."

Theodosia stared at her. "Guy . . . ?"

"Guy Thorne, Reginald's partner in the restaurant. You met him yesterday, probably even talked to him. Remember? The red-haired fellow?"

Right, Theodosia thought. *The man who was so hot to move Reginald Doyle's body.*

Meredith took a few more quick sips of tea and then stood up. "You've been terribly kind, but now I'm afraid I must rush off. I need to deal with all of this aftermath."

57

"Of course," Theodosia said as she walked Meredith to the door. "And Drayton and I would be delighted to join you for dinner tonight."

"Thank you, dear," Meredith said. She turned, about to favor Drayton with a finger wave, when she suddenly spotted a colorful poster hanging on the wall. Curiosity lit her face. "What's this?"

Theodosia touched a hand to the poster she'd created for their *Gone with the Wind* Tea. She'd used the image of a distraught Scarlett O'Hara silhouetted against a bright-red sunset.

"It's a poster to advertise the *Gone with the Wind* Tea we're hosting tomorrow."

"Would you believe that's one of my absolute favorite books?" Meredith exclaimed. "And I adore the movie, too. Always so thrilling. I've probably seen it at least twenty times."

"Then perhaps you should come to our tea. I know seating is still available," Theodosia said.

For the first time, Meredith's mood seemed to brighten.

"I think I'd like that. And maybe I could bring Fawn along."

"Do that."

Meredith nodded. "This tea party sounds

like a welcome diversion. Something that might help cheer us up."

"Then we look forward to seeing both of you," Theodosia said. She watched Meredith go, her heart feeling sad and heavy for everything poor Meredith had recently endured. Then she went back to the front counter, where Drayton and Haley were whispering to each other.

Haley straightened up. "That was Meredith?"

Theodosia nodded.

"She's so pale and skinny. What does she live on?"

"Probably kale smoothies," Theodosia said.

"Do you think there's such a thing as kale tea?" Haley asked.

"Bite your tongue," Drayton said.

5

Drayton dumped two heaping scoops of Assam into a blue-and-white Chinese teapot, added a pinch for the pot, and said, "Are you going to help Meredith?"

It was late morning, and Theodosia was busy clearing her tables and setting them for lunch.

"I don't know. I'd like to, but the whole situation does feel a bit . . . odd."

"Because we were right there, front and center? Because you were the one who discovered Reginald's body?"

Theodosia lifted a shoulder. "Maybe."

Drayton studied his floor-to-ceiling shelves filled with tea tins. Then he reached up and grabbed a tin of Nilgiri. "I think you should help Meredith."

"I imagine you do, seeing as how you were such good friends with Reginald. And because the two of you served together on the board of directors at the Heritage

Society."

"There's that. And it also feels as if something bizarre is going on."

"The murder *and* the fire."

Drayton stared at her over his tortoiseshell half-glasses. "Two horrific events that occurred within hours of each other. I mean, what are the chances?"

"Practically zero to nil. Which is why *you're* about to get dragged into this pretty little mess as well."

Drayton measured Assam tea into a second teapot. "What are you talking about?"

"Meredith invited us to have dinner with her tonight at Trollope's. I think she wants to get our take on everything that's happened and noodle around some ideas."

"Ideas about suspects?"

"Maybe. Probably."

"What did you tell her?" Drayton asked.

"I said we'd love to come."

"And then what?"

"I don't know. I guess we'll have to figure it out as we go along."

In the kitchen, Haley added a judicious shake of black pepper to a bubbling pot of crab chowder as she went over the day's menu with Theodosia.

"I'm also baking eggnog scones," Haley

said. "Our customers always go gaga over those. Especially when we serve them with gobs of strawberry jam. And for lunch, I've got Hawaiian tea sandwiches, Greek salad with black olives and feta cheese, red pepper quiche, and my fabulous crab chowder. The crabmeat, I'm happy to say, was freshly picked from blue crabs just this morning."

"It all sounds delicious," Theodosia said. "Especially your chowder."

Haley gave her chowder a final stir, then banged her wooden spoon against the side of the pot as if playing a timpani drum. "Now that the weather's starting to cool, I'm going to add lots more chowders and stews to our menu."

"Frogmore stew?" It was one of Theodosia's absolute favorites and a low-country staple.

Haley grinned, reached a hand out, and bumped knuckles with Theodosia. "That's a given, girlfriend."

"How are we set for tomorrow?" Theodosia asked. "For our *Gone with the Wind* Tea?"

Haley took a step backward, held a hand to her forehead, and said, with as much drama as she could muster, "I'll think about it tomorrow. After all, tomorrow is another day."

"Very funny."

Then she snapped back into go-getter Haley mode. "Didn't Drayton share the menu with you? I gave it to him, like, two hours ago."

"He's in one of his busy-tizzy moods. I'll check with him later."

But Drayton wasn't the only one who was busy. When the big hand and the little hand both struck twelve, a whole gang of anxious customers began streaming into the tea shop.

Theodosia seated guests, recited the menu, took orders, poured tea, and generally hustled her buns off, all the while feeling a pang of regret that she hadn't asked Miss Dimple, their bookkeeper and occasional server, to come in and help.

Oh well, at least she'll be here tomorrow.

Drayton saw Theodosia's plight and, in between bagging up take-out orders and brewing tea, did the honor of stepping in to refill teacups. Of course, being a dedicated tea sommelier, he couldn't resist dispensing a few choice words of tea lore as well. But lunch went off without a hitch, and thankfully, by the time one thirty rolled around, things at the tea shop had settled down to a dull roar.

"What a crazy day so far," Theodosia said.

She rested her elbows on the counter, leaned forward, and arched her back. For some reason, she had a knot in her right shoulder. From the recoil of her gun yesterday? Or was it just garden-variety tension?

"I've been going slightly batty myself," Drayton said. "Between sit-down customers and take-out orders, it's been . . ." His words suddenly trailed off as he gazed past Theodosia. Then he said, "Bless my stars, it's Timothy."

Theodosia spun around to find Timothy Neville, the executive director of the Heritage Society, shrugging out of his Burberry trench coat and hanging it on their brass coatrack. Though Timothy was an octogenarian, he had the mental faculties and spryness of someone thirty years younger.

"He wants something," Drayton said under his breath.

"I wonder what?" Theodosia said.

They found out about two seconds later when Timothy crooked a gnarled finger and suggested (ordered?) that they sit down with him. Besides being elderly, Timothy was fussy, imperious, and demanding, which meant he rarely minced words.

"We need to get to the bottom of this," Timothy said, once they'd all settled at a table near the window. His dark eyes were pools of intensity as he leaned forward, spare and angular in his bearing.

"You're talking about Reginald . . ." Drayton began.

"Yes, I'm talking about Reginald," Timothy said with a staccato burst. "What else would have me this upset?"

Theodosia smiled. She knew that beneath Timothy's crusty, cranky exterior there beat the kind and generous heart of a true Southern gentleman. He just kept it carefully hidden most of the time.

"What can you tell me about the circumstances?" Timothy asked. "Kindly enlighten me. I know you were both guests at Creekmore Plantation yesterday."

So Theodosia and Drayton quickly sketched a detailed version of Reginald Doyle's getting shot during the bird hunt, as well as a description of the fire that engulfed the plantation house later that night.

"You don't find these back-to-back disasters suspicious?" Timothy asked.

"Are you kidding? We find them *beaucoup* suspicious," Theodosia said.

Timothy's spindly fingers beat a nervous rhythm against the table.

"What are you going to do about it?" he asked.

"Do?" Drayton asked, fingering his bow tie. He was suddenly at a loss for words.

"Let the sheriff's investigation take its course," Theodosia said.

Timothy was already shaking his head.

"Not good enough," he said. "Realize, please, that Reginald Doyle was a dear personal friend of mine. He was also a former board member and major contributor to the Heritage Society. Reginald practically underwrote the entire Audubon Show this past June."

"I know you two are close," Drayton said. "*Were* close."

"Reginald sat on our board of directors for a dozen years," Timothy said. "Almost as long as you have, Drayton. When Reginald finally resigned last year, his CFO, Bill Jacoby, was kind enough to take his place."

"Where exactly are you going with this?" Theodosia asked. Reginald Doyle's curriculum vitae was no doubt interesting, but it wasn't advancing their conversation. And Theodosia figured — no, she knew — that Timothy had come with an agenda.

Timothy tilted his head and cocked an eye at Theodosia, giving the faint impression of a wily magpie.

"Reginald Doyle confided in me that he

66

planned to bequeath Creekmore Plantation to the Heritage Society," Timothy said.

That little bombshell definitely made Theodosia and Drayton sit up straight and take notice.

"Bequeath?" Drayton stammered. "You mean give it to the Heritage Society as a gift? Wait, are you saying that Reginald wrote this bequest into his last will and testament?"

"Whoa," Theodosia said. "What about his wife, Meredith? Wouldn't Reginald have wanted *her* to inherit Creekmore Plantation? Or his son, Alex?"

"Not necessarily," Timothy said.

"Could they contest Reginald's will?" Theodosia asked. "Would they?"

"Not if it was drawn up as an irrevocable trust," Timothy said. He pursed his lips and added, "Although, in my experience, very few wills are completely ironclad."

"Let me get this straight," Theodosia said. "Doyle intended to leave his plantation home to the Heritage Society and not his immediate family." She was having trouble wrapping her head around what felt like an enormous slight. Had Reginald Doyle really been of sound mind when he arrived at that decision?

"I'm not sure how much of the plantation

is still standing after last night's fire," Drayton said.

"Doesn't matter," Timothy said. "The surrounding land is worth a small fortune."

"How much of a small fortune?" Theodosia asked.

Timothy didn't hesitate. "Four or five million."

Drayton let loose a low whistle.

"Is this a done deal?" Theodosia asked. "Did Doyle actually *change* his will? Do you know for sure that the Heritage Society was named sole beneficiary?"

"At this point I *don't* know," Timothy said. "Since it was only talked about." He cocked an index finger at Theodosia and then at Drayton. "That's what I want you two to find out."

"Gracious," Drayton said.

"Who knew about this possible change in bequest?" Theodosia asked.

Timothy shook his head. "I don't know. I assume his family must have been informed; certainly his attorney would be privy. Maybe even business associates."

Drayton cupped his chin in his hand, as if deep in thought. "If Reginald changed beneficiaries, could that have been a factor that led to his death — or the fire?"

Theodosia's mind had already made the

leap. "How could it not?" she said.

Theodosia was sitting at the computer in her small office, using Google Earth to search the countryside outside Charleston, when Drayton walked in.

"I brought you a cup of tea," he said. "That new Ceylonese green tea. The leaves have been steamed so the flavor is very fresh and crisp."

"Thank you." Theodosia kept her eyes locked on the screen.

"What is it you're doing?" Drayton tipped his head sideways, trying to get a look at the screen. "Are you working on ideas for that Paris and Pearls Tea Party we talked about?"

"I'm using Google Earth to pull up a satellite photo of Reginald Doyle's plantation."

Drayton pursed his lips, as if that kind of technology was far beyond his comprehension. Which it probably was. "You can actually do that?"

Theodosia tapped her screen. "Just finished." She hit print, and her printer began its quiet chatter. "See? Now I've got a map. The plantation and the surrounding area."

Drayton walked around her desk and stood behind her. "It looks more like Area

51." Then, "Wait, *why* are you doing this?"

"Because I intend to do some exploring."

"Ah, you mean investigating." A flicker of excitement rose in Drayton's eyes.

"Well, yes."

"So you *are* going to help Meredith." Drayton seemed oddly pleased. "And you did take Timothy's request to heart."

"Only because this new information about Reginald's will raises the stakes a lot higher." Theodosia paused. "And truth be known, I want to satisfy my own curiosity."

6

With printed map in hand, Theodosia set out to visit Blue Moon Lavender Farm first. The place wasn't hard to find; it was only three miles down the road from Creekmore Plantation. And then there was that heady lavender aroma that seemed to perfume the air. Theodosia slid down her driver's side window, inhaled deeply, and decided the scent was probably just as intoxicating as that magical poppy field in *The Wizard of Oz.*

Theodosia turned her Jeep down a gravel driveway that was marked with a purple-and-white sign that said, BLUE MOON LAVENDER FARM, RETAIL SHOP AND TOURS. Just past a small stand of cherry trees sat a white clapboard house, a large white barn, and two smaller buildings also painted white. Stretching beyond all that were fields of lavender. With bright sunlight winking down, the lavender plants looked like bouncy purple clouds.

As Theodosia stepped out of her Jeep, two inquisitive black-and-tan German shepherds bounded over to greet her. Ears perked, eyes sparked with intelligence, they looked like a couple of canine gatekeepers.

Uh-oh, I hope they're friendly.

"Don't mind them," a woman's voice called. "They're just very curious."

So am I, Theodosia thought as she turned to find a pretty dark-haired woman striding toward her.

Susan Monday? Has to be.

Susan Monday was wearing a denim jacket, blue jeans, and a pair of dark-green Wellie boots. She exuded the confident, satisfied air of someone who worked outdoors and was proud of it.

"The female's named Galatea and the male is Cerberus," the woman said. Her voice was light and melodic, her manner warm and welcoming.

"Ah, the heart-stealer and the guardian of Hades."

"You know your Greek mythology," Susan Monday said.

"Some of it anyway," Theodosia said. She stuck out her hand. "Hello, I'm Theodosia Browning."

The woman smiled as she shook Theodosia's hand. "Susan Monday, nice to meet you."

"The Lavender Lady. You certainly have a lovely farm here. How many acres?"

"Sixty, though it's not all under cultivation," Susan said. "And if you're thinking about a tour, our harvesting season is mostly over. That all happens in spring and summer. Right now we're busy pruning our plants." She paused. "But our retail store is open if you're interested in lavender bundles or sachets."

"Actually, I've come for a little information," Theodosia said.

"Oh?"

"I was a guest at Creekmore Plantation yesterday."

Susan Monday didn't seem one bit surprised by Theodosia's words, but her expression shifted immediately.

"Oh dear, that must have been terribly shocking." Her brown eyes crinkled as she shook her head. "Sheriff Burney stopped by late yesterday afternoon to tell me about the shooting and ask a few questions. I still can't fathom why someone would hate poor Reginald Doyle so much that they'd shoot him like . . . like some rabid animal."

"You knew him well?"

"Mostly just as a neighbor. But Reginald

73

was a friendly neighbor, and so was his wife, Meredith." Now Susan looked even more unhappy. "And for a hunting accident — or whatever it turns out to be — to happen so close to my property, it's almost too bizarre. I feel almost . . . I can't say responsible . . . but strangely complicit in a way." She turned an earnest gaze toward Theodosia. "You know what I mean?"

"I think I do. And you also heard about the fire?"

"One of my retail assistants filled me in on all the local gossip first thing this morning. Awful. Just awful. Creekmore is such a beautiful old place. I think it might even be listed on the South Carolina Historic Properties Record."

"I understand that Reginald Doyle was involved in a major dispute with one of your neighbors."

"That would be Carl Clewis," Susan said with slightly raised brows.

"Something about a creek?"

Susan nodded. "First, Clewis claimed he needed to divert water from Axson Creek for the purpose of irrigating a piece of his land. Then he said he was trying to reinvigorate some old rice fields. Growing Carolina Gold and all that. Then his story changed big-time when he began building an exclusive enclave of million-dollar homes." She stopped and thought for a moment. "I imagine Creekmore Plantation got its name because of that creek."

"Sounds plausible. So this water issue was definitely an ongoing problem between Doyle and Clewis?"

"It's been a huge bone of contention. I know both Doyle and Clewis filed lawsuits and went to court several times. Both parties were always lobbying the county commissioner for his learned opinion."

"Was there ever any kind of ruling?" Theodosia asked.

"I have no idea. But maybe, with Doyle deceased . . . his family will let the matter drop and Clewis will get his way?"

"Possibly," Theodosia said. "And you were in a land dispute with Doyle as well?"

"The orphan strip." Susan waved a hand. "It's nothing really. Certainly not worth quibbling over."

"That's good to know." Theodosia glanced toward one of the smaller buildings. "You mentioned something about a retail shop?"

"Come take a look," Susan said.

Theodosia followed Susan, Galatea, and Cerberus over to the gift shop. When they stepped inside, the place smelled like heaven.

"Oh my goodness," Theodosia exclaimed. "This scent in here is absolutely incredible." She had a brief, poignantly sharp memory of her mother, gone now for almost twenty years, sitting at a dressing table and dabbing on lavender perfume. Then the image slipped away.

"It's relaxing in here, yes?" Susan asked.

"I feel so relaxed I could lie down and take a snooze," Theodosia said.

"That's pretty much the whole idea behind lavender. Besides being lovely to look at, scientists have studied lavender and determined that it has calming and anti-anxiety properties."

"I can feel them at work right now." Theodosia laughed.

Susan stepped behind a small white counter where three lavender candles burned next to a large stack of lavender soap. The rest of the gift shop was jammed with all sorts of lavender products as well as various gift baskets.

"As you can see, Blue Moon Lavender Farm sells lavender in bundles as well as lavender sachets, candles, soaps, essential oils, and culinary buds," Susan said.

"What about lavender tea?" Theodosia asked.

"I've been thinking about adding lavender

tea to our gift offerings."

"I have to confess, I own a tea shop, the Indigo Tea Shop, in Charleston."

Susan grinned. "I thought I recognized your name. You've done a couple of TV appearances, am I right?"

"I've been lucky to get the publicity, yes."

Susan grabbed a package of lavender buds and pushed them across the counter into Theodosia's hands. "Then you have to take these back to your tea shop and . . . I don't know . . . blend them into a tea? Can you do that?"

"My tea sommelier can with ease," Theodosia said. "In fact, I'd like to feature some of your lavender products at a special tea luncheon we're having this coming Saturday. A lavender tea. Actually, now that we've finally met, I'd like to invite you to be part of it."

Susan was genuinely surprised. "Me?"

"You're the lavender expert, aren't you? The Lavender Lady?"

"You keep calling me that, but it's the first time anybody's ever done so." Susan smiled. "But I like it. And I'm intrigued. What would I have to do at this lavender tea party?"

"Allow us to use your lavender buds in a special tea. Maybe give a quick talk about lavender and all its amazing properties. And be our guest of honor."

"I would adore that!" Susan enthused. "We could even give your guests some lavender sachets as favors."

"This is beginning to sound more and more perfect," Theodosia said.

"Come into the back room and I'll put together a goody bag for you."

Theodosia followed Susan Monday into her workshop.

"This is fascinating," Theodosia said as she looked around.

Hundreds of bundles of dried lavender hung from a network of wooden lattices. Woven bushel baskets held more bunches of dried lavender. In fact, there seemed to be an ethereal purple-blue haze hanging in the air.

"We grow a dozen different varieties of lavender on the farm thanks to the help of our pollinator bees," Susan said. "Once the plants have fully bloomed, we cut them by hand, tie them into bundles, and allow them to dry for five to six weeks."

As Theodosia glanced around the workroom, she noticed a gun propped against the far wall.

"You have a gun." The words just popped impulsively out of Theodosia's mouth.

"For varmints," Susan said as she stuffed a dozen bundles of lavender into a clear plastic bag.

"Varmints come after your lavender?"

Susan stopped her work and eyed Theodosia carefully. "No, but they do come after my chickens."

Theodosia breathed an inward sigh of relief. Susan had a legitimate reason for owning a gun. "Chickens. You have chickens."

"Just a dozen. Rhode Island Reds. But you'd be amazed how many foxes, coyotes, and weasels drop by to gaze longingly at them."

Ten minutes later, Theodosia called Drayton as she drove along in her Jeep.

"Susan Monday is all in for our Lavender Lady Tea this Saturday."

"That's for sure what we're calling it now? And Miss Monday is a good fit for us?"

"I think so. She's lovely and quite charming. Plus, she gave me tons of lavender so you can blend lavender tea to your heart's content."

"So after conversing with Miss Monday, you no longer view her as a legitimate suspect?" Drayton asked.

"I don't think she ever was."

79

"That answer doesn't sound very definitive," Drayton said.

"Well, I meant it to be. So here's the plan: We'll add Susan's name and a little blurb about her when we send out reminder e-mails to all our tea guests."

"I have no idea how to do that," Drayton said.

"Just write up something quick and fun, and have Haley send it out. She knows how."

Theodosia's next stop was Carl Clewis's farm. But when she pulled in, she realized it wasn't really a farm at all. There was a large, stately brick home, probably built within the last five years, a detached four-car garage, and two expansive barns with adjacent paddocks. So, maybe a horse ranch?

The man who came out to greet Theodosia wasn't Clewis. He introduced himself as Willis, the handyman. No last name given.

Theodosia quickly introduced herself and asked to speak with Mr. Clewis.

"Mr. Clewis isn't here right now," Willis said. He was tall and lean with a pinkish, weathered face. Suspicious eyes peered at her above knife-blade cheekbones.

"Do you know where he went?" Theodosia asked.

80

"I didn't ask him, because it's none of my business."

"Do you have any idea when Mr. Clewis will be back?"

"No, I don't."

"What can you tell me about the Axson Creek situation?"

"I don't know anything about that."

"Is that a fact?" Theodosia could tell by the smug expression on the man's face that he was lying to her. And kind of enjoying it, too.

"That's a fact."

Theodosia handed Willis one of her business cards. "Will you please tell Mr. Clewis that I stopped by?"

The handyman looked at her card and smirked. "You want to talk to him about tea?"

"Not exactly." Theodosia fixed Willis with a steady gaze. "I need to ask Mr. Clewis a few questions concerning Reginald Doyle."

The man's dirty thumb casually flicked a corner of her white card. "Doyle. That's the man who got shot."

"No," Theodosia said. "That's the man who got murdered."

Theodosia drove along, dipping in and out of pine forests, reeling in the sunlight dappling the small ponds that she passed. A dozen miles away, as the crow flies, was Cane Ridge Plantation, where her father had grown up, where her aunt Libby now lived. Theodosia remembered happy childhood summers spent there — running around at dusk, catching fireflies in mason jars, fishing for catfish and bluegills in the streams that wound through the woods.

Spending summers there, running unfettered through the woods and swamps, was one of the reasons Theodosia drove a Jeep Cherokee. The Jeep allowed her to venture off-road, to power her way into woods and forests where an ordinary car couldn't go. There she could gather up wild grapevines for wreaths, forage for purslane, bullbrier, golden chanterelle mushrooms, and even wild pears. Sometimes she'd find abandoned bird nests and would bring them back to the Indigo Tea Shop to be repurposed as holders for small tea-themed note cards, enameled teacup necklaces, and tiny cameos on gold chains.

As she passed the main gate of Creekmore Plantation, Theodosia decided, at the very last minute, to turn in and see what was going on. She juked her steering wheel hard, made a wide, careening turn, and found herself bumping down the gravel driveway.

When Theodosia arrived at the main house, she was amazed at how much activity was already underway. At least a half-dozen trucks and vans were parked helter-skelter around the property, with workers scurrying everywhere. Judging from the signage on the vans, these were tradespeople who'd been called in to assess water damage as well as check the foundation, the building's structural integrity, the wiring, and whatever else might need fixing.

And, yes, there was Alex Doyle, surrounded by a tight little scrum of men who were all dressed in overalls or canvas workwear and brandishing clipboards.

This is good for Meredith's sake. Alex isn't wasting any time.

As Theodosia approached Alex, the group of workmen scattered and Alex turned in her direction. Recognition suddenly dawned on his face, and he smiled broadly.

"Miss Browning," he said.

"Theodosia," she said.

"Theodosia, then." Alex gave an all-encompassing wave toward the main house. "As you can see, we're in the initial stages of rebuilding. Give it a few months and this old place will be good as new."

"That's wonderful to hear," Theodosia said. "I take it the water and smoke damage

83

wasn't as extensive as your mother first thought?"

Alex closed one eye. "Oh, it's bad. But the good news is that everything can be dealt with. Remedied. Gonna cost some serious money, though."

"It always does." Theodosia paused and gently touched Alex's arm. "I know I said this last night, but I'm so very sorry about your father. You have my deepest sympathies."

Alex bobbed his head. "Thank you, that's kind of you. We're all still sort of . . . what would you call it . . . *processing* everything that's happened."

"I spoke with your mother this morning."

"Mom." Alex grimaced. "She's completely devastated."

"Yes, she is."

"But she'll deal with it. She's as tough as they come."

Maybe she is. I certainly hope she is.

"And how is Fawn doing?" Theodosia asked.

"Oh, Fawn." Alex gave an offhand wave. "She's around here somewhere."

"I hope she's feeling better. She seemed awfully upset last night."

"She gets that way. Nerves, I guess. But she'll be fine."

84

"Have you spoken with Sheriff Burney today?" Theodosia asked.

"He dropped by, yeah."

"Is there any news? Has he developed any kind of suspect list?"

Alex glowered. "On the contrary. Burney showed up here and asked a lot *more* questions. It's frustrating beyond belief, because I've already told him everything I know!"

"I'm sure you have," Theodosia said.

But Alex wasn't finished. "It feels like some strange, menacing phantom wafted onto our property, killed Pop, started the fire, and then . . . poof . . . stole away into the night."

But murder and arson are committed by real people, Theodosia thought to herself. *Not a mysterious phantom that disappears in a sulfurous cloud.*

It was gradually dawning on Theodosia that she and Alex were having a slightly strange, disjointed conversation. But maybe that was just Alex. Maybe he was still terribly shaken up by the murder and the fire.

Theodosia planned to ask Alex about Reginald's will. It had been on the tip of her tongue, but now she decided it might be too much for him. So, instead, she just said, "I'm so very sorry all this happened, Alex."

Alex nodded and mumbled, "Thank you.

Please . . . will you keep in touch with Mom?"

"I will."

"She needs all the moral support she can get."

It was only after Theodosia had driven a few miles down Rutledge Road that she began to wonder . . . If Alex and Meredith *knew* that Creekmore Plantation had been willed to the Heritage Society, would they bother rebuilding?

Perhaps Timothy's question had been answered after all.

7

Trollope's Restaurant looked like it had been airlifted, lock, stock, and barrel, directly out of High Street in Windsor, England, and plunked down right in the middle of Charleston.

The place was Olde English and charming in the way that theme restaurants often are. There were brocade tapestries, wooden ceiling beams, brass plaques, pewter tankards, Toby mugs, numerous coats of arms complete with eagles and lions, and crackle-glazed oil paintings of three-masted schooners struggling through raging seas. Hanging above the de rigueur oversize stone fireplace was a pair of antique pistols. Interesting.

"Have you eaten here before?" Theodosia asked Drayton as they wove their way through a maze of very large and heavy dining room tables, headed for Meredith's reserved table.

87

"Only once. I ordered a steak, and when it arrived, it was the size of a cow."

Meredith saw them coming and jumped up to greet them. Tonight she wore a black pantsuit made of some sort of slithery material and a pair of diamond earrings that Theodosia figured had to be four, maybe even five, carats all told. And stunning.

"Drayton, Theodosia, do come here!" Meredith chirped. She reached out, clutched their hands, and fluttered in close to administer hasty air-kisses.

"This is a lovely restaurant," Theodosia said as she settled into a chair that, with its bright purple brocade cushion and gilded arms, slightly resembled an English throne.

"Very elegant," Drayton said.

Theodosia smiled to herself. She knew that faux Henry VIII was not exactly Drayton's idea of elegance. He was more of a Chippendale and Hepplewhite sort of fellow.

But Meredith seemed pleased by his remark. "As you know, Reginald was a confirmed Anglophile. We were forever taking trips to merry old England to purchase furniture and antiques for this restaurant and for our home." She pointed at the tabletop. "You see these pewter chargers?"

"They're beautiful," Theodosia said, even

though they resembled enormous metal Frisbees.

"Handmade by craftsmen in Sheffield," Meredith said. "And the glassware is genuine handblown Cumbria Crystal, which is the exact same lead crystal that was showcased on *Downton Abbey.*"

Meredith stopped suddenly, her demeanor downshifting from slightly manic to suddenly sober.

"Oh dear, I suppose I shouldn't rattle on about such inconsequential things when my poor Reginald is lying on a metal table at Doake and Wilson Funeral Home."

"Nonsense," Drayton said. "You've just experienced a terrible series of shocks to your system. You're entitled to act however you want."

"You're very kind," Meredith said. She gazed at Theodosia and smiled. "You, too."

"I paid a visit to two of your neighbors today," Theodosia said. *Might as well jump right in.*

Meredith managed a hopeful smile. "So you are investigating?"

"At this point, it's more like asking questions," Theodosia said.

"Isn't that the same thing?" Meredith said. "So, what . . . ?" It was obvious she was anxious for any and all information that

89

Theodosia might have gleaned.

"I spoke first with Susan Monday at her lavender farm and then to Mr. Clewis's handyman, Willis," Theodosia said.

Meredith picked up her menu. "Carl Clewis himself wasn't available?"

"If he was, I didn't see him," Theodosia said.

Meredith unfolded a pair of half-glasses and put them on. They were sparkly and shaped like cat eyes.

"We should probably order."

Meredith gave a nod to a waitress who wore a dress, laced corset, and frilled cap that made her look like a scullery maid character straight out of the local Renaissance fair.

"Just so you know, the beef Wellington here is superb," Meredith said.

"Then that's what I shall have," Drayton said.

Meredith and Drayton both opted for the beef Wellington, while Theodosia ordered the grilled salmon.

"And we'll need a bottle of wine. Where's Guy?" Meredith twisted around in her chair. "Oh, there he is." She lifted a hand and waved excitedly. "Guy. Oh, Guy!"

Guy Thorne was standing two tables away when he heard Meredith calling his name.

He turned, flashed a cheesy smile, and held up an index finger. A minute later he arrived brandishing a bottle of wine and a corkscrew.

"I generally let my sommelier attend to this task," Thorne said, looking the part of a bon vivant restaurateur in his sparkling-white shirt and sharp black tuxedo. "But because this is a bottle of Château Margaux, I intend to do the honors myself."

He inserted the wine opener, extracted the cork, and set it in front of Meredith for inspection.

Meredith picked up the cork and gave a perfunctory sniff. "Guy, you remember Theodosia and Drayton, don't you?"

"We met informally yesterday," Thorne said, "but were never properly introduced."

"I'm sorry," Meredith said, as she made hasty introductions.

Theodosia, of course, had recognized Guy Thorne immediately. He was the red-haired fellow who'd been so insistent about carrying Doyle's body away from the murder site. She wondered if Thorne had something to hide or if he was just a type A personality. Or both.

"I'm very sorry about your partner's death," Theodosia said to Thorne.

"Thank you, it's been a tough blow to deal

with," Thorne said as he moved around the table, pouring wine into their stemmed glasses. "Everyone here is completely heartbroken — waitstaff, chefs, kitchen people. We're like one big family." He straightened up and snapped his fingers imperiously to signal the busboy for a wine bucket.

"We really are," Meredith said while Thorne played the genial host.

"You know Trollope's is named after a British fellow named Anthony Trollope," Thorne said.

"An English novelist of the Victorian era," Drayton said. "Yes, I know."

Dinner was good, not great. Maybe because Guy Thorne had joined them and talked incessantly, maybe because the food was heavy as well as being heavily sauced.

"Theodosia and Drayton have agreed to look into Reginald's murder," Meredith said as she slathered butter on her popover.

A dark shadow passed over Thorne's face and then it was gone. "And why is that?" he asked.

"Because I trust them," Meredith said. "And because Theodosia has a history of poking around and discovering little clues and inconsistencies. She's even solved a couple of murders."

Thorne turned a flat-eyed gaze on Theodosia. "Isn't that an interesting talent to have cultivated. So, what are you looking for in this particular case? Or should I ask, *who* are you looking for?"

"I'm not sure yet. So far I've only had brief conversations with Susan Monday at the neighboring lavender farm and with Carl Clewis's handyman," Theodosia said.

"Clewis. Now there's a slimy devil if you can ever get to see him," Thorne said with some relish. "I wouldn't trust him as far as I could spit a rat."

"Guy, please," Meredith said, putting a hand on his arm.

But Thorne was not to be deterred. "No, really. You know as well as I do that Clewis isn't only mean-spirited, he's a liar and a cheat. Look at all the friction he caused by damming up that creek."

"Somehow I don't think Mr. Doyle was murdered over a dammed-up creek," Theodosia said.

"No?" Thorne said.

"Do you see?" Meredith said. "Do you see how insightful Theodosia is?"

"Indeed," Thorne said. "We must keep a careful eye on her." He swallowed a final bite of steak, set his fork down, and gazed around the table. "Dessert, anyone? It's a well-known fact that Trollope's serves the absolute best chess pie in all of Charleston."

"No, thank you," Theodosia said, thinking that Thorne might do well by serving himself a slice of humble pie.

After dessert, coffee, proffered cordials, and brandy, Theodosia was more than ready to leave the restaurant. Unfortunately, rather than noodling ideas around, Guy Thorne had pretty much steered the conversation in the direction he seemed most comfortable with. That is, his theory that Reginald Doyle had been accidentally shot with a stray bullet and that the subsequent fire was probably the result of faulty wiring.

Thorne was pitching his heart out, trying hard to sell his story, but Theodosia wasn't buying it. Neither was Drayton.

Now they stood in Trollope's foyer with its dark wood paneling and checkerboard floor of black-and-white tiles, saying good night, thanking Meredith for the lovely dinner and Guy for the excellent Bordeaux.

A moment later, as Guy draped Meredith's coat around her shoulders, Drayton pulled Theodosia aside and said, "Do you believe any of Thorne's theories?"

"Not a one," Theodosia said.

"I thought not." Drayton sighed and said, "Listen, I'm going to escort Meredith back to her suite at the Lady Goodwood Inn. See if I can pull something more out of her."

"Shall I give you two a lift?" Theodosia asked.

Drayton shook his head. "No, you go on home. We'll walk. It's only a block or so, and I suspect the fresh air will do Meredith good."

Theodosia lifted an eyebrow. "And help you digest that whopping dinner?"

Drayton curled a lip. "Only time will tell."

"Okay, see you tomorrow."

When Theodosia turned to the coat check desk, the young woman who'd been managing it had stepped away. Giving a small shrug, not really worrying about protocol, she ducked in and grabbed her jacket. It was then that her eyes fell upon a small painting that was hung on the wood-paneled wall. Two men engaged in a pistol duel. Theodosia leaned forward and read the notation at the bottom of the frame. *The 7th Earl of Cardigan firing his pistol at one of his former officers.*

Dueling pistols.

An idea suddenly ignited in Theodosia's brain.

Pulling on her jacket, she ran back into the restaurant. The main dining room was dark and almost deserted. Candles flickered;

none of the waitstaff were in sight. Just two tables of people with their heads together, engaged in quiet conversation.

Perfect.

Theodosia moved swiftly toward the fireplace. Then, without hesitation, she stepped up onto the stone hearth, reached up, and ran a hand over the tops of both pistols.

Dusty. They hadn't been used in ages.

Feeling slightly foolish and a little bit disappointed, Theodosia hopped down and silently clapped her hands together. So much for that idea.

"Theodosia," a low voice called to her.

Startled, Theodosia turned to find Guy Thorne staring at her with a look of strange intensity.

"Come join me for a drink in the bar," he said. "A nightcap. We have some forty-year-old tawny port that we reserve for special guests."

"No, thank you," Theodosia demurred. "It's late and I really need to get home."

And I have a boyfriend. A serious boyfriend who is a detective first grade in the Charleston Police Department's Robbery and Homicide Division.

Thorne moved closer and put a hand on Theodosia's arm.

"Excuse me?" she said, pulling away.

96

"Relax. This isn't about drinking or making a pass or anything like that."

Theodosia's brows knit together. "I'm sorry, what exactly are you driving at?"

Thorne balanced on the balls of his feet, and his expression remained fairly intense, as if he was working up to something important. Then he said, "You know about Meredith, don't you?"

Theodosia was instantly on alert.

"What about Meredith?"

A low buzzing started up inside Theodosia's head. It was the kind of electrical pulse you felt right before a severe storm. A sort of crackling energy flooding the universe.

"About her prowess with a gun," Thorne said.

Oh no. Please, no.

"Meredith happens to be a crack shot," Thorne said in a rush. "She won the South Carolina Women's Game Shooting Competition three years in a row."

Theodosia gave a slow reptilian blink. Was Thorne making this up? Was this some crazy ploy to curry favor with her? She stared into his intense, hooded eyes. No, she didn't think so. For one thing, Guy Thorne looked drop-dead serious.

Okay, I'll bite.

"Handguns or long guns?" Theodosia asked.

"Both."

"Did you tell Sheriff Burney about this?"

Thorne's head bobbed. "I absolutely did, because I figured it might be relevant."

Theodosia shifted nervously as she continued to stare at Thorne. "So why are you telling me?"

"Because you're supposedly" — he crooked his fingers into air quotes — "looking into things."

"Mr. Thorne, you seem to be implying that Meredith shot her own husband."

Thorne reared back. "No, no," he hastened to say. "All I'm saying is she *could* have shot him. That it's a possibility." When he saw the look of consternation on Theodosia's face, he said, "Listen, I happen to like Meredith. I like her a lot. I suppose she's become my de facto business partner now that Reginald's dead. But the facts are the facts, and there's no getting around the truth that Meredith is extremely adept at handling weapons."

Theodosia's immediate impulse was to be suspicious of Thorne's sly accusation. Was it possible that Thorne was trying to deflect blame from himself? Maybe. Still, this new revelation about Meredith was both unnerv-

98

ing and intriguing.

Okay, I'll go along with this for the time being. Play a little liar's poker.

"Would Meredith have had a reason to kill Reginald?" Theodosia asked.

Thorne gave an offhand shrug. "I don't know. Money? Inheritance?"

Theodosia digested this. She knew that money — namely, greed — was the critical motivating factor that drove most criminal acts.

Thorne dropped his voice to a low growl. "Plus, they weren't getting along all that well."

This last bit of information sounded preposterous to Theodosia. When she'd seen Reginald and Meredith together — right before Reginald was killed — they'd appeared to be an extremely loving couple.

Theodosia decided to toss out one of her cards.

"I heard a rumor that Reginald was going to leave Creekmore Plantation to the Heritage Society."

Thorne wasn't a bit surprised by Theodosia's statement.

"That might have been the original plan," Thorne said. He glanced around to make sure no one was listening, then added, "But

I know for an absolute fact that Reginald
never got around to putting it in his will."

8

Earl Grey was restless tonight. Theodosia's dog paced about the kitchen in her small cottage, walking back and forth, back and forth.

Click. Click. Click.

His toenails scritched and scratched against the tile floor.

"I'm sorry about the way the kitchen looks," Theodosia told her dog. "But if we're ever going to have new cabinets and counters, we're going to have to put up with this mess."

Earl Grey just stared at her. With his limpid brown eyes, fine-boned muzzle, and expressive ear flicks, he could pretty much communicate anything he wanted. And tonight he wanted an explanation.

"It's the reclaimed wood," Theodosia explained. "We're waiting for the cabinet-maker to strip it out of a barn that's being torn down. There's some problem." She reached over to Earl Grey's treat jar, pulled out a jerky strip, and gave it to him. "I don't know the *exact* problem, but it should be resolved within the next few days. I hope." Fact was, she was tired of dealing with this mess, too.

Earl Grey chewed, swallowed, and stared at her again.

"That's it, that's all I know," Theodosia said as the phone rang. She picked it up, expecting it to be Drayton, calling to complain about a severe case of heartburn.

It wasn't Drayton.

"I understand you were a guest at Creekmore Plantation yesterday," came a warm, familiar male voice.

"Where did you hear that?" Theodosia asked. It was Pete Riley, detective with the Charleston Police Department, barbecue aficionado, occasional sailor, and boyfriend extraordinaire.

Was this man privy to every nit and nat of information in the county?

"Please. I'm a detective first grade."

"Speaking as a professional, then, do you have any advice for me?"

"Yes. Stay out of it."

"How do you know I'm even in it?"

There was a warm, rumbling laugh, and

then Riley said, "Because I know you, my dear."

"Well, yesterday's shooting party did turn into a bit of a catastrophe," Theodosia said.

"I can just imagine." Riley paused. "Here I run off to Hilton Head for one lousy weekend of golf with my buddies, and when I get back I find you up to your ears in another murder investigation."

"I'm not up to my ears," Theodosia said lightly. *Yet.*

"Then you've waded in hip deep. The point being, I'd prefer you keep your distance. From what I've heard so far, this is going to be a nasty, complicated case."

"What have you heard?" Theodosia asked.

"See? There you go."

"I'm just curious."

"I know you are," Riley said. "But just . . . no."

"Come on," she joked. "I'm not trying to interrupt the space-time continuum; I'm just looking for a little information."

Theodosia thought back to when she'd first met Pete Riley. He'd showed up to interview some witnesses after a particularly nasty incident — actually, it was a poisoning — at a fancy tea party. He'd been polite, diligent, and circumspect even when he questioned a particularly skeevy waiter who was a possible suspect. Then, at the end, when he'd finally spoken with Theodosia, there had been a tiny spark. Not Fourth of July rockets, not yet, but a tingle, a hint of interest. Then, when Riley had asked all his questions, he'd closed his notebook, smiled at her, and said, "Is Browning your married name?" That's when she knew she'd be seeing him again. And again and again. And calling him Riley. Not Pete, not detective, just Riley. Because it just worked for them.

"Let's go out for dinner one evening this week," Riley said, abruptly changing the subject. "Grab a table in a dark corner, order up a little wine and candlelight. Do it up right. The full Monty."

"I'd love that."

"Okay, I'll make reservations."

When Theodosia got off the phone with Riley, she straightened up the kitchen as best she could, ran upstairs, and changed into leggings and a hoodie. When she came back down, she brewed a pot of chamomile tea, poured out a cup, and carried it into her living room. She was eager to relax in her cozy cottage with its stone fireplace, exposed beams, mishmash of French and English furniture, and Aubusson rugs. She settled into a chintz-covered chair, sipped her tea, but still found herself at sixes and sevens.

Earl Grey had shadowed her every step of the way and was now staring at her intently.

"What?" Theodosia asked.

Earl Grey sat down and continued to stare at her. He was part dalmatian, part Labrador. In other words, a very clever-at-getting-his-way Dalbrador.

"You want to go for a walk."

At hearing the word *walk,* Earl Grey's tail thunked eagerly against the floorboards.

"Mrs. Barry didn't run you around the block enough times today?" Mrs. Barry was Earl Grey's dog walker and doggy day care person.

Earl Grey stared at the back door as if he were Uri Geller and the intensity of his gaze could cause the door to magically fly open.

"I know, I've been gone for the past two days, and for that I apologize. But just a quick walk, okay? It's getting late, and I've got to be at the tea shop early tomorrow." She was already reaching for Earl Grey's leash.

Two minutes later, they were out the back door and hurrying through the lush foliage of Theodosia's small backyard. A month ago, Drayton had come over and trimmed one of her juniper trees into the shape of a bonsai. A cloud bonsai he'd called it, pruned to reveal bits of trunk with fat clusters of needles fashioned into large, poufy, cloud-like shapes. Then he'd brought over something called a Taihu rock. It was a light-gray humpy-bumpy rock with unusual squiggles and holes that resembled a miniature mountain and looked spectacularly good sitting next to her small fishpond.

"You guys okay in there?" Theodosia asked as she bent over to gaze into the pond, where a half-dozen goldfish swam around slowly. "Never can be too careful."

Raccoons had swooped in more than once to make this their own personal sushi bar, so Theodosia and Earl Grey had to remain ever vigilant.

Seconds later, they were out the back gate and jogging down a dark alley, Theodosia's footfalls echoing in the night, Earl Grey's collar jingling an accompaniment. They ran down Tradd Street, crossed over to Legare, and kept going.

As Theodosia passed one of dozens of churches that gave Charleston the moniker of the "Holy City," she glanced up at the lighted clock tower. Just then, the hands struck ten o'clock, and ten melodic chimes bonged out.

They continued their run down King Street past the Charleston Library Society.

Tendrils of fog were beginning to drift in from Charleston Harbor, creating a halo effect around the streetlamps and softening the outlines of houses, wrought-iron fences, and the occasional marble statue. Charleston, a city that was already highly atmospheric, looked positively magical when blessed with this softer, less distinct outline.

As Theodosia sprinted along, her legs and shoulders began to warm up and she felt the first blip of feel-good endorphins kicking in. She decided to keep going, and it wasn't long before she found herself running past Trollope's and then the Lady Goodwood Inn. She wondered if Drayton was still inside the inn, being his most solicitous and trying to ease Meredith's troubled mind with soothing words. Then Theodosia decided it was way too late for all of that. Drayton was probably puttering around at home by now, listening to an opera, or sitting in an easy chair reading his beloved Dickens.

Running past the front entrance to the Lady Goodwood Inn, Theodosia was struck by how lovely the place was. A circular drive led to an entrance fronted with white Doric columns and a green canvas awning. Each side of the entrance was flanked by a half-dozen palmetto trees.

Theodosia hadn't visited the inn for some time and wondered if they'd repaired the solarium after flying debris from a disastrous summer storm had punched holes in several of the windows. She cut through the parking lot and circled round the building, enchanted by this lovely brick edifice with its elegant white shutters and tangles of green ivy that curled halfway up the sides of the structure.

Then she spotted the solarium. Yes, it had definitely been repaired. Several new octagonal-shaped frosted windows had been put in place, and now they glowed warmly from the inside lights. Faint outlines of large potted palms and hanging plants were also visible, making the solarium look like some kind of human terrarium. In fact, Theodosia could even see faint outlines of two people moving about inside.

How lovely, Theodosia thought as she slowed down to enjoy the moody, almost otherworldly, glow of the place.

And that's when a pair of raised voices suddenly started up and caught her attention. Snatches of conversation from the two people — she thought it was a man and a woman — made it sound as if they were arguing rather vehemently. Then the woman's voice rose to a shrill octave that startled

Theodosia beyond belief, because the voice sounded exactly like Meredith Doyle — a very upset, freaked-out Meredith Doyle!

Could it really be Meredith in there?

Theodosia stepped onto the brick patio, Earl Grey padding along beside her. She didn't exactly want to eavesdrop, knowing it was wrong, but she was drawn in by her curiosity.

Curiosity killed the cat, a voice in Theodosia's head warned.

Yes, and someone killed Meredith's husband.

Could it have been Meredith herself who fired the deadly shot? Had Meredith actually been desperate to rid herself of Reginald? Guy Thorne had certainly implied such a thing.

Theodosia tiptoed closer, weaving her way past outdoor tables with collapsed Cinzano umbrellas that were folded flat like bat wings.

Standing just inches from the frosted glass now, Theodosia could make out a ghostly outline of spider plants hanging inside.

And the outlines of two people.

For a moment she worried it might be Drayton arguing with Meredith. But no, that couldn't be. He was surely home by now.

The pair continued to argue, but now they'd lowered their voices, almost as if they were suddenly nervous that someone might be eavesdropping.

Like me.

The two figures moved closer to the frosted windows, their shadows wavering and lengthening, as if they were leaning forward and attempting to peer outside.

Theodosia held her breath. Didn't move a muscle. She waited ten, twenty, thirty seconds, eyes closed, not daring to move. Finally, she leaned forward and put an ear to the glass.

But by then the people inside had disappeared.

9

Tuesday morning tea service had barely gotten started when Theodosia leaned across the counter to Drayton and said, "I think I might have a definitive answer for Timothy."

"You mean about Reginald's will?" Drayton asked. He popped a miniature wicker basket inside a red teapot, added a scoop of gunpowder green tea leaves, and stared at her expectantly.

"According to Guy Thorne, Reginald never got around to signing his will."

"You spoke to Guy Thorne about this last night? After we left?" Drayton asked.

"Um, he pulled me aside, yes."

Drayton put a hand up and gently touched his cheek, as if deep in thought. "So Creekmore Plantation has *not* been bequeathed to the Heritage Society."

"Not according to Thorne."

"And you believed him?" Drayton asked. "It's hard to take seriously a man who dresses like a Fleet Street tout."

Theodosia suppressed a smile and said, "I gotta tell you, Thorne seemed fairly certain about the state of Doyle's will."

"Then our dear Timothy is going to be extremely disappointed."

"There's more," Theodosia said. "I haven't even gotten to the severely weird part yet."

"What are you talking about?" Now Drayton's curiosity was beginning to amp up.

Theodosia dropped her bombshell.

"Guy Thorne thinks Meredith could have shot her own husband."

Drayton's entire body jerked spasmodically and then went ramrod stiff, as if he'd been poked hard with an electric wire then tossed into a bathtub full of ice. "No!" he cried.

"Well, yes. The thing is, Thorne claims that Meredith is a crack shot. That she took first place in something called the South Carolina Women's Game Shooting Competition. And she did it several years in a row."

"That sounds suspiciously like the demented ravings of a guilty man."

"That's what I thought at first, too," Theodosia said. "That Thorne was trying to throw up some kind of smoke screen. Then I looked up the shooting competition on the Internet last night. Thorne was right.

Meredith was the big winner three years in a row."

"I had no idea Meredith enjoyed that sort of prowess with a gun. What you say is beyond chilling."

"So," Theodosia said. "My question to you is — would Meredith shoot her own husband? *Could* she shoot him? And if so, why?"

"I . . . I don't know." Drayton looked stunned. "I'm still trying to digest all these different bits of information."

"Along with last night's dinner?"

Drayton gave a subtle eye roll. "With apologies to Lord Wellington, remind me never to order his beef again."

"Okay, break it up, break it up," Haley said. "I got a delivery coming through." She elbowed her way to the counter, balancing a large silver tray that was piled sky-high with blueberry muffins, banana bread, and lemon scones.

"Looks as if someone's been busy," Theodosia said.

"Yes, obviously, but these baked goods have to last us all day," Haley warned. "Because . . . because now I have to rush back into the kitchen and focus every drop of energy, every molecule I have, on whipping up a fabulous luncheon for our *Gone with the Wind* Tea."

Theodosia held up a finger. "About that menu . . ."

"Drayton has it," Haley called over her shoulder as she disappeared into the kitchen like a wisp of smoke.

Theodosia shifted her focus to Drayton. "It's a good menu?"

Drayton put his thumb and index finger together. "Perfection. Rather amusing, too."

"Tell me."

"I'd rather you tell me more about Meredith and her modern-day Annie Oakley antics."

"That's it. That's the extent of what I know based on Guy Thorne's say-so and a few stats on the Internet," Theodosia said. She paused as the front door flew open and Miss Dimple rushed in. Just barely over five feet tall, she was round, plump, and had a halo of silver-white hair. If you called central casting and asked for the perfect sweet-faced grandma, they'd send over Miss Dimple.

"Am I late?" Miss Dimple asked with wide-eyed eagerness as she toddled up to the counter.

"Your timing is perfect," Drayton said.

"We're just happy you could help out today," Theodosia told her.

Miss Dimple waved a hand. "Pish-posh.

You know I adore being part of the Indigo Tea Shop gang. And today — this *Gone with the Wind* Tea that you're hosting — is an absolute thrill." Her face puckered into an adorable grin. "If I remember correctly, we're all going to assume the role of a character from the book?" Then, without pausing to take a breath, she said, "Can I please, *please,* be Aunt Pittypat?"

"Who else could fill such a critical and demanding role?" Drayton asked.

Miss Dimple turned to Theodosia. "And I'll just bet that Drayton's going to be Rhett Butler."

Theodosia's eyes twinkled mischievously. "Who else could you see playing such a rogue?"

"Not another soul!" Miss Dimple declared. "Although Drayton does seem to be the perfect gent." She grabbed a long black Parisian waiter's apron and slipped it over her head.

"You see," Theodosia said to Drayton, "she doesn't know you like I do."

Drayton managed a crooked smile. "So I'm *not* a perfect gent?"

"You're a gent," Theodosia allowed. "Just not always a perfect one."

They all got busy then as more customers arrived for morning tea. Scones, muffins, and banana bread were served along with traditional jams, jellies, and Haley's homemade Devonshire cream.

"The Devonshire cream goes best with these lemon scones?" Miss Dimple asked, pointing to Haley's tray.

"Yes, and I've been serving the banana bread with pear butter," Theodosia said.

"I have a pot of Rum Raisin Biscotti tea ready for table four," Drayton said.

"Sounds delicious. Is that one of your special blends?" Miss Dimple asked.

"No, you can thank Tea Forte for that one."

At eleven o'clock, just as Theodosia had delivered a pot of toasted coconut oolong to table two, Bill Glass sauntered into the tea shop. Glass was the writer, photographer, and publisher of his own local tabloid, *Shooting Star.* The paper was glitzy, dishy, and weirdly popular with that segment of the populace who delighted in having their garden parties, cocktail events, and fancy soirees splashed across his front pages in colorful but slightly off-register photos.

Theodosia elbowed her way past Glass to get to the counter. "What are you doing here?" she asked him. Between handling a roomful of customers, checking on Haley's progress in the kitchen, and fretting over their upcoming luncheon, she had her hands full. Everything had to be perfect, right?

Glass flashed a lopsided smile at her. Dressed in a khaki photojournalist's vest and combat fatigues, with two Nikons and a shabby scarf draped around his neck, he had continued expectations that he'd be taken for a war correspondent.

"What's going on?" Theodosia asked, looking at his quasi-military outfit. "Are you sneaking into Kabul? Expecting to be dropped out of a Black Hawk helicopter?"

Glass ignored her sarcasm and said, "I was hoping you'd spill the beans about the cold-blooded murder that took place this past Sunday at Happy Farm."

"Not on your life," Theodosia replied. She grabbed two teapots and carried them to tables five and six.

When she circled back to the counter, Glass tried again.

"Come on, tea lady, you were right there for the grand bloodbath, weren't you? And if I recall correctly, you're the snoopy one who likes to plop herself right in the middle of a good mystery — right?"

"Not at all," Theodosia said.

Glass leaned closer. "I'll bet you've picked up all sorts of juicy information that my readers would love to drool over."

"You're talking to the wrong person."

"Who should I talk to, then?" Glass asked. "Meredith Doyle?"

His words stopped Theodosia cold. "No," she said sharply. "You leave Meredith alone. She's got enough problems without you badgering her."

"You mean because she's one of the suspects?"

"Why on earth would you think that?" Theodosia tried to keep her voice perfectly neutral.

Glass's smile was smarmy and self-assured. "I have my sources."

Theodosia didn't want to waste precious time verbally jousting with Bill Glass, so she poured him a take-out cup of Darjeeling and placed a lemon scone in a waxed paper bag.

"Here," she said, shoving everything into his hands. "A takeaway tea party. Have fun. Enjoy."

"Is this a subtle way of asking me to leave?" Glass opened the bag and took a big bite out of his scone. "Oh yeah, tasty."

"I'm afraid we're frantically busy and have to prepare for an event tea. So, yes, kindly leave us to our mania," Theodosia said. She was firm with Glass but not unkind.

"Okay, tea lady, but I'll be back," Glass said. His mouth was so crammed full of pastry it sounded like, *I'll buh buk.* In fact, he was still chewing vigorously as he strolled toward the front door.

Theodosia watched as Glass pulled open the door, cried, "Whoops!" and did a comical sideways maneuver to allow a messenger carrying a ginormous cardboard box to step through the doorway.

"Wow," Glass called back to her. "Looks like you guys got some kind of supersized delivery." He waved. "Okay, see ya." Nobody waved back.

Theodosia was happy to see that her rented costumes from Big Top Costumes over on Fulton Street had arrived.

"Whatcha got?" Miss Dimple asked as Theodosia tipped the messenger then muscled the large box onto the counter.

"Our costumes are here," Theodosia said. *Thank goodness.*

"Is there one in there for me?"

Theodosia opened the box and pulled out a canary yellow dress with puffed sleeves and a flouncy, ruffled skirt. "Here you go," she said, handing it to Miss Dimple. Her hand dipped back into the box. "Oh, and a fan to go along with it."

"What if the dress doesn't fit?" Miss

Dimple stage-whispered. "I don't exactly have my girlish figure anymore."

"The dresses all lace in back," Theodosia said.

"Thanks be praised."

A second later, Haley was also there, sniffing around. Haley loved a good theme party as much as the next guy.

"Got a costume for me, too?" Haley asked.

Theodosia pulled out a peach-colored dress and passed it to Haley. "How about this one?"

"Fab," Haley said as she held her costume against her and smiled.

Theodosia glanced at Drayton, who'd been suspiciously quiet. "We've got a costume for you, too, Drayton."

Drayton frowned. "Great Caesar's ghost, you don't expect *me* to wear a costume, do you? What if I spilled tea on it? What if I . . . ?"

"Get with the program, Drayton," Haley said. "We're all wearing costumes." Sweet little Haley could be a stickler for order, a little martinet issuing commands, when she wanted to be.

"I'd feel foolish," Drayton said.

Haley laughed. "Good grief, Drayton, it's only a tie and tails. It's not like we're asking you to strip to your skivvies and put on a bright-yellow SpongeBob costume or something."

"SpongeBob?" Drayton said. "What is . . . ?"

"Aw, forget it," Haley said.

Drayton poked a finger in her direction. "Gotcha."

Once their morning customers had departed, everyone buckled down to make sure the tea room was perfect for lunch. Tables were draped in white linen tablecloths, shawls were placed artfully across the backs of chairs, and table centerpieces consisting of pots of magnolias, lace fans, diamond earbobs (faux, of course), and copies of Gone with the Wind were added to the tables.

Theodosia selected silver candelabras and added white tapers, then chose Chelsea Garden dinnerware by Spode and Gorham Buttercup sterling flatware to add even more Southern grace to their tables. She always tried to create the perfect tea shop experience for her guests. In Theodosia's mind, teatime wasn't a luxury at all, but a basic requirement for both body and soul.

Moments later, amid raucous laughter and a few groans, they all slithered into their costumes. Theodosia ended up wearing a green-and-white dress, similar to the one Scarlett O'Hara wore to the Twelve Oaks barbecue, Haley looked splendid in her pink dress, Miss Dimple was the picture of a fine Peachtree Street doyenne, and Drayton wore his tie and tails like a true Charleston gentleman.

As the pièce de résistance, a life-size cutout of Rhett Butler was placed near the front door.

"Stand over there next to Rhett," Haley instructed Drayton. "I want to get a picture of the two of you."

"There's a top hat here, too," Theodosia said, pulling a hat from the bottom of the box.

Drayton put it on obediently, then stood next to Rhett and draped an arm over his cardboard shoulder.

"Hurry up and take the picture," Drayton begged. He was fast losing his good humor.

"Just one more," Haley said, adjusting her camera phone. "Smile now. I want to make sure I get a really good shot of you guys to post on our Facebook page."

Drayton's smile turned to absolute shock. "Post on our . . . Wait! . . . What?"

10

After considerable coaching and kibitzing from Theodosia, Haley, and Miss Dimple, Drayton stood at the front door greeting their guests with "Good morning, ladies," as he tipped his hat and gave a roguish wink.

Theodosia smiled, checked off guests' names from her list, then led them to the appropriate tables, where Miss Dimple hovered with steaming pots of tea. The guests had come for tea, and by golly, she was going to make sure they were served their tea — fresh and hot and aromatic.

Theodosia greeted Brooke Carter Crockett, the owner of Hearts Desire Jewelers, as well as Maggie Twining, her Realtor, and Angie Congdon from the Featherbed House B and B down the block. Then another dozen of her regulars showed up — Jill and her daughter Kristen, as well as their friends Linda and Judi and Jessica.

Finally, when almost all the guests were

seated and the Indigo Tea Shop buzzed with excitement and friendly conversation, Meredith and Fawn arrived.

They weren't exactly garbed in old-fashioned mourning clothes, but they were wearing dark tailored clothing, and their demeanor was fairly subdued as Theodosia led them to a table for two near the window that looked out upon Church Street. She hoped this lovely view would help lift their spirits.

"Thank you," Meredith said as she took her seat. "I'm praying this tea party will be a welcome prescription for us. A quiet respite in what's been a horrid couple of days." She smiled faintly at Fawn, who nodded obediently.

"Is there any news?" Theodosia asked. "Anything at all?" She told herself she wasn't prying; she was simply curious. Especially after Guy Thorne's shocking revelation last night, coupled with the argument she'd overheard outside the Lady Goodwood's solarium.

Meredith smoothed her skirt and pursed her lips. "Perhaps," she said.

"Tell her," Fawn urged. "Tell Theodosia what's going on. You asked for her help, practically begged her. Now you've got to keep her in the loop."

"What's going on?" Theodosia asked. *Something happened?*

Fawn shot a meaningful look at Meredith, who still seemed reluctant to say anything.

"Then I'll tell her," Fawn said. She gazed at Theodosia with a determined expression on her normally placid face and pushed back a hank of curly brown hair. "As of this morning, Sheriff Burney is officially investigating Jack Grimes, the caretaker."

You could have knocked Theodosia over with a feather.

"Jack Grimes!" Theodosia exclaimed. "Investigated for murder?" She was practically sputtering now. "But I thought Grimes had been with your family . . . that he'd worked at Creekmore Plantation for *ages.*" She looked pointedly at Meredith. "In fact, when I saw your husband and Grimes together this past Sunday, organizing the group, getting the dogs and gear all set up, I had the feeling they were quite close."

"They were. At one time," Meredith said.

"He's the one who shot Pop," Fawn said under her breath. "I just know it."

"We don't know anything for sure," Meredith said in a cautionary tone. But she didn't look like she was about to rush to Grimes's defense anytime soon.

"Here now," Miss Dimple said, coming

125

up to the table, a teapot in each hand. "You have your choice of Lapsang souchong or a black tea citrus blend. What's it to be, ladies?"

"The citrus blend," Meredith said. "For both of us."

As Theodosia wandered through the tea shop, greeting her guests, checking to make sure everyone was comfortable and cozy, she couldn't help but think about Meredith and her prowess with guns.

Meredith could have been the shooter. Or, for that matter, so could Guy Thorne. There was something about Thorne that was . . . unsavory. But now, strangely enough, the blame seemed to have tipped in the direction of Jack Grimes. So . . . with several key suspects on the line, she had a lot to think about. But first, there was a tea party that needed hosting.

Thankfully, Drayton already had the audience well in hand.

"Ladies," Drayton said as he stepped to the center of the tea room, "if I could have your attention please." The tea room instantly quieted down. "Scarlett O'Hara may have demanded that her biscuits and gravy be taken back to the kitchen so she could eat her fill at the barbecue, but I can guarantee" — he glanced around the tea room

— "that once you hear today's luncheon offerings, you won't want to send anything back."

Now there was hearty laughter.

Drayton gave a sweeping bow and said, "Theodosia, will you do the honors?"

This was Theodosia's cue to step into the middle of the room.

"Welcome, everyone," she said, her voice ringing out clear and strong. "I'm delighted you could join us today for our first-ever *Gone with the Wind* Tea. Because Ashley Wilkes famously said he liked to see a girl with a healthy appetite, we'll be starting our luncheon service with a sweet potato scone accompanied with honey and jam."

There were giggles and a spatter of applause.

"Fiddledeedee," Theodosia said. "It sounds as if you like everything so far." She gave a deep curtsy and continued. "We'll follow with an apple-pecan salad, and for your main entrée, we'll be serving our famous Twelve Oaks barbecue sandwiches with caramelized onions. For dessert, you shall have your choice of Georgia peach cobbler or Scarlett O'Hara cake — this particular cake being a rich red velvet cake highly reminiscent of Scarlett's infamous red dress."

127

There were audible sighs along with appreciative murmurs.

Then Drayton stepped in again and said, "For your sipping pleasure, we'll be pouring my special peach and black tea blend as well as peach iced tea."

That was the signal for Miss Dimple and Haley to emerge from the kitchen, balancing trays with the first course. They served piping hot sweet potato scones along with honey and jam while Theodosia patrolled the tea room, checking every detail, making sure everyone was not only satisfied, but thoroughly enjoying themselves.

"I love your dress." Theodosia's friend Brooke grabbed her arm and pulled her in close. "In that frock you look like you're ready to dance up a storm with the Tarleton boys."

"But first I have to stomp my foot and throw a plaster figurine at Rhett," Theodosia responded.

"I love it!" Brooke shrieked.

"Excuse me, ladies, but did I hear my name mentioned?" Drayton drawled. "I hope it was in a favorable context."

"You make a very dashing Rhett Butler," Brooke told him.

Drayton tipped his hat. "Thank you kindly, ma'am."

The luncheon was a hit. After the scones, the apple-pecan salads were eaten and exclaimed over, and then the barbeque sandwiches drew absolute raves. Haley had outdone herself with her topping of caramelized onions sautéed in a spicy, honeyed sauce. The barbecue meat, served on puffy, oversize buns, was both sweet and savory, imparting just enough heat that guests drank cup after cup of tea.

"It's all going awfully well, don't you think?" Drayton whispered to Theodosia.

"Couldn't be better," she whispered back.

In no time at all, they were ferrying their dessert courses of peach cobbler and red velvet cake to all their guests.

Except for Meredith.

When Miss Dimple brought two pieces of cake to Meredith's table, she shook her head adamantly and rose from her chair. Then she gave an imperious glance about the tea room and crooked a finger at Theodosia.

Who, me?

Theodosia hurried over to Meredith's table. "Is there a problem? A different dessert or sweet that I can bring you instead?"

"Not a thing, dear," Meredith said. "Your food and hospitality have been absolutely unparalleled. It's just that I have to leave."

"I'm sorry to hear that. You're going to

miss out on a couple of truly sinful desserts."

"Give my share to Fawn," Meredith said. She pulled a fur scarf around her neck and tied it. "Unfortunately" — she dropped her voice to a low whisper — "I have to deal with certain arrangements." She carefully enunciated the word *arrangements* as if she were discussing classified CIA documents.

"The funeral," Theodosia said.

Meredith shook her head. "It won't be a funeral per se. My idea is to create an event that's far more upbeat. Such as . . . a memorial."

Same thing, Theodosia thought.

"It's scheduled to take place at the Heritage Society this Thursday morning," Fawn said. She'd already dug into her red velvet cake and showed no intention of abandoning her dessert to leave with Meredith.

"So I was wondering," Meredith continued as she patted the scarf at her neck. "Could you possibly cater a small luncheon for us? I mean, transport the food — maybe tea sandwiches and such — from here to the Heritage Society? Set it up and make it look elegant?" She peered at Theodosia expectantly. "Would that be a problem?"

"Not at all. We've catered dozens of events at the Heritage Society," Theodosia said.

"They even have a small kitchen that's quite serviceable."

"Wonderful," Meredith said. "That's one problem solved."

"How many people will be attending this, uh, memorial?"

"I'll have to let you know, dear. Right now I'm . . ." Meredith glanced at her bejeweled Chopard watch as she started for the front door. "I'm terribly late."

More tea was poured, and a few guests even opted (begged) for a second dessert, which Haley was happy to oblige. By one thirty, two-thirds of the guests had departed, and the final third was milling about the tea room, shopping for tins of tea, jars of honey, and quilted tea cozies, as well as admiring shelves of giftware and the wall filled with grapevine and teacup wreaths.

Theodosia positioned herself behind the counter, where she could ring up purchases, thank departing guests, and remind a few of them about the Lavender Lady Tea on Saturday.

When only a handful of guests were left, Theodosia noticed that Fawn was one of them. She was perusing the label on one of the T-Bath products but going about it in a somewhat listless fashion.

131

Oh no. Problem?

Theodosia stepped away from the counter and walked over to join Fawn.

"Fawn, you seem suddenly pensive," she said in a kind, concerned voice. "Are you okay? Would it help to talk about it?"

Fawn stared at Theodosia, then a strange, crooked smile appeared on her face. "You think I'm upset about Reginald, don't you?"

"Aren't you?" Theodosia asked.

Fawn shook her head, her long gold earrings swishing against her neck. "My father-in-law and I weren't particularly close."

"Okay," Theodosia said. Then what could be wrong? Where was this conversation going? Was it about to turn into some sort of confessional? Because it seemed as if Fawn wanted to say more. A lot more.

Finally, she did.

"It's just that . . . things haven't been good at home," Fawn said.

"You mean at Creekmore?" Theodosia asked.

"I mean between me and Alex," Fawn said. She was suddenly swallowing hard and struggling to hold back a flow of tears.

"Oh, honey," Theodosia said. "All newly-weds have problems in their first year of marriage."

"But Alex has a temper," Fawn whispered.

132

"A really horrible temper."

Theodosia's heart immediately went out to the girl. "Fawn, why don't you come with me." She took Fawn by the hand and led her back to the office. When Fawn was settled in the big, cozy brocade chair they'd dubbed the Tuffet, Theodosia handed her a box of Kleenex tissues and said, "Is there anything I can do to help?"

Fawn shook her head. "I don't think so."

Theodosia plunged ahead anyway. Because clearly something was wrong.

"Fawn, do you . . . Are you . . . in an unsafe environment?" There, she'd spoken the dreaded words.

Fawn's chin quivered. "I don't know. Maybe."

"Honey," Theodosia said as she watched a sudden torrent of tears spill down Fawn's face. "Is Alex . . . He hasn't been physically abusive to you, has he?"

"He hasn't hit me, if that's what you mean." Fawn gave a loud hiccup as she dabbed at her eyes. "But he screams at me all the time. Tells me how stupid and ridiculous I am."

"That's abuse," Theodosia said. Her heart ached for the poor girl. How fast could verbal abuse turn into physical abuse? Probably in the blink of an eye. "Have you told

133

anyone about this? Talked to Meredith? Someone in your family? A close friend?"

Fawn shook her head. "Not yet. But I'm seriously thinking about leaving Alex. I can't take it anymore." Her eyes were sorrowful, and her alabaster complexion looked even paler.

"That's an awfully big step. Have the two of you considered seeing a marriage counselor?"

"I asked Alex to go to counseling with me, but he refused to even consider it. Said it would be a blight on his family name." Fawn picked out another tissue and blew her nose with a loud honk.

"There's no shame in going to counseling, to get an expert's help or opinion. If you'd like, maybe I could —"

A door slammed way at the front of the tea shop, followed by a harsh shout and then loud, pounding footsteps. Seconds later, Drayton's voice was raised in warning.

"Don't, sir," Drayton cried out. "Kindly do not —"

Theodosia's office door suddenly blew open!

Fawn let out a piercing shriek as Jack Grimes loomed in the doorway. His face glowed high-blood-pressure red, and in his

134

scruffy leather jacket, he looked like a refugee from a motorcycle gang.

Theodosia was on her feet in a heartbeat.

"What do you think you're doing?" she cried. "How dare you come bursting into my office like that!"

Grimes ignored Theodosia as he stumbled the rest of the way in. He was obviously a man hell-bent on a mission. His eyes burned with fury; his breath poured out in angry rasps. Grimes stared at Theodosia for a single hot moment, then he turned and pointed an accusing finger at Fawn.

"You!" Grimes shouted. "Do you know what your sniveling rat of a husband just did? He *fired* me!"

Theodosia held up both hands in a calming gesture, even though her nerves were strumming wildly.

"Whoa, whoa, whoa! Calm down, Mr. Grimes. Kindly show a modicum of respect here." Theodosia glanced past Grimes and saw a white-faced Drayton hovering in the doorway, just in case a show of force was required.

But Grimes wasn't about to settle down or pay one whit of attention to Theodosia. He was feverish with rage and poised to aim his vitriol directly at Fawn.

"Alex had no right to fire me!" Grimes

cried. "Because he isn't the one who's in charge. He hasn't inherited Creekmore Plantation *yet!*"

"Please, stop this immediately," Theodosia ordered. "Take a deep breath and try to calm down."

Grimes shook his head as if a horde of angry bees were buzzing around him.

"Now Sheriff Burney is questioning *me* about your father-in-law's death," Grimes spat out forcefully.

"You don't know that Sheriff Burney regards you as a suspect," Theodosia said. She was struggling to maintain an even tone, hoping to set a calming example.

Grimes stared at Theodosia and pulled his mouth into a grim line. "But I *do* know," he said. "This girl's dirtbag of a husband pointed his finger at me. Me!" He let loose another angry snort. "Jiminy Crystal, I've been working for Mr. Doyle for going on six years! I've been loyal to the man, been his employee and his *friend*! Do you really think I'd *murder* him?"

Fawn, who'd pulled herself into a tight little ball to ward off Grimes's rage, suddenly uncoiled herself and jumped up to face him.

"You could have! You might have!" Fawn shouted at Grimes.

"I didn't!" Grimes cried.

Fawn glared at him. "You don't know *any*thing. You have no *idea* what's going on!"

"Don't get snippy with me, Mrs. Fawn Doyle, to the manor born," Grimes yelled back. "I happen to know you used to work as a *waitress* at Buster's Bar over in Folly Beach. You weren't such a grand lady back then, no, sir. Not until you married Mr. Fancy Pants Alex Doyle!"

"I don't have to listen to your ridiculous ravings!" Fawn cried. "I don't have to listen to any of this crap!"

Fawn threw her head back, and just for a moment, Theodosia thought she was actually going to spit in Grimes's face. Instead, Fawn gathered herself together and stormed out of the office, brushing brusquely past Grimes and then Drayton, her high heels clacking loudly as she crossed the tea room floor.

Suddenly, Grimes looked like the air had been punched out of him.

Theodosia jumped on what she perceived as a possible opportunity to restore some measure of civility.

"Mr. Grimes, if you could find it in yourself to calm down, we could discuss these events rationally." She drew a deep breath. "Perhaps over a cup of tea?"

11

"I don't know what got into me," Grimes said. He was sitting directly across from Theodosia in the chair Fawn had just vacated. His right leg jiggled with nervous energy, but his head was bowed contritely, and he'd dialed back his anger.

"You were upset," Theodosia said. "You weren't thinking clearly."

Grimes lifted his head and swiped the back of his hand across his mouth. "I thought I was."

"That's the crazy thing about being blindsided by bad news. It hits you like a ton of bricks, and you never know how you're going to react. Hot, cold, whatever. Now . . ." Theodosia tapped a finger insistently against her desk. "Why exactly did Alex fire you?"

"I dunno," Grimes mumbled.

"Think hard. Try to recall his exact words," Theodosia said. "He must have given you some reason."

"He didn't." Grimes raised a hand and scratched the top of his head. "But I've been thinking . . . maybe by firing me, by trying to make me look guilty, he was trying to set me up?"

A lot of that going around, Theodosia thought to herself.

"You think Alex might have been trying to set you up for Mr. Doyle's murder?" Theodosia asked.

Grimes's thin shoulders hitched up a notch. "Yeah, maybe. I don't know." He exhaled slowly. "But please believe me when I say this: I didn't murder Mr. Doyle. And I sure didn't start that house fire."

"Knock, knock."

Startled by the interruption, they both glanced up.

"Pardon me," Drayton said, "but I've brought your tea." He stood in the doorway, holding a steaming cup and saucer in each hand. "A nice Fujian silver."

"Thank you, Drayton," Theodosia said as he passed her one of the cups of tea.

"And Mr. Grimes," Drayton said as he bent forward a trifle stiffly. "Tea for you, sir?"

"Uh, thank you," Grimes said, accepting the teacup from Drayton somewhat shakily.

"Will you be needing anything else?"

140

Drayton asked. With brows raised, he looked pointedly at Theodosia.

"We're good for now," Theodosia told him.

Drayton gave a perfunctory smile. "Just call if you need me." He turned and walked out, deliberately leaving the door wide open.

Theodosia took a sip of tea and said, "You mentioned that Sheriff Burney questioned you this morning?"

Grimes nodded. "Right after Alex fired me. It was like they had it all set up."

"Perhaps they did. Or maybe Sheriff Burney was just doing his job, covering all the bases. Did he ask you more questions about the murder?"

Now Grimes ducked his head, looking sheepish. "Mostly he wanted to dig into my past." He drew a shaky breath. "I know it's not good."

"What's not good about it?" Theodosia asked. Was there some nasty secret lurking in Grimes's background that she should know about?

Grimes took a sip of tea and said, "The thing is, I have sort of a criminal record. But it's from a long time ago, when I was just a kid. Boosting cars and . . . but that's not important. Mr. Doyle, he knew all about that nonsense and hired me anyway. He

141

came to trust me." Grimes let loose a shuddering sigh. "There's no way I'd have ever brought harm to that man."

"How did you get along with Meredith?"

"Fine, I guess. I didn't deal with her all that much."

"Were you aware of her shooting skills?"

Grimes nodded. "Oh yeah. She knew her way around firearms, that's for sure. Mr. Doyle was real proud of her, too. That lady could drill the right eye of a woodchuck at three hundred paces."

"That's quite amazing," Theodosia said, though Grimes's confirmation of Meredith's shooting skills had sent a slight chill oozing through her veins.

"She's a real pip," Grimes said.

"Tell me about the neighbors," Theodosia said. "I understand there was a terrible dispute going on between Reginald and Carl Clewis."

"It was more than a dispute. Those two guys despised each other."

"Do you know why?"

"All I know is that Clewis dammed up part of the creek. It didn't seem like a big deal to me; then again, it wasn't my land that got messed with."

"And Susan Monday? At the lavender farm?" Theodosia asked.

Grimes crossed his arms. "I never had any dealings with her at all."

"Let's get back to your accuser, Alex Doyle. He obviously filled Sheriff Burney in on your background."

Grimes nodded. "You got that right."

"And Alex might have fingered you as a suspect. But did Sheriff Burney take him seriously?"

"Seriously enough," Grimes grunted. "Because he sure asked me a lot of questions."

"I'd say it's obvious that you never got along with Alex."

"Alex is a spoiled rich kid who never did an honest day's work in his life!" Grimes blurted out. In an instant, his fire and fervor had once again bubbled to the surface.

"Now he's gone and fired you," Theodosia said.

"But he had no right. I guess I've gotta have a sit-down with Mrs. Doyle. She's the one in charge now. She's the one who says who stays and who goes," Grimes said. He blinked rapidly and added, as more of a question than anything, "Or maybe *you* could help me with these crazy accusations?"

Theodosia set her teacup down with a sharp *clink*. "Let me ask you something that might sound a trifle strange. Do you think Alex is a violent person? Does he have a violent temper?"

Grimes narrowed his eyes. "Are you kidding? Alex and Fawn fight like tigers all the time — day in and day out. You should hear those two once they get started, screaming at each other."

Theodosia leaned back in her chair. "Really?" This was completely unexpected. Fawn had made her rocky relationship sound extremely one-sided. As if Alex was the hotheaded spouse frothing with rage, the one who initiated all the disagreements.

Grimes was still shaking his head. "If you ask me, I don't know which one of them is crazier."

"What's the verdict?" Drayton asked, once Jack Grimes had left.

"Yes," Miss Dimple exclaimed. "Who's the guilty party?" She gave an excited little shiver and said, "Drayton's been feeding me snippets about the murder. And all the possible suspects." Miss Dimple was a fan of *Murder, She Wrote* and a rabid *Clue* player.

"Unfortunately, pretty much everyone seems to have had a motive to bump off Reginald Doyle," Theodosia said. "We've

144

got a virtual clown car full of suspects."

"So you haven't narrowed anything down yet," Drayton said.

"I'm not even close. But get this, Jack Grimes just asked for my help," Theodosia said.

Drayton lifted an eyebrow. "Help with . . ."

"To try to disentangle him from Alex's accusations."

"You *should* help him," Haley said suddenly. She was crouched nearby on her hands and knees, shoving white pillar candles into the lower half of a wooden cupboard.

"Pray tell, why is that?" Drayton asked her.

"Because I think he's sorta cute in a bad boy kind of way," Haley said.

Theodosia was amused in spite of herself. "Haley's a sucker for any guy in a leather motorcycle jacket," she said.

Drayton shook a warning finger at Haley. "Don't you dare get flirtatious with that man, do you hear me?"

"Why not?" Haley asked. She stood up and grabbed a plastic tub of dirty dishes off a nearby table. Held it in front of her like a shield. "Just because *you* think he's dangerous."

"That's exactly right. Grimes could be a

murderer!" Drayton cried.

"Hmm," Haley said, drawing the expression out thoughtfully. "Grimes didn't strike me as any kind of stone-cold killer."

"That girl!" Drayton exclaimed once Haley had disappeared with a few quick steps and a flip of her hair. "You can't tell her anything." He grabbed a teapot, thunked it down hard on the counter, and poured himself a cup of tea.

"Be careful," Miss Dimple cautioned. "If you tell Haley not to do something, she'll dig her heels in even deeper. She's stubborn that way."

Drayton frowned. "Sometimes dealing with her is like being a parent."

"Still, you have to go easy," Miss Dimple said. "She is an adult. You have to let her figure things out for herself."

Drayton gazed at Theodosia. "With all the excitement, I don't suppose you've had a chance to call Timothy yet. To tell him the bad news?"

"You mean tell him that the Heritage Society probably isn't going to inherit Reginald Doyle's property? No, I've been putting that off," Theodosia said.

Drayton looked distracted. "I suppose I could call him."

"Thank you."

"I'm going to go in your office and . . ." Drayton continued to mumble as he wandered off, his cup of tea in hand.

Miss Dimple stared at Theodosia, her gaze a mixture of worry and curiosity.

"You'd better be careful, too," she said as she folded her yellow dress and placed it back inside the cardboard box. "From everything Drayton's told me, this is a tricky case."

"You're afraid I might get in over my head?" Theodosia asked.

"I'm afraid you *are* in over your head."

By the time Drayton emerged from Theodosia's office, Miss Dimple had gone home, the closed sign was hung on the front door, and Theodosia had managed to straighten up the tea shop, getting it halfway back to normal.

"What did Timothy say?" Theodosia asked.

"He's extremely disappointed. Obviously," Drayton said. "The Heritage Society is still down when it comes to donations."

"But Timothy's not surprised about being left out of Reginald's will?"

"I think, deep down in his heart of hearts, Timothy knew it was too good to be true."

"No hard feelings, then? Timothy's still

amenable to allowing Reginald's memorial service to take place at the Heritage Society?"

"It's all set," Drayton said. "The Great Room at ten o'clock on Thursday. But Timothy did inquire about possible suspects."

"What did you tell him?"

"I had to play it straight. I told him that both Meredith and Alex have a vested interest in Reginald's property and finances. That Jack Grimes had access and opportunity, as did a half-dozen others. And that Reginald had ongoing land disputes with Carl Clewis and Susan Monday."

"And don't forget about Guy Thorne. He stands to be the sole partner now at Trollope's Restaurant."

"I did mention Thorne."

"What we should do is put our heads together and make a hit list. Then under each name we should check off different factors like opportunity, motive, and relationship to the victim," Theodosia said.

Drayton thought for a moment, then said, "Come over to my house tonight, and we'll do exactly that."

"Are you serious?" Theodosia had been half-kidding.

"Why not? By the by, I'll also fix us a nice dinner. Show you what a confirmed bachelor can accomplish when he sets his mind to it."

"You're on."

"Bring Earl Grey along, too. My little Honey Bee will adore the company."

for can accomplish when he sees his hand

12

Earl Grey was strutting his stuff this Tuesday evening. He was feeling frisky, straining at his leash, as he and Theodosia walked down the back alley on their way to Drayton's house.

"You know you're going to have a play-date tonight with your friend Honey Bee, don't you?" Theodosia asked him. Drayton's dog, Honey Bee, was a Cavalier King Charles Spaniel that they'd found wandering the streets of North Charleston. The poor little thing had been hungry and homeless when Drayton took her in. Now Honey Bee lived in the lap of luxury, ensconced in Drayton's elegant, antique-filled home a few blocks away.

Theodosia tightened up on Earl Grey's leash as she cut down Longitude Lane, one of Charleston's famed single-lane alleys. It was dark and a little spooky because it was so narrow, and the moss-covered cobblestones were also tricky to navigate. But oh, the scenery! They strolled past mysterious-looking rounded doorways that were set deeply into ivy-covered stone walls. Step through one of those doors, however, and you'd find yourself in a spectacular Charleston backyard filled with carefully tended gardens, reflecting pools, and marble statuary. This was also the historic alley that cotton wagons had rumbled down in the eighteenth century, and where a Revolutionary War cannon had once been unearthed. Now, visitors in the know came to admire its quaintness and charm.

In fact, one such visitor was strolling toward them right now.

"Be good," Theodosia admonished Earl Grey. Then, her serene smile turned to utter surprise when the person stepped into a circle of lamplight and she saw who it was.

"Fawn!" Theodosia cried out. "Is that you?"

Fawn, who'd been sort of dawdling along, stopped dead in her tracks, startled at encountering another person in the alley. Then, as recognition dawned, she stared, openmouthed, at Theodosia.

"Theodosia?" she finally said.

"Yes."

Fawn glanced at Earl Grey.

"You have a dog."

"This is Earl Grey," Theodosia said.

Fawn took a single step closer, looking flustered, and said, "I think I might owe you an apology."

"For what?" Theodosia asked. She knew darned well what Fawn was referring to, but those were the first words that popped out of her mouth.

Fawn looked down at her shoes in embarrassment.

"I think I might have been overly dramatic at your tea shop this afternoon. And then, that argument I had with Jack Grimes . . . well, I apologize if I caused you any distress."

"Fawn, *you* seemed like the one who was in distress."

Fawn shook her head. "Oh, not really."

Theodosia brushed aside Fawn's words. Clearly, the girl was downplaying the entire episode.

"Fawn, if you're in trouble — and I'm referring to the problem between you and Alex that you shared with me earlier today — then we need to get you some professional help."

Fawn just stared straight ahead at Theodosia. She seemed a little dazed, a little out of it.

"I shouldn't have brought any of that up. I was wrong to unburden myself on you." Fawn picked at an invisible piece of lint on her sweater.

"Fawn, are you feeling okay? Because what you told me about Alex was very upsetting. And the way you reacted to Jack Grimes . . ."

Fawn pursed her lips and shook her head. "It's nothing I can't handle. Really. I shouldn't have said a word to you. Shouldn't have bothered you at all."

"It's no bother. And everything you divulged seemed quite serious."

Theodosia focused carefully on Fawn. The girl seemed changed tonight. Perhaps because her attitude now seemed more indifferent? Theodosia wasn't sure she and Fawn were even communicating on the same frequency.

"You know what? I can handle it," Fawn said. "All I really want to do is get out of my marriage unscathed, be done with the whole thing. Because that family . . ." She stopped and shook her head.

"Fawn, what did you mean when you told Jack Grimes that he didn't have an inkling of what was going on?"

"Nothing," Fawn said. She started to walk away. "I meant nothing by it."

153

"Fawn . . ." Theodosia called after her. But Fawn was already gone. Melted into the gathering mist.

By the time Theodosia got to Drayton's house, she felt hopelessly confused by Fawn's mixed messages. Did Fawn genuinely need help? Or had the girl been overly theatrical — as she'd claimed?

Standing on Drayton's side piazza, ringing his doorbell, Theodosia decided that she'd better tell Drayton about . . .

"There you are! And precisely on time!" Drayton exclaimed as he pulled open the door. He was still wearing a coat and tie — his self-imposed dress code — as a sharp volley of barks erupted directly behind him. Earl Grey suddenly lunged past Theodosia, slipping through the doorway and practically knocking Drayton head over teakettle. Then Earl Grey's barks joined Honey Bee's in a rising canine chorus of excited yips and yipes.

"At least they're happy to see each other," Drayton said, as he led Theodosia into his kitchen.

"Maybe we should put them in the backyard? Let them run wild and burn off some of that energy?"

"Good idea," Drayton said. He opened

another door, and the two dogs surged out into his fenced backyard.

"Will your bonsai be okay?" Theodosia asked. Drayton had a small patio and a thin ribbon of green lawn. The rest of the yard was taken up by a Japanese pavilion, fish-pond, groves of tall bamboo, winding gravel paths, and all manner of benches and pedestals where his prize Japanese bonsai were on display.

"As long as the dogs don't chew any plants down to their nubbins, we'll be fine," Drayton said. He stepped over to his stove, where two pots bubbled enticingly.

"Whatcha got going there?" Theodosia asked. She was suddenly hungry. It had been a long, trying day.

"I'm making pasta with a cream sauce of sun-dried tomatoes and country ham."

"Sounds delish." Theodosia gazed about Drayton's elegant little kitchen. The stove was a six-burner Wolf gas range, the sink was custom hammered copper, and the cupboards were all faced with glass, the bet-ter to show off his collection of teapots and Chinese blue-and-white vases.

"Is that new?" Theodosia pointed to a tall blue-and-white vase decorated with clouds and fanciful dragons.

"Just got it last week, as a matter of fact.

Like it?"

"It's gorgeous."

"Ever since the *Empress of China* arrived in New York Harbor in 1785 with her hold full of blue-and-white pots, collectors have been in love with these beauties." Drayton smiled, nodded, and grabbed a wooden spoon.

"Anything I can do to help?" Theodosia asked.

"Actually, yes." Drayton handed her a pair of oven mitts. "You can drain the pasta while I finish off my sauce. I need to add a touch more cream."

Theodosia ferried the pan of pasta to the sink and dumped it into a waiting colander.

"It's also critical to add my strips of ham at the very last moment," Drayton said as he fiddled away, "because I don't really want to cook them, just warm them ever so slightly."

"Okay, pasta's drained. Now what?" Theodosia asked.

"I'll take it from here." Drayton mounded pasta in two majolica bowls and topped each nest with generous amounts of his finished ham and sun-dried tomato cream sauce. They carried their bowls into an adjoining dining room, where candles flickered on the table, a nice Barollo wine chilled

156

in a wine bucket, and a loaf of warm, crusty French bread was nestled in a sweetgrass basket.

"This is so formal," Theodosia said as she sat down.

"Formal is good," Drayton said. "Most people today are too *in*formal. They've forgotten or forgone some of the little niceties when it comes to dining."

"I think that's what brings folks to our tea shop."

Drayton nodded. "You're exactly right. There's a genuine hunger for the graciousness of a tea experience. The white linen tablecloths, the polished silver, the good china . . . people love it. You might even say they crave it."

"To say nothing of our food."

"And our tea," Drayton said. "With our international selection of fresh, whole-leaf teas, there isn't another tea or coffee shop in town that even comes close."

Drayton poured out glasses of red wine, and they enjoyed their pasta then, talking easily, chatting about friends, about the upcoming Ghosts & Galleons boat parade for Halloween. They did not mention the very dead Reginald Doyle, nor did they talk about possible suspects. That would all come later. For now, it was enough to sit on velvet-tufted chairs and enjoy fine food and wine in Drayton's lovely and sophisticated dining room with its crystal chandeliers, damask draperies, and Sheraton sideboard.

"Music," Drayton said, suddenly springing up from his chair and heading for his stereo. "We've been so busy talking and eating that I forgot all about it."

He dropped a needle on a record, and lovely music from a suite of violins immediately filled the house.

"What is that, Mantovani?" Theodosia joked.

"I'll have you know it's one of the *Mystery Sonatas* by Biber."

"Mystery," Theodosia said. "As in murder mystery."

"We haven't talked about that yet," Drayton said as he returned to the table.

"Maybe we should." Suddenly, the events of the past three days came flooding back to Theodosia.

"Let me clear first. Then we can enjoy some cookies and dessert tea in the library," Drayton said.

"Let me help."

They carried their dishes into the kitchen, dumped them into the dishwasher (Drayton's one concession to all-out modernity), and brought the two dogs inside. Drayton

158

brewed a pot of black currant tea, and they carried that, along with a small plate of ginger-cardamom cookies, into the library.

"I sure do love this room," Theodosia said as she flopped into one of the cushy leather chairs that faced his marble fireplace. "It must be heavenly to laze around here on rainy days." Her eyes took in his walls of leather-bound books, a painting of an English countryside, and a few antique tea caddies.

"I lucked out with this house," Drayton said. "Even though it's well over one hundred sixty years old, it's solidly built and has everything I could want, and then some. Even the library shelves are original built-ins, so I didn't have to endure endless days of sawdust and shuffling workmen."

"Like I am now?"

"Well, I didn't mean it quite that way," Drayton said.

"I know you didn't." Theodosia took a sip of her tea and said, "I ran into Fawn Doyle on my way over here."

"Where was she running off to?"

"That's the strange thing. She seemed to be out wandering."

"Trying to clear her head?"

"I suppose, though she acted rather strangely."

"I think it runs in the family," Drayton said. "You've obviously noticed how needy Meredith is."

"High-maintenance," Theodosia said.

"Still, it's greatly appreciated by everyone that you've agreed to look into Reginald's murder."

"Even though I haven't turned up much of anything so far."

"Say now." Drayton bent forward and plucked a magazine off a small round table. "Have you seen the new issue of *Southern Interiors Magazine*?"

"Is it the one featuring your house? No, I haven't seen it yet." Theodosia curled a hand. "Gimme, gimme." She'd given Drayton styling advice during the photo shoot and was eager to see the final result.

Drayton handed Theodosia the magazine and watched, almost shyly, as she eagerly thumbed through it.

When Theodosia got to the middle section, she said, "OMG, Drayton. They gave you the center spread!"

Drayton looked pleased as he fingered his bow tie. "Yes, I believe they did."

Theodosia studied the photographs. They were rich and warm, showcasing his rooms to perfection.

"The photos came out beautifully," Theodosia said. "Just look at this shot of your dining room. It's gorgeous. And the one of you posing in front of the fireplace. You're the epitome of a perfectly dapper Southern gentleman." She lowered the magazine. "You could get an agent, do some modeling."

"I hardly think so," Drayton said, trying to downplay her praise. "As you well know, I had major reservations about opening up my home to such a large readership. Now I have to admit I was wrong. This entire spread has exceeded my expectations."

Theodosia was delighted that the photos captured the Southern aristocratic elegance of Drayton's home yet still managed to make it look cozy and homey.

"The text is beautifully written, too," she said. "Descriptive and filled with details, but not overly flowery. You see, not every magazine is as tacky as *Shooting Star.*"

"Thank goodness for that."

Theodosia set the copy of *Southern Interiors Magazine* back on the small table and picked up a copy of *Charlestonian Magazine.* "Since when do you subscribe to this one?"

Drayton shrugged. "I don't. It just started appearing one day."

"You must be on some sort of comp list," Theodosia said as she flipped through the colorful city magazine. "Kind of interesting, though." She paused at the restaurant section and looked at the listings. Turned the page to the *New Restaurant Feature* section. Scanned the article, blinked, and stared again at what she was reading.

"What?" Drayton asked.

"Holy cats!"

"What?"

"Did you ever hear of Mr. Toad's Restaurant?" Theodosia asked.

"No, why?"

"It's brand-new. Apparently, just opened. And you'll never guess who the owner is."

"Clearly, I haven't a clue."

"It's that Carl Clewis person that Reginald Doyle was at war with."

Drayton leaned forward in his chair. "You're not serious."

Theodosia thumped two fingers against the page. "I can't make this stuff up."

"Let me see."

Theodosia passed the magazine to Drayton and watched as he pulled his tortoise-shell half-glasses from a jacket pocket.

"How very strange," he said, as he skimmed the article.

"Now I ask you," Theodosia said, "what motive would Carl Clewis possibly have had for getting rid of Reginald Doyle?"

Drayton glanced up at her, looking slightly owlish in his glasses. "Besides making the Axson Creek thing go away?"

"That's right."

"By the facetious tone in your voice, I imagine you're hinting that perhaps Clewis tried to make a competing restaurant go away, too?"

"It's certainly possible," Theodosia said. She thought for a moment and said, "But the thing is, Charleston's become such a foodie town, what with all the new restaurants, bistros, and craft breweries. So how exactly would Carl Clewis benefit from making just one single restaurant disappear?"

"Where is this Toadies located?" Drayton asked.

"Mr. Toad's."

"Whatever," Drayton said as he searched the article. "Oh, here it is. The place is on King Street."

"Same street as Trollope's Restaurant," Theodosia said.

"Which is strangely interesting."

"Maybe it's time I talked to Carl Clewis in person."

"Do you really think that's wise?" Drayton asked.

Theodosia gave a wry smile. "Probably

not. But it's time somebody got his side of the story."

Theodosia returned home with a very tired, played-out Earl Grey, a list of suspects surrounded by question marks, and a hunger to finally meet the elusive Carl Clewis.

It seemed to Theodosia that almost everyone had a motive, almost everyone carried a deep, dark secret. There were lots of moving parts just like . . . well, just like in an official police investigation.

But any more investigating and theorizing would have to wait until tomorrow, though she wasn't sure when or how she could work it into her busy schedule. Right now it was time to retire upstairs to her reading nook, immerse herself in a few chapters, and slip off to bed.

"C'mon," she said to Earl Grey as he followed her upstairs. "Time to hit the hay."

Theodosia kicked off her shoes and padded into her tower room. She loved it here. There was always the warm, familiar aroma of tea and fresh flowers along with an undertone of her Chanel No. 5.

She was also well aware of the *hygge* trend that was still sweeping the country. *Hygge* was the Nordic notion of creating a space that fostered a feeling of coziness and contentment. In fact, she'd been way ahead of the curve when she designed her combination upstairs bedroom, reading nook, and walk-in closet. She'd long been a fan of soy candles, cashmere blankets, feather beds, fresh flowers, and drinking tea out of china cups. Add to that vintage French fabrics, colors of pale peach, alabaster, and light blue, a few antique quilts, and loads of pillows . . . and presto, instant Southern-style *hygge.*

Theodosia took off her gold hoop earrings and dropped them onto a Florentine tray. Then she settled into her easy chair to read. Two minutes in, she heard the throaty rumble of a sports car in the alley down below. Earl Grey barely lifted his head, but she stood up and peered out her window.

Headlights strobed brightly, then a sleek, dark shape shot down the driveway that bordered her yard. It was her neighbor coming home. The hedge fund guy who lived in the rather opulent Granville Mansion directly adjacent to her much smaller (and more tastefully appointed, she thought) Charleston cottage.

Yes, Robert Steele, owner of the somewhat questionable Angel Oak Venture Capital Fund, was pulling into his driveway in his brand-new Porsche 911 Carrera.

Theodosia sat back down. Steele was a bachelor — a very man-about-town bachelor. And his frequent comings and goings were an obvious testament to his popularity with Charleston's single ladies.

13

Theodosia propped open the front door of the Indigo Tea Shop, the better to welcome in the shafts of sunlight that filtered down through puffy, pink clouds and lit up the whole of Church Street. Cars buzzed by, a bright-yellow horse-drawn jitney clip-clopped past, and goldfinches and chicka-dees pecked at the handful of crumbs that Haley had tossed out onto the sidewalk.

It was Wednesday, midweek, and Theo-dosia was feeling surprisingly upbeat and optimistic. Yes, she still had a mystery to unravel, but she was confident that she would soon be able to put some of the pieces together. That's if Sheriff Burney and his investigators didn't get there first.

Drayton stuck his head out the door and smiled at her. "Lovely day, isn't it? Lower humidity and much cooler this morning. You can feel a snap in the air. One season melting into another."

"There's no beating Charleston in the springtime when the blooms are popping like crazy," Theodosia said. "But autumn is awfully special, too."

"Which brings to mind a few verses by the English poet James Rigg."

"And those are?"

Drayton, never one to miss a chance for a poetic recitation, began:

Now Nature dons her tawny gown,
And to her rest doth creep:
She's laid aside her Summer crown,
And sadly slinks to sleep.

"Lovely," Theodosia said. She was always amazed by Drayton's encyclopedic knowledge of English poetry.

"So maybe it's time to spice up our tea offerings?" Drayton said. "Toss some cranberry-orange black tea into the mix? And perhaps Keemun tea with bits of black currant and also some cardamom tea?"

"You'll get no argument from me."

Theodosia trusted Drayton's judgment implicitly. When he declared that an extra fancy Formosan oolong was the perfect complement to Haley's chai and chocolate scones, there was no disputing it. Or when he paired gunpowder green with spicy Asian food. Exquisite. Or Assam tea with custard or lemon. Drayton knew his teas, and he knew exactly how each one could subtly enhance whatever food it was served with.

Back inside, Theodosia set the tables with her favorite Villeroy & Boch French Garden place mats, then added small plates plus matching cups and saucers in Royal Albert's American Beauty pattern. She was trying to decide between silver or brass candlesticks when the phone rang. Figuring it was an early morning take-out order, she skipped across the tea room, grabbed the receiver, and said, "Indigo Tea Shop, how may I help you?"

"Theodosia!" came a strangled cry.

Theodosia almost didn't recognize the voice at first. Then, in a tentative, almost disbelieving tone, she said, "Meredith, is that you?"

"It's . . ." There was a series of choking sounds, then, "Yes, it's me."

Meredith sounded so bad that Theodosia figured something terrible had happened.

"What's wrong?"

"Everything!" Meredith wailed. "Fawn went out for a walk last night and never came home!"

That bit of news rocked Theodosia back on the heels of her Cole Haan loafers.

169

"You mean that Fawn never made it back to her and Alex's house?"

"She did not. Now . . . like, five minutes ago, I received a call from the Coast Guard. They told me they discovered Alex's sailboat — his J/22 — floating in Charleston Harbor. It was bobbing around like some kind of crazy cork, practically heading out to sea!"

"Wait. What?" Theodosia was still trying to process this startling burst of information. "Are you saying . . . is the Coast Guard saying . . . that Fawn disappeared out of the sailboat?"

"Yes!" Meredith cried. "That's exactly what the Coast Guard suspects! Because the really horrible thing is, Fawn's purse and sweater were found in the sailboat's small cabin. But there was no sign of *her*!"

"Dear Lord, I ran into Fawn last night on my way to Drayton's house," Theodosia said.

Meredith pounced on Theodosia's words. "You did? Really? Did Fawn tell you where she was going?"

"Fawn told me she was simply out for a walk. Mulling things over, trying to clear her head." Theodosia hesitated. "Actually, Fawn struck me as being somewhat despondent."

"Oh no," Meredith quavered. "That does

170

not sound good at all."

"Did you know that Fawn and Alex haven't been getting along?" Theodosia asked. "That Alex has been verbally abusive to her?"

There was a long, drawn-out silence, and then Meredith said, "That can't be true. They're newlyweds. They adore each other."

"Fawn stuck around after the tea yesterday and confided in me that she and Alex were having serious problems."

"This is the absolute first I've ever heard about any kind of rift in their marriage," Meredith said. Then, with renewed firmness in her voice, she said, "No, that simply isn't possible. Fawn and Alex are completely in love." She let loose a heart-wrenching sob. "And now Fawn's gone!"

Theodosia decided a discussion about Fawn and Alex's failing marriage wasn't important right now. What was critical was finding Fawn.

"Tell me what's being done to locate Fawn," Theodosia said.

Overhearing Theodosia's words, Drayton suddenly appeared at her shoulder.

"What's going on?" he asked.

Theodosia held up an index finger.

"Does Sheriff Burney know about this?" Theodosia asked. "That the sailboat was

171

found floating in the harbor and that Fawn is missing?"

"Something happened to Fawn?" Drayton asked, the expression of concern on his face suddenly turned to genuine worry.

"I was about to call Sheriff Burney, but then the Charleston police intervened," Meredith said. "Apparently, the Coast Guard called the police, which was why I got a call from one of their detectives. They're going to notify Sheriff Burney and decide who's got jurisdiction over this. Oh, and Alex is supposed to meet with someone, but I . . . oh, good heavenly days, I feel like my sanity is completely ripping apart."

"Does Meredith want us to come over there?" Drayton asked.

"Do you want Drayton and me to come over there?" Theodosia asked. She'd just seen Miss Dimple walk through the front door and breathed a sigh of silent relief. If necessary, Miss Dimple could handle morning tea.

"Would you?" Meredith managed to choke out. "I'm at Divine Design right now. My shop on Royal Street."

"Of course. Just let me tell —"

But Meredith had already hung up.

"We have to leave," Theodosia said to Miss Dimple before the poor dear had even

172

slipped out of her coat. "Can you mind the tea shop for an hour or so?"

Drayton had already taken off his apron and was buttoning up his tweed jacket. "Maybe not even that long," he said. "And it shouldn't be that busy."

Haley came wandering out of the kitchen, wiping her hands on a towel and looking curious. "You guys are leaving?"

"Just for an hour at most," Drayton said. "Can you handle things?"

"Um . . . sure," Haley said. "Is this about Meredith?"

"It's about Fawn," Theodosia explained. "She's gone missing."

Haley's eyes went wide. "Then I guess you'd better hurry!"

"I knew it," Theodosia said as they bumped down the back alley in her Jeep, then turned onto Church Street. "I knew that poor girl was despondent. If only I'd said something . . . or *done* something last night. Interceded somehow."

"You couldn't have known Fawn was going to jump in a sailboat and . . ."

"And what?" Theodosia asked as she gunned her engine to run a yellow light and ended up clipping a red one. The fact that Fawn might have thrown herself overboard into the harbor was too horrible to even contemplate.

"I don't know." Drayton shook his head. "I don't know."

Divine Design was located in a tall red-brick building with white shutters and large windows that faced the street. The window display featured a contemporary group of swoopy chairs, an ostrich leather footstool, a silver floor lamp with a geometric lampshade, and a tall cylindrical clay vase that looked like it had straw stuck to the outside.

"This doesn't look like the refined taste of an Anglophile," Theodosia remarked to Drayton as they peered in the window.

"Yes, it's mostly contemporary," Drayton said. His lack of enthusiasm spoke volumes.

A bell over the door *ding-dinged* as they pushed their way into a store that was filled with leather accent chairs, sleek lacquered console tables, faux fur ottomans, and Barcelona chair wannabes. An array of bold, contemporary art hung on crisp-white walls.

"Drayton! Theodosia!" Meredith sang out when she saw them.

She was seated at the back of the store on a dusty rose–pink chair that looked almost like an old-fashioned settee that a Chinese empress might ride in. Only this one was updated and sleek.

174

"Bless you folks for coming," Meredith said. Rather than get up, she held out both hands in greeting as Theodosia and Drayton approached.

Drayton reached out and clasped one of Meredith's hands. Theodosia hung back, studying the two men who stood on either side of Meredith, flanking her like a pair of palace guards. One was her son, Alex; the other was a man she recognized but didn't really know.

"Dear Drayton, dear Theodosia," Meredith cooed. "Thank you for coming. Alex didn't believe me when I said you'd come rushing over."

Theodosia glanced at Alex. "Really," she said.

"And this other wonderful man here is Bill Jacoby, Reginald's business partner at Celantis Pharmaceuticals."

"Nice to meet you," Theodosia said, shaking Jacoby's hand. He had a pleasant hangdog face and an extra twenty pounds hanging over his belt. Jacoby was ambling, loquacious, and friendly, in the manner of a Southern politician.

"Actually, we crossed paths this past Sunday," Jacoby said.

Theodosia snapped her fingers and pointed at him. "You were the man in the

175

tan Carhartt jacket." She'd warmed to him instantly that day. He'd been both sensible and caring.

"I'm the one who didn't actually hunt," Jacoby said. "I'm what you might call a gentleman farmer. I was there more for the food and spectacle than anything else."

"It certainly *did* turn into a spectacle," Meredith said in a crabby voice. "Didn't it?"

"Is there any word on Fawn?" Theodosia asked. She had to remind herself why they'd come rushing over.

"Nothing!" Meredith cried.

"Only the sailboat was found and towed in," Jacoby said. He leaned down and patted Meredith's hand gently, trying to be solicitous, hoping to help keep her calm.

"Was Fawn a good sailor?" Theodosia asked.

"She was terrible!" Alex cried. "Never learned how to swim, scared to death of the water. That's why we're so crazed about our boat being found."

"With her sweater and handbag on board," Meredith added. She started to sniffle, so Jacoby dug into his jacket pocket and offered her his handkerchief. Meredith wiped at her nose, then poked a finger in Theodosia's direction. "You were the last one to see her."

"You were?" Jacoby gaped at Theodosia.

"I was walking my dog, heading over to Drayton's house last night for dinner," Theodosia explained. "And I ran into Fawn in Longitude Lane."

"You said she looked all mopey and sad?" Meredith asked.

"I knew it," Alex said. "Fawn falls into these downer moods once in a while. She gets very melancholy."

"When I talked to Fawn yesterday afternoon, she was beyond melancholy," Theodosia said to Alex. "She was angry and upset."

Alex frowned. "Upset about what?"

"About you," Theodosia said.

"I can hardly believe that," Alex said. "Fawn was actually fairly upbeat yesterday." He was downplaying Theodosia's words, trying to blow her off.

But Theodosia stuck to her guns.

"Fawn told me that the two of you had been fighting a lot. Arguing," Theodosia said.

"That's absolute nonsense," Alex said.

"Jack Grimes told me the same thing," Theodosia said.

Two red blobs of color rose on Alex's cheeks, and his eyes transformed into a pair of hard, dark marbles. "You're going to take the word of a murder suspect?" he sputtered.

"Actually," Theodosia said, "you're all suspects at this point."

Alex gasped. "You can't mean that!"

"Miss Browning is right," Jacoby said, nodding thoughtfully. "It's not only reasonable; it's logical thinking."

"We are *not* suspects!" Alex shouted at Theodosia. "How dare you come in here and toss out these wild, unfounded accusations."

"They're not really that wild," Drayton said.

Alex glared at Drayton. "Go ahead, take *her* side."

"I'm not taking anyone's side," Drayton explained. "Meredith asked Theodosia to look into things, and that's pretty much what she's been doing. The fact of the matter is, everyone who was at Creekmore Plantation on Sunday remains a suspect until they can be safely eliminated."

"Makes sense to me," Jacoby said. He glanced at Meredith. "Meredith? What do you think?"

Meredith gave a faint nod. "I suppose I can see the logic in that."

"Thank you," Theodosia said. She turned

178

to face Alex. "Where were you last night?"

Alex fixed her with a murderous glare. "This is unbelievable. You're asking about *me*?"

"Alex was with me last night," Meredith said quickly. "He stayed at the Lady Goodwood Inn. In a room adjacent to my suite."

"He was there all night?" Theodosia asked. She glanced at Drayton, who flashed her a dubious look. He thought it sounded strange, too.

"Alex dropped by to see me around seven," Meredith said. "We ordered room service . . ."

Theodosia did a quick calculation in her head. She'd run into Fawn around seven fifteen. So it looked as if Alex was in the clear. In this instance anyway. That's if they were both telling the truth.

"Go on," Theodosia said to Meredith.

"The thing is, we started talking about Reginald, about the damage to the house, and I got extremely upset," Meredith said. "Alex saw right away that I needed a shoulder to cry on, so he stayed with me." Tears dribbled from her eyes. "Maybe if I hadn't been so emotional . . . so needy . . . none of this would have happened. Alex would have been home, taking care of Fawn like a good and loving husband."

"I've *always* been there for Fawn," Alex said.

Theodosia studied Alex. "So you called Fawn early on and told her you were going to stay with your mother?"

"Of course I did."

"And what was Fawn's reaction?"

Alex projected an air of absolute innocence. "She was perfectly fine with it. She knew that Mother's been feeling incredibly vulnerable."

"Perhaps Fawn was kidnapped," Meredith said. "And then forced into the sailboat."

"That sounds a bit far-fetched to me," Bill Jacoby said.

"But it could have happened that way," Meredith said.

"It sounds as if there might have been foul play," Theodosia said. "Now we need to track down the sequence of events and figure out what happened." She wondered if she could call Riley and pump him for information? It might be worth a shot.

"We must focus our efforts on getting Fawn back," Drayton said.

"There are people out there who wish great harm to our family," Alex said. "People like Carl Clewis, maybe even Jack Grimes."

"I suppose that's possible," Jacoby said.

"Or even the Lavender Lady," Alex said.

Drayton glanced at Theodosia, then said, "What about Guy Thorne? At the restaurant."

Meredith looked shocked. "You think Guy could have had a hand in any of this?"

"I suppose we can't rule anyone out," Alex said.

Theodosia focused on Meredith. "Did you know that Carl Clewis opened a restaurant called Mr. Toad's? And that it's only a block away from Trollope's?"

This time Meredith was totally gobsmacked. "What?"

"That lousy scumbag!" Alex cried. "He's moving into our territory?" He looked like he was ready to spit a mouthful of tacks.

Theodosia thought about all the suspects they'd named so far, and she knew that both Meredith and Alex had to be tossed into the mix as well. One of them might not be telling the truth.

"Oh dear," Meredith fussed. "You have no idea how much this has disrupted my life. I used to host my book club, I used to garden . . ."

"And you used to shoot," Theodosia said. She wanted Meredith to know that she was well aware of her unique talent.

"I did," Meredith said without missing a beat. "But now it's all gone — poof! —

everything's been rendered meaningless now."

"Not everything," Alex said. "You still have your decorating business."

"As if that's supposed to sustain me."

Alex glanced at his watch and cleared his throat. "I'm sorry, Mother," he said, "but I need to leave." He glanced at Theodosia, Drayton, and Jacoby and said, "I've got a meeting with the police. They want me to try and help fill in some of the blanks for them concerning Fawn."

"You go do that," Meredith said. "But call me later, will you?"

Alex nodded. "Of course."

"He's such a good boy," Meredith said, once Alex had left.

Jacoby pulled his mouth into a sharp grimace. "Still . . . I remember how upset Alex was when he thought Reginald might be leaving Creekmore Plantation to the Heritage Society."

"That's a moot point now," Meredith said. "Water over the dam. Now Alex is poised to eventually inherit Creekmore."

"I suppose a son generally does inherit from his father," Drayton said.

"Oh, Alex isn't Reginald's son," Meredith said.

The three of them gaped at Meredith in

surprise.

"He's not?" Theodosia said. "Then what . . . ? Who . . . ?" She stopped abruptly, truly at a loss for words.

14

"Alex is from my first marriage," Meredith said. "Alex's father is deceased. He died while playing golf at Turtle Point Golf Club. Got struck by lightning on the seventh hole and was fried to a crisp."

"How awful," Theodosia said, trying to block that image. Still, with this startling new information, her mind was suddenly exploring all sorts of possibilities. Not all of them good.

"Tragic," Drayton said. "But when you remarried, Alex and Reginald got along well?"

"I always thought they did," Meredith said. "Yes, there were some minor squabbles along the way. When Alex flirted with dropping out of Charleston Southern University and becoming a tattoo artist. And then, when he decided to marry Fawn, Reginald thought Alex might be marrying beneath himself . . ."

"Did Reginald actually *say* that to Alex's face?" Theodosia asked. She was incredulous. How could anyone be so mean and hurtful?

"I'm afraid he did," Meredith said. "But then it all seemed to work out fine and dandy. Until . . . well . . . until now. Now Reginald is gone and our dear Fawn is missing." Meredith's face sagged again. "My whole family seems to be crumbling around me, and there isn't a single thing I can do!" She started to cry softly.

"Now, now," Jacoby said. "You've got your family at Celantis Pharmaceuticals. We're always going to be there for you."

"But what if something changes?" Meredith held a hankie to her nose and blew into it. "What if the company goes public? What if that IPO you people have been talking about really happens?"

"That's basically pie in the sky and not going to happen for a very long time. Now don't worry, Meredith, you know you'll be taken care of. There's no reason to be so upset."

"I have another question," Theodosia said. Meredith blew her nose. "Yes?"

"What does Alex do?"

"Do?"

"You know, for a living," Theodosia said.

185

"Oh, well, Reginald got him a job at Wentworth Bank. He's an executive there, a financial wunderkind."

"And he's doing what, exactly?" Theodosia asked.

Meredith started to cry again. "Alex is a junior loan officer. But he's working his way up."

"Perhaps Meredith should go back to her hotel suite and lie down?" Drayton suggested.

"Yes. Yes, I think she should," Jacoby said. "In fact, I'll take her there myself." He turned toward Meredith. "Meredith, honey, do you want to go back to the hotel?"

Meredith gave an offhand shrug. "I suppose. Since there's no definitive news about poor Fawn. But let me . . . let me grab a few things out of my office first."

When Meredith disappeared, Theodosia said to Jacoby, "Will Meredith be okay? Financially, I mean?"

"She'll be more than okay," Jacoby assured her. "Meredith stands to inherit all of Reginald's shares in the company as well as a seat on the board of directors." He looked thoughtful and added, "She'll end up a very wealthy woman."

"So according to Bill Jacoby, Meredith

stands to inherit a great deal of money," Theodosia said to Drayton as they drove back to the Indigo Tea Shop.

"And property. Real estate," Drayton said.

"Don't forget Trollope's Restaurant. I suppose Meredith owns half of that place now."

"I don't think she cares about any of that at the moment."

"Meredith's losing her focus," Theodosia said. "Between the murder, the fire, and now Fawn's disappearance, she's having a lot of trouble coping."

"I can understand why. There are so many strange disparate issues at play."

"I know," Theodosia said. "The whole thing makes my eyeballs hurt." She drove along, thinking about all the craziness they'd been drawn into, then said, "How do you feel about Meredith's revelation that Alex isn't Reginald's biological son?"

"You could have knocked me over with a feather. First I've ever heard of that," Drayton said.

"It could certainly give Alex motive. He's filled with so much acrimony, it's practically shooting out his ears."

"You think he wanted Reginald out of the way?" Drayton said. "To hurry up his inheritance?"

"And then there's Fawn."

"Where do you suppose she disappeared to?"

"Hopefully, she's not at the bottom of Charleston Harbor," Theodosia said.

"That's too horrible to even contemplate," Drayton whispered. He glanced over at Theodosia. "Please, Theo, tell me you're not going to quit this investigation."

"If I was going to quit, I'd have quit when I was ahead."

"So . . . your answer is no?"

"Does it look like I'm ahead?" Theodosia asked. She turned from Atlantic Street onto Church Street. "There's something I forgot to tell you. Something that, looking back now, could be relevant."

"What's that?"

"Monday night, after we had dinner at Trollope's, and after you walked Meredith back to the Lady Goodwood Inn . . ."

"Hmm?" Drayton said.

"I took Earl Grey for a run. In fact, we passed by the back of the Lady Goodwood Inn where they built that new solarium. Anyway, I'm pretty sure I heard Meredith talking to someone in there. Arguing with them."

Drayton's brows knit together. "Well, it wasn't me."

"I figured that. But who could it have

been? Alex? Guy Thorne? Jack Grimes? Somebody else?"

"You mean there might be someone we don't even know about who factors into this investigation? This murder?"

"Could happen."

Drayton didn't look happy. "Good grief."

By the time Theodosia and Drayton got back to the Indigo Tea Shop, midmorning tea was well underway.

"We had a customer who requested a pot of Darjeeling tea," Miss Dimple told Drayton in a hushed voice. "And I suddenly panicked, trying to figure out the brewing time."

"So what did you do?" Drayton asked.

Miss Dimple tapped a finger against her forehead. "Then I remembered that you once told me a First Flush Darjeeling should only be brewed for about three minutes. And that the water temperature should be just short of boiling. So that's what I did." She gave an eager smile. "And that was right, huh?"

"It's spot-on," Drayton said. "You're a very quick study."

"Anything else to worry about?" Theodosia asked as she slipped an apron over her head.

"No, that's about it," Miss Dimple said. "Oh, and we had a huge take-out order for scones. Angie Congdon from the Feather-bed House called and asked for three dozen scones along with Haley's famous pear butter."

"Did Angie pick them up yet?" Theodosia asked.

Miss Dimple nodded. "The scones walked out the door ten minutes ago. Now Haley is baking a brand-new batch for lunch."

"I think I'll go check on her," Theodosia said.

"What's going on?" Haley asked. "Did you guys find Fawn? Or figure out what happened to her?"

Theodosia stepped into their small kitchen. The air was redolent with baking scones while a pot of French onion soup bubbled on the stovetop. "I'm afraid not."

"Do you think she drowned?"

"Drowned? No, I don't think so." Theodosia wasn't sure why she thought Fawn might be somewhere else; she just did. You could call it a hunch, intuition, or just plain hope.

"There's something important that I gotta tell you," Haley said as she stepped away from her stove. Her hands moved anxiously

190

as she twisted her white apron into knots.

"What's wrong?" Theodosia scooped up an errant carrot stick and munched it.

"I heard something about, you know, that dead guy's partner. The one who pretty much runs Trollope's Restaurant."

"You mean Guy Thorne?"

Haley nodded vigorously. "That's the one. Yup."

Theodosia was instantly on alert. "Haley, what did you hear?"

"Rumor has it that Thorne is way behind in paying his bills. That he owes a lot of money to food and liquor suppliers all over town."

"Who's been spreading those rumors? Wait, how exactly did you come by this information?"

"Most of Trollope's suppliers are the same ones we do business with."

Theodosia digested this new information along with her carrot stick.

"So you're telling me that Guy Thorne is seriously hurting for money."

"Apparently so," Haley said. Then, "Doesn't the FBI list financial stress as a key motivating factor when it comes to murder?"

"Haley! Where did you pick up *that* bit of information?"

Haley gave a sheepish smile. "From you?"

Lunch got underway with a menu that featured mushroom quiche, French onion soup, shrimp salad with Haley's special tomato-dill dressing, cream cheese and green olive tea sandwiches, and chicken breasts with caper sauce. Theodosia was pleased that Miss Dimple was there to help out. With the addition of more take-out orders, plus two large tables of guests from the Windsor Tea Club, they were busy, busy, busy.

Then, when the Indigo Tea Shop was practically filled to capacity, Delaine Dish came strolling in.

"Theo-*do*-sia," Delaine sang out in her pay-attention-to-me voice. "I am so *crunched* for time I can barely breathe! Plus, my dear niece Bettina is with me today, so if you could seat us immediately, *s'il vous plaît,* we would be most grateful."

"Delaine . . . yes," Theodosia said. Delaine was perpetually crunched, stressed, tense, or jittery. Her adorable and well-stocked boutique, Cotton Duck, kept her in a state of high anxiety, as did her work with various charities, her rotation of boyfriends, her cats, and all her imagined emergencies. Delaine spoke too rapidly, peppered her sentences with italics and exclamation marks, was a notorious flirt, and chronically worried about her weight. Today her small frame was squeezed into a sample size 0 white knit dress that showed off her prominent collarbone and hip bones to perfection.

"This is *sweet* of you to work us in without a reservation," Delaine said breathlessly as Theodosia led them to a table. "We *so* appreciate it."

"Not a problem," Theodosia said, because it really wasn't. She focused her gaze on Bettina, who'd recently graduated from the Fashion Institute of Technology in New York. Bettina had a coltish figure and luminous brown eyes. Her hair, which a few months ago had been curly and brown, was now shorter, spiky, and streaked with highlights (undoubtedly Delaine's doing). Delaine had also coaxed Bettina into an intense internship that could only be considered slave labor.

"How are you doing, Bettina?" Theodosia asked.

"Good," Bettina said.

"Still having fun?" Theodosia knew that Bettina was working her tail off at Cotton Duck, trying her best to gain hands-on experience in retail sales and merchandising.

"It's been really cool. Aunt Delaine is an excellent teacher," Bettina said.

Delaine's pretty, heart-shaped face assumed a slightly pinched expression.

"Best to just call me Delaine. *Aunt* makes one sound so terribly ancient and haggard."

"If you ladies are in a rush," Theodosia said, "may I recommend our French onion soup and a shrimp salad?"

"That sounds great," Bettina said.

"Just the salad," Delaine said.

"How about a couple of cream scones?" Theodosia asked. "Haley just baked a fresh batch."

"Yes, please," Bettina said.

"Carbs." Delaine scowled.

Theodosia circled back to their table a couple of minutes later with a pot of chamomile tea. Though it was more an infusion than tea, chamomile was known to exert a calming effect. And heaven knows, Delaine could use a little calming.

Five minutes later, Theodosia delivered their luncheon orders.

"These scones are low-carb, right?" Delaine asked.

"Uh . . . sure," Theodosia said. How much could a little white lie hurt, anyway? Besides,

194

hers was a tea shop that served traditional scones, muffins, biscuits, crumpets, and breads, along with quiches, salads, soups, and whatever entrée Haley deigned to whip up. None of them — not Theodosia, not Drayton, not Haley — had a paleo-keto-vegan bone in their body.

"And what is this?" Delaine asked. "Raspberry jam?" She was already slathering a gob of it on her scone along with a generous helping of Devonshire cream.

"It's cranberry-orange marmalade."

Delaine took a bite, chewed hungrily, and said, "I heard via the grapevine that you've been poking your nose into Reginald Doyle's murder."

"Where did you hear that?" Theodosia asked.

Delaine gave a little sniff. "Around." Then added, "Did you know that Meredith and Fawn are customers of mine? Good customers. I actually dressed both of them for the Opera Ball last spring. Oh, you should have seen Meredith in her de la Renta gown. So sleek and pretty . . . to *die* for."

"You probably haven't heard this piece of news yet, but Fawn has gone missing," Theodosia said.

Delaine flapped a hand, seemingly unconcerned. "Why am I not surprised? It's about time Fawn dumped that stick-up-his-backside husband of hers."

"It's not quite that simple," Theodosia said. "Nobody knows where Fawn is. They found an empty sailboat bobbing around in Charleston Harbor this morning, and her family is extremely worried."

"That's awf—" Bettina started to say. But Delaine interrupted her.

"I'm sure Fawn will turn up *somewhere,*" Delaine said. "She always struck me as a savvy and highly resourceful girl. Oh, Theo, dear, do you have our reservations for your Lavender Lady Tea on Saturday? I e-mailed you the other day. We're absolutely *dying* to taste Drayton's special blend. And did you hear that Franny Moultrie has been keeping company with a man who's *ten years younger* than she is? Isn't that totally cray-cray? And why do some women have all the luck?"

Theodosia was mildly interested in sticking around and listening to Delaine's gossip and musings until a new customer walked through her front door and surprised the heck out of her. It was Susan Monday, the Lavender Lady herself. Theodosia hurried over to greet her.

"Susan," Theodosia said. "Welcome to the Indigo Tea Shop."

"If I'm going to be part of your Lavender Lady Tea this Saturday, I figured I'd better brush up on my tea shop knowledge," Susan said.

"How would you like to start with lunch?" Susan grinned. "That would be fantastic. I was hoping you'd say that."

Theodosia seated Susan Monday on the far side of the tea shop, away from Delaine and Bettina, where there wouldn't be any distractions. Then she brought Susan a pot of Formosan oolong tea, a strawberry scone with Devonshire cream, and a shrimp salad.

"Your place is so adorable," Susan said between bites. "I love the wooden floor and beamed ceiling. And this food is delicious! I'm not sure what I was expecting — maybe an oversize bran muffin like in those hustle-bustle coffee shops — but this is fantastic. As good as what's served in any of the fancy bistros around town. Maybe even better!"

"We have an even more elaborate menu planned for Saturday," Theodosia told her.

"Saturday," Susan said, squinting at her. "Just what would you like me to do?"

"After we welcome our guests and detail the menu, I'd like you to do a two- or three-minute talk on lavender. About its relaxing properties, how it can be infused in tea and food and lotions, that sort of thing."

"I can surely do that."

"Then we'll have you sit at one of the larger tables so you can chat with our guests, get acquainted, and answer any questions."

"That sounds like fun," Susan said. She broke off a piece of scone, slathered it with jam, and said, "The lavender tea isn't the only reason I showed up here today."

"Oh?"

"Here's the thing. Sheriff Burney came to my farm yesterday afternoon and asked me a whole bunch of questions."

"What kind of questions?" Theodosia asked.

"About my farm and its borders. About the orphan strip of land. How well I got along with Reginald Doyle and my other neighbors. And, this is kind of strange, but he wanted to know if I owned a pistol."

Theodosia's heart caught in her throat as she asked, "Do you?"

15

Susan shook her head vigorously. "No. And I never have." She fixed Theodosia with a mild, questioning gaze. "Why do you think the sheriff interrogated me like that?"

"Probably because Reginald Doyle was killed with a pistol," Theodosia said.

Now Susan looked anxious. "Is someone pointing a finger at me? Trying to make me a suspect in Doyle's murder?"

"There's a lot of finger-pointing going on right now," Theodosia said.

"By Meredith Doyle? Or her son, Alex?"

"It's possible they could have mentioned your name," Theodosia hedged. "Meredith is terribly upset and super stressed right now. I'm sure you've heard that her daughter-in-law, Fawn, is missing?"

Susan shook her head. "I did not know that."

"The Coast Guard found Fawn and Alex's J/22 floating in the harbor."

Susan put a hand to her mouth in shock. "Do they think she drowned?"

"It's possible. Anyway, Alex is one of the suspects — well, he is to me in any case."

"He is? For sure? Why?"

"Because I know for a fact he wasn't getting on very well with Fawn."

"That's . . . so bizarre. Weren't they newlyweds?"

"They are . . . were."

"So a murder, a fire, and now a possible drowning. This has turned into a complicated situation, hasn't it?" Susan said.

Theodosia gave an uneven smile. "You have no idea. So, to circle back and answer your question, Alex could have easily pointed a finger at you and whispered nasty innuendos in Sheriff Burney's ear."

"Wow." Susan thought for a moment. "Is it possible that Alex murdered Reginald? And then made Fawn disappear?"

"I have no proof of anything like that, but Alex does seem to be stirring the pot like crazy — pointing out potential suspects and then throwing up smoke screens to shield himself."

Susan looked grim. "Lies and innuendos are not what I need right now. I haven't shared this with many people, but my goal is to open a small shop called Lavender &

Lace right here in Charleston. If word gets out that I'm a suspect in a murder case, it won't do my reputation any good. Landlords won't want to rent to me, customers will avoid me like the plague. I'd be cooked before I even got started!"

"I don't believe Alex has spread the sort of rumors that would damage your reputation," Theodosia said.

"Maybe not yet. But he could. I mean, what about my lavender farm? That place means everything to me. A ripple of nasty rumors could hurt me there as well." Susan's brows knit together. "I've poured my heart and soul into Blue Moon Lavender Farm, working hard to build my reputation, taking extra care with the pruning and harvesting. And I *never* use dangerous pesticides like some of my neighbors do, because I care *passionately* about the environment."

"I can see that," Theodosia said.

Susan was wound up and venting like crazy. "Did you know that right here in South Carolina, all over the low country, the Pine Barrens tree frog is now on the endangered species list?"

"I had no idea."

"Most people don't, and it makes me *crazy* that nobody cares about God's tiny crea-

201

tures," Susan said.

"I hear you," Theodosia said. "I'm forever rescuing turtles when they crawl across a roadway."

Susan gave a faint smile. "Blessings on your head for that."

"Susan Monday seems like a lovely woman," Drayton said to Theodosia. She'd introduced him to Susan on her way out.

"Susan is being questioned by Sheriff Burney," Theodosia said.

Drayton's eyes flicked up to her and he did a double take. "I can't imagine why. For goodness' sake, the woman grows *lavender* for a living. She's probably the calmest, most serene person in the county."

"Susan also comes across as a slightly radical environmentalist."

"That's a good thing, is it not? To be concerned about polar bears and bee populations and whatnot?"

"Susan Monday alluded to one of her neighbors using pesticides and not caring about the environment. I'm wondering now if she was referring to Reginald Doyle."

"Theodosia, what are you getting at?" Drayton asked.

"What if Susan Monday shot Reginald because she considered him an environmental disaster?"

Drayton poured hot water into a Wedgwood teapot, swished it around, and then dumped it out.

"I thought you told me we had nothing to worry about with Susan Monday," he said.

"That's before she went all radical tree-frog-hugger on me," Theodosia said.

Drayton gazed at her. "And now she's coming to our tea party on Saturday."

"Look at it this way," Theodosia said. "At least we can keep an eye on her."

Miss Dimple was handling early-afternoon tea with such care and skill that Theodosia took the opportunity to sit down at one of the tables, enjoy a cup of soup, and read the newspaper. She was halfway through Section A of the Charleston *Post and Courier* when Detective Tidwell ghosted into the tea shop.

Not only was Burt Tidwell big and burly like a Kodiak bear, he had the grouchy disposition of one that had been awakened mid-hibernation, one who hadn't enjoyed his full complement of z's.

"Imagine my surprise this morning when a report from the Coast Guard came across my desk," Tidwell said in an almost accusatory voice. He was wearing a bagged-out tweed jacket that barely stretched around him and voluminous slacks. His feet, however, were neat and small, like a dancer's.

Theodosia looked up from her newspaper to find his dark beady eyes staring at her as he slouched his way to her table.

"It concerned a recovered sailboat and a possible drowning," Tidwell continued. "And now I find that *you* were a guest of this particular woman's family when her father-in-law was murdered." He drew a deep breath. "And when their plantation home caught fire shortly thereafter."

"How do you know about this?" Theodosia asked as she folded her paper.

"Informants, police reports, and" — Tidwell tapped one chubby finger against the side of his head — "my own singularly unique radar."

"Plus you've been talking to Sheriff Burney."

"There is that. May I sit down?"

Without waiting for an answer, Tidwell dropped his bulk into the chair directly across from Theodosia.

"Am I to believe you are meddling?" he asked.

"No, but I have been asked by the family to look into things," Theodosia said.

"And a fine job you've done. Now Fawn

Doyle is missing, presumed drowned." Tidwell looked almost gleeful as he said it.

"Excuse me, I did not have anything to do with *that.*"

"But you're involved," Tidwell pressed.

"So far, more as a peripheral witness to these various disasters."

"Talk to me. Bring me up to speed."

So Theodosia gave Tidwell a sort of Cliffs-Notes version of her take on the shooting of Reginald Doyle, the flash fire at Creekmore Plantation that same night, and Fawn's confession to her yesterday afternoon that Alex was an abusive husband.

"It's only been three days, and you're intricately entwined in any number of serious situations," Tidwell marveled. "All of which might result in assault, felony, or murder charges."

"I've actually been at this awhile longer than that. And I *don't* know anything about possible charges," Theodosia said. "I'm only trying to help the family."

"Help, she says," Tidwell muttered.

Theodosia was about to fire back at Tidwell, but she managed to stop herself and peer at him. "Are you hungry? Can I offer you a scone and a pot of tea?" She knew that sugar was the magic ingredient that would soften him up and calm him down.

Maybe even pry loose a few details she wasn't privy to yet.

"Might you have any of those delightful flowering teas?" Tidwell asked.

"I'm sure we have some stashed away on Drayton's magic shelves. And would you prefer a cream scone or a strawberry scone?"

"Hmm . . . such a difficult choice."

Theodosia stood up from her chair. "I'll bring you one of each."

"Perfect."

Five minutes later, Theodosia delivered Tidwell's tea tray to the table and then plopped back down across from him. She poured hot water into the clear glass teapot that held the Chinese flowering tea, and together they watched as the buds unfurled.

"Lovely," Tidwell said. He gave a perfunctory smile, sliced his scone lengthwise with his butter knife, and delicately slathered on an enormous dollop of Devonshire cream. It was done with such precise skill and care, it was like watching a doctor perform microsurgery.

"What is . . . ?" Tidwell pointed to the small glass compote jar on his tray.

"Cranberry-orange marmalade. It's something new we're trying," Theodosia said.

"Ah." Tidwell seemed pleased by the tasty addition.

Theodosia reached across the table, grabbed his teapot, and poured an amber stream of tea into his teacup. "I think this has steeped long enough."

"Thank you."

Theodosia smiled sweetly. "And by the way, was there a bullet recovered from Reginald Doyle's body?"

Tidwell sipped his tea slowly, then said, "I understand the medical examiner did remove a 9mm bullet."

"So the shooter used a pistol." Theodosia thought about Doyle's body lying on a stainless steel table, the ME going about his business as if it were just another day at the office, just another routine shooting, which it probably was. Probing the wound with a toothed forceps, pulling out a slug, and then dropping it into a metal tray with a hard clank. A shiver oozed up her spine. Sometimes her imagination could be a little too vivid.

"What mystifies me," said Tidwell, "is the report on the unmanned sailboat that just came across my desk. I'm guessing I need to ask Alex Doyle any number of questions."

"Good. And while you're at it, could you please beat him silly with a rubber hose for me?" *Because I really worry that Alex might be the guilty party.*

Tidwell took a bite of scone, chewed thoughtfully, and said, "We really don't do things like that."

Theodosia sighed. "Right."

Once Tidwell had finished his scones (with great relish) and left (grumpy as usual), Theodosia strolled into the kitchen, where Haley was putting away the last of the luncheon leftovers.

"Got some leftover soup here if you'd like to take it home with you," Haley said.

"No, that's okay. What I actually came in here to talk to you about is tomorrow's funeral luncheon. The catering part."

"Yup. I'm on top of it."

"And you're sure you can handle everything okay? I know I'm putting a lot on your plate."

"Actually, I just have to make the scones and sandwiches. *You're* the one who has to put them on plates."

"You know what I mean. I'm concerned because you've got the Sugar Arts Show tomorrow afternoon. And I know you're counting on entering one of your fondant sculptures. So I guess what I'm asking is, are you sure you have time? I don't want this funeral luncheon to compromise you in any way. I mean, Miss Dimple will be here

208

to help out again, but . . ."

"I'm chill. I can handle everything just fine," Haley said. "I'm planning to finish my piece tonight at home and then add a few last-minute touches, like, an hour before the contest starts. So, yeah, I'm pretty sure I can manage everything. Hey, I always do, don't I?"

Theodosia slipped her arms around Haley's shoulders and gave her a warm hug. "Haley, you always manage with class and grace."

"I do?" Haley looked pleased by Theodosia's praise.

"You're our shining treasure," Theodosia said.

Back out in the tea room, Drayton was fussing with his teapots and Miss Dimple was serving afternoon tea to two tables of customers. Theodosia looked around and smiled. With a few rays of afternoon sun prisming in through the wavy glass windows, the tea room looked positively enchanting. And, once again, she thanked her lucky stars that she'd somehow ended up in just this perfect spot.

After college, Theodosia had worked as an account executive at a midsize marketing firm. During her time there, she realized she had a knack for understanding how to market and promote products. She'd worked with software companies, banks, even some retail accounts. But, eventually, her best efforts had been for herself. After six years, she'd taken stock of her career and decided she needed something that was a little more tangible, a little more . . . nourishing to the soul. She hit upon a tea shop because tea was just beginning to come out of the closet. Tea shops were sprouting up around the country like mushrooms, women were eyeing Granny's antique china in a whole new light and bringing it out of the cupboard, hats and white gloves suddenly had renewed cachet.

So. A tea shop.

Theodosia had set about finding a small building, renovating it — but not too much — and imbuing it with the cozy, elegant touches she thought a proper tea shop should have. After that it was all PR, word of mouth, a few lucky TV appearances, and a lot of hard work. The tea shop had grown in popularity along with their burgeoning catering business, and her website was doing a bang-up job in retailing all of Drayton's special house blends.

Theodosia had even been offered the opportunity to write a weekly tea column but had turned it down because she didn't think she could devote the proper amount of time to getting it perfect. To Theodosia, perfect was everything.

"What are you thinking about?" Drayton asked, causing her reverie to suddenly burst like an errant soap bubble.

"I think . . ." Theodosia said. "I think I'm going to duck out and take a look at that sailboat."

Drayton looked askance. "The J/22? The one the Coast Guard found floating in the harbor? What could you possibly discover by looking at that?"

"That's the thing, Drayton. You just never know."

16

Theodosia drove over to the Charleston Yacht Club, checked in at the clubhouse office, and discovered that Alex Doyle's J/22 not only had been towed back here, but was now moored in its regular slip. She quizzed the harbormaster about what condition the boat was in when it was returned, then went outside, crossed a sandy patch of grass, and walked out onto Dock 3.

Where she immediately felt at home.

Theodosia had been a sailor all her life and reveled in the excitement of skimming across silver waves with the wind whipping your hair and sea spray hitting your face. To her it spelled heaven. Freedom. And here she was, back at one of her favorite haunts, waves lapping, boats bobbing all around her, halyards clanking noisily but reassuringly against their masts.

Walking down the dock, she saw this was where most of the smaller sailboats were docked. Here was a Marblehead 22 tugging at its moorings, over there a BayRaider, and farther down a CW Hood 32 with its huge open cockpit.

When Theodosia arrived at Berth 24, she stopped and took a careful look at Alex's sailboat. She knew the J/22 was a popular, fixed-keel racing sailboat — a boat that was easy to sail because it was amazingly stable. It was also excellent for poking around the harbor and nearby inlets on weekends. Because the boat looked to be in excellent condition, she figured it had to be on the newer side. Maybe only a year or two old.

Bought before Alex's marriage to Fawn? Probably.

Theodosia glanced around, saw no one watching, and stepped onto the boat. It dipped slightly then leveled out. Everything seemed to be in order. Lines stowed, cabin locked, mast rigid. She wondered how Fawn had managed to rig the boat all by herself late at night. If Fawn was frightened of boats, terrified of the water, how had she been able to run a twenty-four-pound sail up a twenty-foot mast, cast off, and then carefully navigate her way out of the marina and into Charleston Harbor proper. All under cover of darkness.

The answer was . . . she couldn't. There

had to be an accomplice. Or a better explanation.

Theodosia studied the boat with a discerning sailor's eye, trying to figure out what might have taken place here. She glanced fore and aft and saw a small trolling motor attached.

Okay, maybe this explains it.

Theodosia touched a hand to the stern and leaned forward to get a better look at the motor. And as the sun popped out from behind a puffy cirrus cloud, she saw a glistening streak on the shiny red top side of the motor.

Streak of what?

Reaching out, Theodosia swiped two fingers across the spot. And felt . . . something slippery and viscous. Like a smear of gasoline.

Someone had fired up this motor recently. Yes, the Coast Guard had brought this boat back in, but they would have *towed* it back in.

So who had motored this boat out into the harbor? Fawn? Alex? Or someone else?

Theodosia pondered this new mystery as she drove down Queen Street. She'd planned to go on home from there. But, at the last minute, she decided to take a

214

detour. She crossed over Legare and turned down King Street. Her heart beat a little faster as she realized she was taking on another investigation today . . . that of paying a visit to Mr. Toad's Restaurant.

Carl Clewis had been a mysterious phantom who'd been flitting through the backwaters of the investigation for the last four days. Now it was time to try and corner the man, to actually meet him. Theodosia had looked for Clewis at his farm and been brusquely turned away. But maybe, just maybe, Clewis was spending all his time right here, at his new restaurant.

Theodosia parked in the adjacent parking lot and slipped in the front door. The restaurant was dark and moody, a mash-up of a fig and fern bar and a bistro that favored brass and stained glass. And she could hear the sounds of jubilant voices coming from the bar just off to her left. Must be early happy hour.

A young woman with pink curly hair and a green sheath dress slipped behind the hostess stand and smiled at her.

"Are you here for Double Bubble?" the woman asked.

"Am I . . . ?"

"Happy hour," the hostess said. "Two-for-one priced-well drinks as well as raw oysters

215

for a dollar each."

"I'm tempted," Theodosia said. "But I really dropped by to say hi to Carl Clewis."

"In that case, his office is just down the hall on the left," the hostess said with a smile.

"Thank you. Thank you very much."

Theodosia sped down the hallway before the hostess could ask if she had an appointment. Or if she even knew Carl Clewis.

An engraved brass plaque on the door said MANAGER.

Okay, here goes nothing.

Theodosia drew a deep breath and knocked.

"What?" boomed a voice from inside.

"Mr. Clewis?" Theodosia said.

"Enter if you must," came the voice again. Cranky sounding.

Theodosia pushed the door open and stepped inside. She was surprised to find herself in a small, cramped office with no windows and a buzzing fluorescent light overhead. Carl Clewis himself was seated behind a metal desk pawing through a mountain of paperwork.

"Mr. Clewis?" Theodosia said.

"Where *is* that plumbing permit?" Clewis muttered to himself. "I just had that puppy in my hand."

Clewis was short and stocky, like an ex-wrestler, with fingers that never stopped moving, like insect legs. He wore his hair in an old-fashioned high fade and had a pair of rimless glasses perched on his nose. Finally, after examining another stack of papers, he looked up at Theodosia.

"Are you the city health inspector?" Light bounced off his glasses, giving him an odd, slightly manic look.

Theodosia shook her head. "Afraid not."

"Poore's Liquor rep? Because we've been going through that Vladivostok Vodka like tap water."

"Again, no."

Clewis pursed his lips. "Then who are you and what do you want?" He was obviously impatient and unhappy about being disturbed.

"I'm a friend of Meredith Doyle's."

"Not interested," Clewis said in a flat tone, turning his attention back to his mound of paper.

"Please," Theodosia said. "If you could just spare two minutes of your time?"

"What for?"

"To answer a couple of questions?"

Clewis breathed out an audible sigh. "Concerning what?"

"May I sit down?"

217

Clewis flapped a hand. "Sit. Stand. Whatever."

Theodosia sat down on an uncomfortable metal folding chair and found there was so little room in Clewis's office that her knees rubbed against the back of his desk.

"I wanted to ask about the land dispute that's been going on between you and Reginald Doyle," Theodosia said.

"There is no land dispute," Clewis barked. "Our argument is about a creek. About *water* rights." He lifted his head and peered closely at Theodosia. "So what's this about really? Oh, wait, I bet you think that maybe I was the one who shot that old buzzard?"

"Did you?"

"Doyle wasn't worth the expenditure of ammunition."

"But the two of you were involved in a lawsuit," Theodosia said. "Several lawsuits. Because you dammed up Axson Creek."

Clewis leaned back in his chair and stared at her. "Please. It's nothing people haven't done in the low country for the last hundred years. So what if I dammed up part of the creek? Now it's a gorgeous little pond that I plan to stock with bluegills and rainbow trout. And the current in Axson Creek is still flowing nice and strong, by the way. I saw some canoers paddle by my place just this morning. When you think of all the fishing, swimming, and recreational use that little creek affords — it's a win-win situation all the way around."

"I'm afraid the Doyle family doesn't quite see it that way," Theodosia said.

"And you're . . . Who are you?"

"Theodosia Browning. I own the Indigo Tea Shop over on Church Street."

"My, my, isn't that lovely. In between pouring cups of tea you're looking into poor old Reginald's murder?"

Theodosia gave an abbreviated nod. "Something like that." She realized that Clewis might look mild mannered, but he had the personality of a wolverine.

"Maybe you should redirect your focus and take a good hard look at Reginald's restaurant buddy, Guy Thorne."

"Why is that?" Theodosia asked. She harbored her own suspicions about Thorne and was interested in hearing what Clewis had to say.

"It's possible that Reginald finally uncovered the real dirt on Thorne. And then ended up paying the price."

"Excuse me?"

"I'm saying that maybe Reginald caught Thorne with his hand in the cookie jar." Clewis chuckled. "Wait, you didn't know

219

that Thorne's a notorious gambler? He's been gambling away the restaurant's profits for months. Maybe years."

"How do you know this?"

Clewis cocked his head and pulled his face into an unbecoming smirk. "Bartenders, cooks, and servers are the biggest gossips of all, sweetheart. They hop from job to job, turning the food service industry into a veritable game of musical chairs. Sometimes servers and busboys even work a couple of different jobs at once. Do you see where I'm going with this? Food service folks are privy to all the latest dirt and hot rumors about their coworkers and employers."

Okay, Theodosia decided. *So Clewis is telling me the same thing Haley did. Interesting. Where there's smoke there's fire?*

Theodosia stood up, almost banging her knees. She'd seen and heard enough. Carl Clewis might be correct about Guy Thorne. Then again, Clewis might be a darned good poker player, able to bluff and lie his way through anything.

"Thank you for seeing me, Mr. Clewis."

But Clewis was once again focused on his paperwork. "Bye-bye. Let's not do this again anytime soon."

Just as Theodosia climbed into her Jeep, she

got a call from Drayton.

"Meredith just phoned me and she's completely distraught," Drayton said. "Unhinged, you might say."

"Uh-huh. And where are you?"

"Still at the tea shop. Just finishing up."

"What's the crisis this time?" Theodosia asked as she blew out a glut of air.

"Meredith and Alex were supposed to pick out a coffin for Reginald this morning, but with the developing Fawn situation, they never got around to it."

"I thought Meredith was planning a simple memorial service. Tasteful and dignified," Theodosia said. "I assumed they'd have Reginald cremated."

"Well, it's still going to be tasteful and dignified, but now there's going to be a coffin," Drayton said in a droll voice.

"And let me guess. Meredith needs our help." Theodosia was beginning to wish she hadn't gotten so tangled up in Meredith's problems. One, because Meredith was taking up an awful lot of her time. And two, because she really wasn't getting anywhere.

"Meredith asked if we could pretty please — her words, not mine — meet her at the Doake and Wilson Funeral Home." Drayton paused. "Might you have time for that?"

"I suppose I could make time."

Right after I call Pete Riley and cancel our dinner.

Theodosia didn't need a crystal ball to tell her what was on the docket. "I'm guessing Meredith wants our help in selecting a coffin?"

"Is that too odious a task?" Drayton asked.

"I'll pick you up in ten minutes," Theodosia said. "And to answer your question — yes, it is."

17

Doake and Wilson Funeral Home was located in a redbrick building on Montagu Street. It was basically an old mansion that had been built in the nineteen twenties. Over time, gaudy pillars had been added to the front and a large white stucco building had been tacked onto the back part of it.

Theodosia pulled into the funeral home's small parking lot and decided she really didn't want to know what went on in that white stucco building with the narrow, frosted windows. But as soon as she and Drayton stepped into the funeral home, via a side entrance, the chilled scent of carnations and chemicals pretty much screamed, *Funeral Parlor — Bodies Embalmed Here.*

A thick dark-blue carpet whispered underfoot as they approached an old-fashioned reception desk that held baskets of flowers and a gold gooseneck lamp.

"We're here with the Doyle party," Drayton said in a decorous tone to the gray-haired receptionist who was sorting through a stack of papers. Death certificates?

Theodosia was happy that Drayton was able to handle funereal issues with dignity and grace. She pretty much had to be dragged, kicking and screaming, into a funeral home, whether it be to select a casket or attend a viewing.

The fifty-something receptionist looked up with a sad, practiced smile. "Some of your party is already here. I'll take you downstairs so you can join them in our showroom."

"Showroom," Drayton stage-whispered as they followed the woman down a flight of beige carpeted stairs to the basement. "As if picking out a casket is like buying a car."

But Theodosia thought it might actually be similar to buying a car, since make, model, and price were all important factors.

The showroom, at the end of a narrow hallway, was brightly lit (some would say garish) and filled with caskets in various models, finishes, and sizes.

"You came," Meredith said, as soon as she spotted Theodosia and Drayton. "I knew you would. I told Alex that you would never desert me in my hour of need."

"Don't forget, we're here for you, too,"

Alex said as he and Bill Jacoby rose from where they'd been sitting on an ugly green sofa. They'd obviously postponed THE BIG DECISION until Theodosia and Drayton arrived to cast their vote.

Picking out a casket? To what do we owe this honor? was the thought that screamed through Theodosia's brain. Drayton had other things on his mind.

"Is there any word on Fawn?" was Drayton's first question.

Meredith toddled up to him and practically collapsed in his arms. "Nothing at all," she sobbed.

Theodosia looked past a weeping Meredith to Alex. She wondered what his state of mind was at the moment. Although the look on his face didn't surprise her. Calm? Check. Looking slightly bored? Check that box, too.

"Thank you both for coming," Bill Jacoby said. He looked keenly embarrassed by Meredith's theatrics and Alex's indifference.

"You're quite welcome," Theodosia said. She glanced around at all the coffins on display. Some were propped up against the wall; others rested on raised metal biers. "Have you made any decisions yet?"

Looking a little disheartened, Jacoby pursed his lips and shook his head. "Nope."

But before they got down to the business of selecting a casket, Theodosia had a couple of questions she wanted to get out of the way.

"Alex," Theodosia said, "I didn't know Fawn very well — I barely had a chance to speak with her — but in the short time I did, she told me she was quite unhappy. That she wanted a divorce."

Alex looked shocked. Or maybe pretend-shocked?

"I thought we settled this the other day. Fawn *never* told me she was unhappy," Alex blurted. "Never, ever. You have to believe me!"

"They loved each other very much," Meredith said. "Fawn was a happy-go-lucky girl."

"And another thing," Theodosia said, pressing on. "You mentioned that Fawn wasn't a particularly skillful sailor."

"She wasn't," Alex said. "She was pretty much terrified of boats."

"Yet she managed to start up the motor, maneuver your sailboat out of the marina and into busy Charleston Harbor, and then put up a sail," Theodosia said. "At night.

226

Which is rather interesting."

"It is?" Meredith asked. "Why?"

"Because it makes me think that perhaps Fawn wasn't alone in that sailboat," Theodosia said.

"What exactly are you getting at?" Alex asked.

"Maybe Fawn sailed out there with someone's help. The harbormaster at the yacht club told me the sail was still up when the Coast Guard towed it back to the dock."

"She could have managed it," Alex said.

"Maybe she read a book about sailing, boned up on it," Meredith said.

"Or maybe Fawn managed to sail out on her own and was then picked up by another boat," Theodosia said.

Meredith looked shocked. "You mean Fawn might have been running away from home?" She blinked at Alex. "She wouldn't do that, would she? Tell me she wouldn't do that."

"Of course not," Alex said. But he didn't sound convincing.

"You loved her. We all loved her," Meredith blubbered.

"If Fawn was so dearly loved, then where is she?" Theodosia asked.

"Where is she indeed?" Jacoby asked, rocking back on his heels. He suddenly looked suspicious of his two charges.

Conversation broke off then, devolving into muffled sniffles and a few whispers between Meredith and Alex. In fact, it was blessed relief when the funeral director finally showed up.

"Bob Doake," he said, shaking hands with everyone. "I do apologize for keeping you folks waiting."

Doake was tall, thin, and slightly ethereal-looking. He wore a three-piece pin-striped suit that was a little too sharp. Like maybe he'd been auditioning for the road company of *Guys and Dolls.*

"Have you had sufficient time to look around?" Doake asked. He steepled his fingers together and arranged his features in a faint, decorous smile. "Have you made any decisions yet?"

"We're still looking," Meredith said.

"Take your time," Doake said smoothly. Then, when everyone just stood there, uneasy about making the first move, he said, "Our Granada model is extremely popular for our male clientele." He walked a few steps toward a casket and rested his hand on a pouf of pale-blue lining. "This one has a walnut veneer with satin-covered memory foam and silver handles and fixtures."

Meredith's nose twitched. "It looks a little cheap."

"Then perhaps an upgrade to our Argosy model," Doake said smoothly. He was eager to upsell her for an undoubtedly steeper markup.

Meredith lifted a shoulder. "Eh." She wasn't impressed.

"Let's try to figure out what you *do* want," Theodosia suggested. "The, uh, features that are most important to you."

"A capital idea," Drayton said. He stepped over to a large copper-colored casket. "How about this one?" He looked down, fingered a tag, and read it out loud. "The Bradford model. Stainless steel, continuous weld construction . . ." His mouth twitched. "An adjustable bed."

Meredith shook her head. "No."

"Okay," Theodosia said, feeling like a hostess on *The Price Is Right*. "What about this silver-blue one? It looks kind of spiffy." She thought it looked like an airbrushed Harley-Davidson, but maybe Meredith would think it contemporary and stylish?

"I think I need something a touch more elegant," Meredith said.

"She means more better," Alex said. He was in a bad mood, and it was obvious he couldn't wait to get out of there.

"That one looks nice," Meredith said, pointing to a stainless steel casket. "I like the silk lining with French folds." She turned to Doake. "Do you know, is the lining made of Indian muga silk or mulberry silk?"

"I believe it's mulberry silk," he said.

Meredith wrinkled her nose. "Oh."

"Does it make a difference?" Bill Jacoby asked her. "Is the casket going to be open or closed?"

"Closed," Alex said.

"Open," Meredith said.

Doake looked down at his spit-polished shoes, wisely staying out of the discussion.

Drayton stepped in gallantly to fill the void.

"What would you think about this Luxor model?" he asked, touching the edge of a nearby casket. "The mahogany with brass fittings does lend a subdued but elegant note."

"I don't know," Meredith said. She tapped an index finger against her upper lip, thinking. "It's difficult to choose. My brain isn't working like it should." She spun around and gazed at Alex. "Which casket do you think Reginald would've preferred?"

"I don't know," Alex snapped. "Probably that big, honkin' El Presidente model over

230

there. It would appeal to Reginald's sense of power and grandiosity."

"That's so cruel," Meredith said.

Alex pulled his mouth into a sneer. "But it's the truth."

18

"Alex hated his stepfather," Theodosia said
to Drayton as she drove down Queen Street.
When Drayton didn't reply, she glanced
sideways at him and said, "You did pick up
on his negative vibes, didn't you?"

"Hard not to. But it pains me greatly to
see their family so fractured."

"Well, they are."

They rode along in silence for a few
blocks, then Drayton said, "So you took a
look at the sailboat, did you?"

"That's right."

"Find anything unusual?"

"I think somebody fired up the auxiliary
engine and motored that J/22 out into the
harbor."

"So Fawn didn't suddenly turn into a
crackerjack sailor?"

"Doubtful," Theodosia said.

"You think Fawn had an accomplice?"
Drayton sounded surprised.

"It's possible."

"Strange, isn't it?" Drayton said.

"What is?"

"All of this started with a day of hunting, and now you're *still* hunting."

"Trying to, anyway."

Drayton smiled. "A bird in the hand?"

"If only," Theodosia said.

"Are you . . ." Drayton started.

"What?" Theodosia said.

"Do you have plans for the evening?"

"I was supposed to go out to dinner with Riley tonight, but that got kicked to the curb in favor of our coffin-hunting expedition."

"Oh dear." Drayton looked upset. "I'm so sorry for intruding."

"It's okay, don't worry about it. What did you have in mind?"

"I was wondering if we could swing by the Heritage Society."

"Now?"

"There's a meeting I'm supposed to attend. Well, I technically don't have to attend it; I can simply drop by and cast my ballot."

"What are you voting on?" Theodosia asked.

"Budget. What else?"

"Sure, we can stop there. I don't mind," Theodosia said. "As long as it doesn't take too long."

"Then you come in with me," Drayton suggested. "Tap your foot, glance at your watch. They'll get the message."

"You're making me out to be the bad guy, huh?"

Drayton smiled as he gazed straight ahead. "I could try, but they'd never believe it."

The Heritage Society, that venerable granite building that sat like its own small principality in the middle of Charleston's Historic District, was busy tonight. Lights shone from the windows, cars were parked on both sides of the street in front of it, a small group of people was gathered on the steps.

"The joint's jumping," Theodosia said as she drove by slowly, looking for a parking spot.

"Because there's so much going on. Besides hiring new curators, Timothy is rallying the membership to go out and beat the bushes, try to turn up more big-buck donors."

"Nothing wrong with that." Theodosia knew that many nonprofit organizations were hurting. She served on the board of Big Paws, a service dog organization that was continually desperate for funding.

"Why don't you pull around to the alley?" Drayton said. "We'll sneak in the back way."

"You have a key?"

"Yes, but don't tell anyone."

They parked and went in the back door — click, clack, unlock — which led them right through one of the storage rooms.

"I love it in here," Theodosia said as they walked through the temperature-controlled semidarkness. "Look at all these wonderful pieces. It must be heaven to work here as a curator." Her eyes danced across an old map table, some ladder-back chairs with woven wicker seats, and a few faded oil paintings that were probably waiting to go to the conservation department. Theodosia was a woman who appreciated art — paintings, sculpture, photography, pottery, almost anything that had been lovingly created by human hands. Her tastes also ran to outsider art, as well as the marvelous, handwoven sweetgrass baskets that were so ubiquitous to South Carolina.

They popped out next to one of the meeting rooms and ran into Timothy as he strode down the corridor. His face was not only pinched with worry, but as gray as his three-piece charcoal suit.

Timothy took one look at Drayton and said, "Good, you're here." Then he noticed Theodosia, gave a perfunctory smile, and said, "Hello, there."

"I mean no disrespect, but you're looking a little frantic," Theodosia said to him.

"Probably because I am frantic," Timothy said. "Money, the funds needed to run this place — to pay my staff, keep the lights on, do programming, and make continued acquisitions for our various collections — just keeps getting tighter and tighter."

"Our wealthier citizens do seem to be holding on tight to their money," Drayton said.

"Even in a bull market, donations are markedly down," Timothy said. "I've never seen anything like it. And now that we're not getting Creekmore Plantation, well . . ."

"But you've still got a strong membership base," Theodosia said. "Which I'm sure you can mobilize to attract other members and donors."

"Particularly donors," Drayton said.

"And you're sponsoring that big Edgar Allen Poe Symposium next month," Theodosia said. "That should generate some interest and dollars." She really did try to see the upside of things.

"Hopefully, it will," Timothy said. "I know that Claire Waltho, one of our new curators, has some kind of Halloween event lined up to complement the symposium." He led them past a display of antique Civil War

236

pistols to his office. He unlocked the door and gestured for them to come in and take a seat.

Theodosia loved Timothy's office. It was a combination library and mini museum. His shelves contained leather-bound books and precious antiquities that included rare coins, Greek statues, American pottery, and even a jewel-studded crown that had once belonged to a long-exiled Russian prince.

Once Timothy had seated himself behind his enormous rosewood desk, and Theodosia and Drayton were seated in the leather-and-hobnail chairs directly opposite him, he got down to business.

"Is there anything new that I should know concerning Reginald Doyle's murder?" Timothy asked. "Rumors about suspects? Ripples of mistrust? Heartfelt confessions?"

"I'm afraid not," Drayton said.

"Well, there might be a few things," Theodosia said.

Timothy's sharp eyes shifted in her direction. "Such as?"

"I found out that Meredith Doyle is a crack shot with a pistol, Guy Thorne is gambling away the profits at Trollope's Restaurant, Carl Clewis is an absolute jerk, and Alex Doyle has been a verbally abusive husband to Fawn, who is missing and sort of presumed to be drowned."

Drayton turned and stared at her. "Do you think you left anything out?"

"No," Theodosia said. She wanted Timothy to know that the suspect situation was definitely in flux.

Timothy raised a wrinkled hand and touched a small bronze dog statue that held a stack of papers in place.

"You've been busy."

"Busy, yes," Theodosia said. "Productive, no."

"I heard about the sailboat being found. Do you think Fawn might have drowned?" Timothy asked.

"I'm not sure," Theodosia said.

"Take a guess."

"No," Theodosia said. "No pun intended, but I think there's something fishy going on. I just don't know what it is."

"Do you think Fawn might have been the one who killed Reginald?" Timothy asked.

"Oh no!" was Drayton's shocked response.

"Hard to say," Theodosia said in measured tones. "Fawn was angry at the family; there's no doubt about that. But is she a killer? I'd like to think not."

Timothy's dark eyes sparkled. "Is there any chance Alex might have killed his

238

stepfather and then turned his wrath on Fawn?"

"Alex is certainly angry enough. In fact, he takes turns raging at just about everyone. I suppose he could have killed Reginald Doyle. But Fawn? When push comes to shove . . . killing his own wife? Probably not," Theodosia said. "At least I hope not."

"I say," Drayton said. "This is a terribly unnerving conversation."

Timothy slapped both hands against his knees, then stood up. "Enough of this craziness, then. Drayton, you need to go cast your vote. Our registrar, Eleanor, has all the ballots laid out in the Palmetto Room. Once everyone on the board has voted, she'll tally them up."

They all walked down to the Palmetto Room then, passing the Great Hall, where Reginald Doyle's funeral would be taking place tomorrow morning. Peering into the dim interior of the large auditorium that served a dual purpose as a gallery, Theodosia could see that a semicircle of black folding chairs had already been set up. But no coffin. Not yet.

"Say now," a voice called from behind them. "I didn't expect to see you two again so soon."

Theodosia turned and found herself staring at a smiling Bill Jacoby.

"Timothy twisted my arm, too," Jacoby said. "About the balloting."

"He's good at that," Drayton laughed.

"We're delighted to have Mr. Jacoby on our board of directors," Timothy said. "When Reginald retired and Mr. Jacoby took his place, there was a seamless transition. Not a single missed step."

"Mr. Jacoby's company even gifted us with a nice financial donation," Drayton said to Theodosia.

Timothy plucked at Drayton's sleeve. "Time to vote. Let's not keep Eleanor waiting."

Which left Theodosia facing Bill Jacoby.

"Thank you for your help tonight," Jacoby said. "At the funeral parlor."

"It was the least I could do. I'm just sorry it was so traumatic for Meredith."

"Tomorrow's going to be even more emotional for her. Especially with Fawn still missing."

"Do you think she drowned?" Theodosia asked.

Jacoby's brows scrunched together, his eyes teared up, and he seemed to be on the verge of an emotional breakdown. Then he swallowed hard and managed to pull it together.

"I'm praying that Fawn is safe and sound," Jacoby said. "Wherever she may be."

Theodosia had just dropped Drayton off and was driving down Legare Street, when her phone rang. She dug in her purse, pulled it out, and said, "Hello?"

It was Pete Riley.

"I know we called off dinner tonight, but now I'm hoping — no, I'm holding my breath and praying — that we can somehow get together anyway," he said. "Have a late dinner date."

"Let me check my schedule," Theodosia said. She let two seconds slide by, then said, "Guess what? You're in luck. I just cleared my calendar."

"Meet me at Poogan's Porch in twenty minutes?" Poogan's Porch was a Charleston landmark, a restaurant located in an 1891 home on Queen Street in the French Quarter.

"You got it."

Theodosia managed to get to Poogan's Porch in a record fifteen minutes. But Riley must have called her from there, because he was sitting at a table in their posh-looking parlor, waiting for her when she arrived. Even better, he'd ordered a bottle of wine.

"A cabernet," Riley said as he plucked the

bottle from the wine bucket and poured her a glassful. "Stag's Leap FAY Cabernet. 2014." He grinned. "That's the vintage, not the price."

"Aren't you just full of surprises," Theodosia said. She smiled at Riley across the candlelit table, and her heart skipped a few beats. Tonight he was wearing an oatmeal-colored cashmere sweater paired with blue jeans. A casual look that made him appear more like a college English professor than a homicide detective. Plus, he was tall, fairly intense, and his brown hair carried a few threads of silver at the temples to give him a seasoned look. Yup, she thought, Riley was *so* good-looking. And now here they were, finally able to connect and enjoy a late dinner.

"How'd your day go?" Riley asked once they'd ordered. A bowl of she-crab soup with Poogan's famous buttermilk biscuits for Theodosia, shrimp and grits for Riley.

"Promise you won't get mad if I tell you?" Theodosia said.

"No. But tell me anyway."

"I talked to the Lavender Lady, snuck a look at Alex Doyle's J/22, argued with Carl Clewis, and went shopping for coffins."

"Some folks have all the fun."

"What did you do?" Theodosia asked.

"I got called on the carpet today by our Supreme Allied Commander," Riley said.

"Really?" Theodosia's voice held a questioning note.

Riley's laugh was a warm rumble. "Don't act so innocent. You knew I would."

"No, I didn't," Theodosia said.

"Let me put it this way, part of the tongue-lashing included Burt Tidwell asking me to personally deliver a warning to you."

Theodosia gave him a questioning look. "So this isn't a romantic dinner after all? It's more a romantic warning?"

"Something like that."

"Let me guess, Tidwell wants me to back off."

"*I* want you to back off," Riley said.

"Of course you do."

Conversation halted as the waiter arrived with their dinners, set everything out carefully, and refilled their wineglasses. Then they were caught up in exclaiming over the elegant presentation and the tantalizing aromas rising from their food.

Which, in turn, led to actual eating.

"This is fabulous," Riley managed to say in between bites.

"Mmn," Theodosia responded. With every spoonful of she-crab soup, her mouth was in culinary heaven.

"I take it the soup is good?"

"Some of the best I've ever had." As Theodosia broke open a buttermilk biscuit, Riley hastily reached for the plate of butter and passed it to her.

"Anything else you'd like?" he asked.

Do I dare?

Theodosia nodded. "Do you know if an accelerant was used in the fire at Creekmore Plantation?"

"What!"

"Oh, and could you do a quick check on Carl Clewis for me? See what he was up to the day of Doyle's murder?"

"Are you serious? Asking me to . . ." Riley was practically sputtering. "After the thrashing I just got?"

"Please? They're both awfully important."

Riley stared at her for a few seconds, then nodded. "Okay, but you can only pick one."

"Carl Clewis."

"So that's it. The final, *finito,* finale. One and done, then no more worming information out of me. And I assure you, my dear, our deal is nonnegotiable."

Theodosia just smiled sweetly.

19

Reginald Doyle's simple, dignified memorial service wasn't all that simple and it wasn't particularly dignified. Since nine thirty, people had been pouring into the Heritage Society's Great Hall, moving the spindly black chairs around to suit their needs and circle of friends, greeting one another loudly, and tippy-tapping on their phones.

"Looks like it's going to be a full house," Drayton whispered to Theodosia. "Although I don't see a single soul that I know."

"I think most of these people are from Celantis Pharmaceuticals and Trollope's Restaurant," Theodosia said. "Employees."

"So a mandatory event then. A command performance, heavy on the command."

"Probably."

"Do you know how Haley is coming with the food?"

"Last time I checked she was setting up

the buffet table in the Palmetto Room with the help of one of the Heritage Society interns. And she's using the adjacent kitchen to brew tea. Once the scones and tea sandwiches are all arranged, Haley plans to scoot back to the tea shop. She's exhibiting at the Sugar Arts Show this afternoon, if you recall. So we'll need to get in there to honcho the luncheon as soon as this service concludes."

"This service can't conclude until it starts," Drayton said in a dour tone as he glanced about the room again. "I see people, I see a wooden bier, but there's no coffin."

"Reginald is late to his own funeral," Theodosia said. She glanced about the room, at the clerestory windows that let in small shards of light, at the tasteful display of Audubon prints hung on the far wall.

A shadowy figure hovered in the doorway, then shlumped its way in and sat down heavily in the last row.

Theodosia immediately recognized Bill Glass, who was dressed like a refugee from a nineties'-era consignment shop. Weird khaki vest, grunge-inspired plaid flannel shirt, and pants that were just this side of parachute pants. He immediately began fiddling with his cameras.

A man in a dark three-piece suit — an

usher or maybe one of the Heritage Society's young curators — touched Glass on the shoulder and asked him to put away his cameras. Glass nodded and left the room. But two minutes later, he snuck back in again. When he glanced around and saw Theodosia looking at him, he touched a finger to his forehead in a mock salute.

She ignored him.

Finally, amid the buzz and whispers of the assembled crowd, Meredith arrived on the arm of Bill Jacoby. She wore a black skirt suit, a white silk blouse with a pussycat bow, and a jaunty black veil. She looked, Theodosia thought, like a *Vogue*-inspired Sicilian widow.

Two minutes later, the coffin arrived. Resting on a metal conveyer that had one loose, squeaking wheel, it was rolled into the Great Hall by six somber-looking pallbearers. Theodosia recognized Alex Doyle, Timothy Neville, and Guy Thorne as they struggled to push the gleaming El Presidente model along, but she wasn't sure who the other three men were. Probably executives from Celantis Pharmaceuticals.

Even as the coffin was seesawed into place and transferred to the bier, as a podium was rolled out next to it, the guests surrounding them were still texting and checking their e-mails.

"What are all these people doing?" Drayton asked. "What's on their phones that's so all-fired important?"

"Nothing," Theodosia said. "They're millennials. That's what they do."

"The porch light's on but nobody's home," Drayton muttered.

As Guy Thorne draped a large swag of white lilies over the casket (closed, not open, Theodosia noted), music seeped through the room's speakers. Theodosia recognized the song as "How Great Thou Art."

Finally, a black-suited minister strode into the room and took his place behind the podium. Throats were cleared, a few phones were switched to mute, and Bill Glass began to surreptitiously take pictures. Theodosia could hear the faint *snap, snap, snap* of his camera. She wished she could go back there, pry open that camera, and rip the film out. Except she knew it was a digital camera. Maybe, she thought, some things *shouldn't* be improved upon.

The back row also held a couple of surprise guests who'd snuck into the room and settled themselves onto folding chairs. One was Jack Grimes, the other was Carl Clewis.

Weird, Theodosia thought, *that those two just showed up.* She also decided it could prove to be highly interesting.

The minister opened with a reading from Romans 6:4, *We were buried therefore with him by baptism into death, so that as Christ was raised from the dead by the glory of the Father, we too might walk in the newness of life.*

Then the minister spoke about Reginald Doyle for a while, recounting a sort of time capsule version of Doyle's life, accomplishments, and charitable contributions. He did not mention that the man had been murdered, or that his killer was still out there roaming freely.

Timothy Neville was the next speaker. He spoke for a good ten minutes, praising Reginald's service and devotion to the Heritage Society and sharing a few amusing anecdotes.

By the time Bill Jacoby got his turn to eulogize Reginald, offering even more platitudes, the audience had pretty much tuned out. They were back on their phones.

"Rude," Drayton hissed to Theodosia.

"Tell me about it."

Finally, it was Meredith's turn. She rose shakily from her chair, staggered to the podium, and clutched it with both hands.

"Thank you all for coming," Meredith said in a high, reedy voice, made tight with emotion. "As you're well aware, this is a desperate and challenging time for myself and my family. Losing Reginald . . ." Meredith's voice faltered, and she turned her head away from the crowd, trying to tamp down her tears and gather her thoughts.

Finally, she was able to continue.

"Losing Reginald . . . and then Fawn . . . who we are *still* praying for and hoping will have a safe return . . . this has all been completely unbearable. It feels as if . . ." She touched a hand to her chest. "As if my heart is wound tight with barbed wire. The only bright spot in any of this has been my son, as well as my dear friends, and all of . . ." Meredith's voice cracked again, and this time she simply shook her head. She was not only rambling, she was way too grief-stricken to go on.

Thankfully, the minister bounded up to the podium, escorted Meredith back to her chair, and led the group in a fairly rousing rendition of "Amazing Grace." And then he graciously invited everyone to stay for a light lunch to be served immediately across the hall in the Palmetto Room.

"Oops," Drayton said. "That's our cue."

Theodosia and Drayton popped up from

their seats like a couple of wily gophers and bounded down the center aisle ahead of everyone else. They flew across the hallway and ran into the Palmetto Room, ready to don aprons and get busy. But when they laid eyes on the perfectly arranged tea table, it was clear Haley had already worked her magic.

A dozen three-tiered stands held all manner of tea sandwiches — chicken salad, crab salad, cream cheese with chutney, and parsley and bacon tea rounds. More tiered stands, as well as several large platters, held brownie bites, miniature butterscotch scones, chocolate chip cookies, and fig bars. Haley had also set out a large stack of luncheon-sized plates that were perfect for sandwiches and scones, as well as balancing a small teacup.

"Is this okay?" Brenda, the intern, asked them.

"Magnificent," Theodosia proclaimed. "Thank you for your help. It looks as if we won't have to do much more than smile and encourage the guests to help themselves."

"What about the tea?" Drayton asked.

Brenda pointed to a large silver urn.

"Better taste it," Theodosia said.

Drayton poured a cup and took a taste. "Well?"

"Harney & Sons Silver Needle," Drayton said. "Highly drinkable."

Meredith and Bill Jacoby were the first ones through the line. Meredith was still leaking tears like mad, but Theodosia noticed it didn't stop her from helping herself to an assortment of tea sandwiches and desserts. Jacoby also piled up his plate.

Theodosia and Drayton smiled, answered questions, and poured tea as more people filed through: Alex and a couple of his friends. Guy Thorne and a contingent from Trollope's Restaurant. The Celantis people. Then Jack Grimes and, at the very tail end, Carl Clewis.

Theodosia sidled over to Drayton. "You see the guy with the high fade haircut and glasses? That's Carl Clewis."

"He's the neighbor? The one who dammed up Axson Creek?" Drayton asked.

Theodosia lifted her shoulders. "He claims he improved the creek."

"Did he?"

"Darned if I know."

A thought formed on Drayton's face as he glanced around. "Just think," he said. "All your suspects are gathered together in one place."

Theodosia nodded. "It's slightly reminiscent of a locked-room murder mystery, yes?"

Drayton gave a faint smile. "Agatha Christie."

Just when everything was running smoothly — most of the funeral guests had filed through the line, the food had been greatly appreciated — two loud, quarrelsome voices rose above the gentle hum of conversation.

Theodosia stood up on tiptoes, wondering what was going on. And saw Jack Grimes tap a finger hard against Carl Clewis's chest.

"You ought to be ashamed of yourself," Grimes said loudly. "Why are you even here? Did you come to gloat over the poor man's death?"

Clewis bristled at his words. "I'm allowed to pay my respects just as much as the next person!"

"You know what I think?" Grimes shouted back. "I think you're the one who killed him."

Clewis sneered as he made an angry shooing motion. "Get out of my face, you troglodyte."

"You think you'll get away scot-free?" Grimes cried. "You won't! People are onto you. *I'm* onto you."

Heads turned. Conversation in the room

253

came to a screeching halt as the men continued to rail loudly at each other. Meredith looked like she was going to faint.

"Oh no," Theodosia said. She was about to go over and shush the two men up when Guy Thorne suddenly bulled his way through the crowd and stuck himself right in the middle of the fray.

"He's right," Thorne thundered at Clewis. "There's no way you're going to get away with this." He shook a finger directly in Clewis's face. "You're a murdering scum!"

"Shut up!" Clewis shouted. He was red-faced and angry, losing his composure.

But Guy Thorne was wound up and eager to get his licks in. "You think you're so smart when you're really a simpleton."

Theodosia wondered why Thorne was going after Clewis, then decided that maybe Thorne was trying to throw up a hellacious smoke screen. If Thorne had really gambled much of Trollope's proceeds away, and Reginald Doyle had found out, then maybe Thorne *was* the guilty party!

"Should I do something?" Drayton asked. "Go over and try to intercede?" He looked as if it was the last thing he wanted to do.

Theodosia shook her head. "Let them squabble and have their hissy fit. They'll poop out sooner or later."

And they did. Eventually.

Clewis stormed out. Thorne stormed out. Grimes just stood there and flapped his arms helplessly.

Theodosia went over to talk to him. Grimes looked beyond defeated, as if he'd just lost everything. And the soft spot in Theodosia's heart thought that maybe he had.

"Are you okay?" Theodosia asked.

"Oh . . . not really," Grimes said.

"What are you . . . What will you do now?" Even though Grimes was still a suspect in Theodosia's book, she couldn't help but feel a little sorry for him.

"I'm leaving town, for one thing."

"Where will you go?"

"My brother, Keith, owns a game farm in Clinch County, Georgia, where he raises Bluefaces, White Kelsos, and Lacy Round-heads."

"Those are fancy chickens?" The only chickens Theodosia knew were the ones she generally counted before they were hatched.

"Yup, chickens. I'll go there and help out for a while."

"Good luck," Theodosia said, meaning it.

20

But that still wasn't the conclusion of the memorial service from hell.

In a burst of frantic pomp and pageantry, Meredith had hired a number of what could only be called *attractions* to accompany her dead husband to his final resting place in St. Philip's Graveyard.

The first inkling anyone had of this was the mournful sound of bagpipes. As everyone crowded into the hallway, curious as to what was going on, two bagpipers in tartan kilts and sashes stood there playing a slow Scottish tune.

"Please." Meredith's voice rose as she clapped her hands together. "Everyone, come this way."

And they did.

The pallbearers had reassembled and were now wheeling Reginald Doyle's casket to the front door of the Heritage Society. And there, waiting on the street, was an old-fashioned horse-drawn caisson. Four black horses tossed their heads, anxious to get going, stomping and clopping their shiny hooves.

"Meredith has really gone all out," Theodosia said as the pallbearers loaded the casket onto the horse-drawn caisson.

"Tasteful and elegant has been kicked to the curb," Drayton said, "in favor of a full-blown Barnum and Bailey spectacle. What's next? A court jester? Fire-eaters?"

"Please follow along, everyone. We need to proceed to the graveside service," Meredith urged. She hurried over and took her place behind the caisson and in front of the bagpipers.

"Now what?" Drayton asked.

"I guess we're going to the graveside service?" Theodosia said.

"What about our dishes and teapots?"

"I'll ask the intern to pack everything up for us."

The procession — because that's what it truly was — wound its way down Gateway Walk. They passed through the Governor Aiken Gates, walked around the Gibbes Museum of Art, crossed Meeting Street, and continued along. Gateway Walk was one of Charleston's hidden gems, a ramble

257

through four churchyards that was both contemplative and charming. And with plenty of towering hedges, gardens, marble statues, and memorial plaques along the way, it was also secretive and seductive.

"St. Philip's Graveyard," Theodosia said as the procession halted and the mourners fanned out among dozens of ancient moss-covered grave markers. "Looks like Reginald's going to be buried right here." After the riot of greenery on Gateway Walk, the cemetery felt a little dark, a little too dank.

"I have to say I'm grudgingly impressed," Drayton said. "You have to be a big muckety-muck to have a resting place here. You have to have important *family members* buried here."

Theodosia nodded in agreement. "Old money."

"On the other hand . . ." Drayton cast a watchful eye at the tilting gravestones shaded by oak trees dripping with Spanish moss. "This place . . ."

". . . is supposedly haunted," Theodosia said, thinking about all the legends she'd heard over the years, about the strange sightings that were still whispered about.

"Or so the story goes," Drayton said.

"But you don't believe . . ."

"That's the funny thing about legends,"

Drayton said. "There's often a kernel of truth somewhere."

More prayers were said, another eulogy given, and bagpipes played. Afterward, there was a sort of reception line where all the guests crowded around Meredith and Alex to express their final sympathies.

When Theodosia and Drayton eventually reached the two of them, Drayton gave a respectful nod to Meredith and said, "Tell me, how are you holding up?"

Meredith's face was white as a sheet.

"I don't think I am," Meredith said. She took a half stutter step toward Drayton and curled a trembling hand around his upper arm. "The memorial service . . . that terrible argument . . ."

Drayton gazed at her with deep concern. "Perhaps a spot of tea might help revive you? The Indigo Tea Shop is a mere two doors away, so maybe you could walk back there with Theodosia and me and . . ."

"Have a fortifying cup?" Meredith asked, her voice filling with gratitude. "That would be wonderful." She glanced over at Alex, gave him an offhand wave, and said, "I'm going to the tea shop with Drayton and Theodosia. I'll see you later."

Theodosia had walked a few steps ahead of Drayton and Meredith. So when she arrived at the Indigo Tea Shop and saw Haley standing behind the counter, her first words were, "The Sugar Arts Show. Is your dessert ready to go?"

"No problemo," Haley said. "I put the finishing touches on it this morning. The tea shop's been relatively quiet, too. Only a few takeouts. Miss Dimple and I handled everything with ease."

"Is she still here?" Theodosia asked.

"Just left."

"What time does your entry need to be there?"

Haley consulted her watch. "One o'clock. Then judging starts at two."

"So you've got an hour before you have to leave, and then I'll come join you a little later."

"Wonderful. I can use the moral support."

"You'll do fine. And now I'm going to close the tea shop for the afternoon," Theodosia said just as Drayton escorted Meredith through the door, hung up her coat, and settled her at the nearest table.

"Works for me," Haley said. "I'll even put

out the 'Closed' sign."

Haley hung the sign and went back into the kitchen while Drayton busied himself behind the counter, happy to be back where he was reigning king of his domain.

Theodosia picked up a yellow floral teapot and held it out to him. "Chamomile tea?" she asked. She figured Drayton's number one priority was to calm Meredith down.

Drayton shook his head. "I'm going to whip up a London fog tea latte for Meredith."

"Really." Theodosia watched as Drayton brewed a pot of Earl Grey, heated up some milk and frothed it, then poured the tea and milk into a tall latte glass and added a half teaspoon of vanilla extract.

"You want one, too?" he asked.

"Why not." Theodosia went into the kitchen, assembled a plate of scones, and carried it back to Meredith's table.

Meredith sipped her London fog tea latte in a self-induced teary haze. She was obviously upset and feeling sorry for herself.

"How is your tea?" Drayton asked.

"Hot and delicious," Meredith said. "This is so kind of you. I feel like I've really been through the ringer. First Reginald and then . . ." She made a choking sound. "Fawn."

"I'm sure she'll turn up," Theodosia said. She was enjoying her tea latte as well.

"I'm so fearful that Fawn's poor body will come bobbing to the surface and she'll get snagged in some fisherman's net," Meredith sobbed.

"I think that only happens in B movies," Theodosia said under her breath.

"But perhaps . . ." Drayton started to say. Then he was interrupted by —

BANG! BANG! BANG!

Meredith clutched a hand to her chest, eyes rolling, practically having a brain spasm. "What was that?" she cried. She was a rabbit afraid of its own shadow.

And another BANG! BANG! Someone was pounding loudly and insistently at the front door.

"Honestly," Drayton said. "The 'Closed' sign is out, so who on earth could be that rude and insistent?"

Theodosia walked over and peered out the window.

"It's Delaine," she said. "We may as well let her in, or she'll just keep pounding away until she wears off the paint." Theodosia knew by now that Delaine didn't have an "off" switch.

Theodosia opened the door, and with a triumphant smile on her face, Delaine Dish

262

crowed, "I *knew* it. I just *knew* you were in there."

"That's me, hiding in plain sight," Theodosia said as Delaine bustled past her, leaving behind a whiff of Dior perfume (or was that brimstone?). She wore a cream-colored sheath dress with a mandarin orange wool jacket over it. Her supple leather handbag matched her jacket perfectly.

"What I want to know," Delaine demanded, "is why the Indigo Tea Shop is locked up tighter than a drum. In the middle of the day, for goodness' sake. When you know that customers like myself are *dying* for a light lunch and a spot of tea."

Then Delaine caught sight of Meredith sitting at a table and her face fell. "Oh. Oh no," she said in a plaintive voice. "You poor, poor dear." She touched two fingers to the side of her head. "Silly, ditsy me. I just realized the *funeral* was this morning!"

Meredith nodded wordlessly.

"Oh, sweetie!" Delaine tottered to Meredith's side, taking tiny tight steps in her four-inch stilettos. Then she began cooing and patting Meredith's hands and face, insisting that everything was going to be just fine. Which of course it wasn't.

Meredith pretty much lapped up Delaine's soothing touch and words of comfort. Much

263

like Delaine, she was inner-directed and self-absorbed.

Not really the best traits to guide one through life, Theodosia thought as she watched the two women try to outdo each other in spilling their emotional baggage.

"And I suppose you also know that our dear Fawn is missing?" Meredith cried to Delaine.

"Yes, I did hear that. And about the sailboat being found." Delaine studied her French manicure. Whenever the conversation didn't center directly on her, she tended to drift away.

"We're holding a vigil for Fawn tonight at White Point Garden," Meredith said. "Can I count on you to attend?"

"Well . . . perhaps," Delaine hedged. "Though sea air does tend to give me a dreadful case of sniffles."

This was the first Theodosia had heard of a harborside vigil, and she thought it sounded strange. Better that Meredith and Alex should cooperate a little more with law enforcement. Unless, of course, they were hoping that Fawn would somehow come surfing in on a great wave tonight, surrounded by pink lights and dancing unicorns.

Delaine patted Meredith's hand. "You

know, dear, I thought the world of Fawn. She was such a lovely girl. And one of my very best customers."

Meredith blinked back tears. "Was she really?"

"Oh my, yes," Delaine said. To Delaine, a good customer was one who spent oodles of money.

"I'm sure Fawn will come back to us," Drayton said, adding his two cents to the conversation. "Somehow."

"Do you really think so?" Meredith almost pleaded.

"He just said so, didn't he?" Delaine said. She studied Meredith's tea latte and said, "Say, I wouldn't mind having one of those myself."

"Coming right up," Drayton said as he headed back to his counter.

Meredith focused intently on Delaine. "Let me ask you something. I've been thinking about having a séance. To, you know, see if we could somehow contact Fawn. Do you think that's a good idea?"

"I think it's a *monumental* idea," Delaine enthused. "Maybe you could contact your dead husband as well. He might still be close by, spinning around in the nether-world."

That was enough for Theodosia. She stood

up and walked over to the counter to join Drayton.

"What was Meredith saying?" Drayton asked. He was wiping out a Chinese famille rose teapot. "Something about finances?"

"She was talking about *séances*," Theodosia said, enunciating carefully. "Meredith is all wound up about holding a séance so she can try to communicate with Fawn. And maybe even Reginald."

"Oh my," Drayton said. "I don't like the idea of anything so . . . paranormal."

Delaine overheard him. "It seems perfectly normal to me," she shot back.

Theodosia waited for Drayton to finish making Delaine's tea latte, then carried it over to her. The two women were still batting around the merits of a séance.

"There are so many unanswered questions," Meredith was saying. "Who killed Reginald? Did Fawn really fling herself into Charleston Harbor? Or is the poor girl just missing — maybe kidnapped? Or perhaps she simply fell and hit her head and is wandering around with a dreadful case of amnesia."

Delaine pointed at Meredith. "I think I've seen that exact movie on Lifetime."

"Really?"

But Delaine's eyes were lit up like a

pinball machine. "I think your idea of holding a séance is *fabulous*! It would help find answers to all those pesky questions that are troubling you."

"No, it really wouldn't," Drayton said, sotto voce.

But Delaine was not to be dissuaded. "I know the absolutely *perfect* psychic for the job. Her name is Madame Emilia. The woman is all knowing, all-seeing — she can part the veil on the universe, just like that." Delaine snapped her fingers for added emphasis. Then she glanced around and dropped her voice, as if Soviet spies might be listening in. "Don't you dare tell a soul, but Madame Emilia helped my friend Kitty make an absolute *killing* in the stock market."

Theodosia frowned. Somehow, consulting a psychic, even a Wall Street wizard of a psychic, didn't seem like a particularly smart idea at this point in time. Meredith was too unstable, too vulnerable.

Unfortunately, Meredith was stuck on the idea like slick on a politician. "Then let's do it!" she squealed. Her skinny frame shook like a Chihuahua caught in an ice storm.

"Here's what I'll do," Delaine said. "I'll call Madame Emilia and arrange the whole thing. We'll do it immediately — tomorrow afternoon." She glanced around, immensely pleased with herself. "In fact, we'll do it right here."

"Here?" Theodosia echoed, her voice rising in an almost-squawk.

"This is the absolute perfect place," Delaine said.

"Um . . . why would that be?" Theodosia asked.

Delaine raised her hands as if to bestow a blessing, and her face took on a beatific expression. "Because Fawn was recently a guest here, and you can still literally *feel* the vibrations."

"I think that's Haley running the vacuum in the back room," Drayton muttered.

21

When Theodosia walked into the Grand Ballroom of the Commodore Hotel at two fifteen in the afternoon, she was hit with an aromatic tidal wave of sugar, cinnamon, vanilla, and chocolate (with an exquisite layer of butterscotch thrown in for good measure).

As far as the eye could see, tables were laden with every type of rich, sinful dessert one could imagine. And even though ribbons hadn't yet been awarded, a few hundred guests, gawkers, bakers, chocolatiers, chocoholics, and sugar artists (their white chef's hats bobbing in the crowd) walked the aisles, oohing and aahing over the incredible display of goodies.

Haley spotted Theodosia and rushed to greet her.

"You came!" Haley was bubbling over with enthusiasm.

"How could I not?" Theodosia said.

"When I'm almost positive you're going to take home a ribbon."

"I'm not sure about that. From what I've seen, there's some awfully stiff competition here."

"Let's go take a look."

They strolled from table to table, thoroughly enchanted by the amazingly creative entries.

"The theme this year is Southern Grace," Haley explained. "Which is why even the ballroom is decked out with flowing pink draperies, baskets of flowers, and floral garlands strung on the chandeliers."

"And what are the four categories again?" Theodosia asked.

Haley ticked them off on her fingers. "Wedding Cakes, of course. Then there's a Sculpted Cakes category, Southern Party Treats — those are the cookies, bars, and pies. And then there's my category, Sculpted Confections."

"I still don't know what you came up with," Theodosia said. "After you decided not to enter your sweet tea pie."

Haley grinned. "Then you'd better come and have a look."

They walked past tables with wedding cakes in the shape of castles, flower beds, hearts, pirate ships, and even bottles of champagne. At the Southern Party Treats display they saw cupcakes with swirls of fondant flowers, cookies decorated with sprinkles and twinkles, and all manner of bourbon, pecan, and chess pies.

The display of sculpted cakes gave them pause.

"These are fabulous," Theodosia said.

And they were. Cakes were skillfully made in the shape of hatboxes, guitars, Bibles, angels, circus tents, mystery books, and teapots, as well as Mad Hatter cakes and tipsy cakes with multiple layers that looked like they might become unbalanced at any second.

"But over here's the best," Haley said.

"Must be Sculpted Confections," Theodosia said as her eyes fell upon a garden of tiny mushrooms — all made from fondant and painted with food coloring. There were also fondant hummingbirds in jewel colors, a huge orange tropical fish, a tiger with gleaming green eyes, a shiny red high heel, a bouquet of pink roses, and many more.

"Haley, which one is your entry?"

Haley grinned. "Don't you recognize him?"

Theodosia's eyes roved across the table. She saw a pink elephant, a blue dolphin, a ballerina, and a . . .

271

Wait, is that really what I think it is?

Theodosia was stunned. Haley had created the most incredible and realistic fondant sculpture of Earl Grey that she could ever imagine.

"Is that really . . . ?" She was almost choked up. No, not almost. She *was* choked up.

"Do you like it?"

"Haley, I absolutely love it. It looks exactly like him. Sweet, friendly, alert, and a little bit mischievous. And his coat . . . all those subtle colors . . . How did you manage his coat?"

"I used Satin Ice rolled fondant and mixed the right colors together, just like they recommended. Five parts orange, one part green, and one part red."

"To get . . ."

"That lovely brownish-beige color." Haley's eyes danced with glee. "You really like it?"

"I love it. And I'm positive the judges will, too."

"The judges!" Haley said. "Omigosh, here they come!"

As if arriving on cue, four white-coated, clipboard-yielding judges strolled toward the table. One of the volunteers — they knew this because the woman wore a pink sash that said VOLUNTEER — walked ahead of them to shoo people out of the way.

"Please, everyone, move back at least ten feet," the volunteer urged. "Kindly give the judges an unobstructed view of the tables so they can score all these wonderful entries."

Haley clapped a hand to her chest. "This is so exciting."

Theodosia was about to respond to Haley when a voice in her right ear whispered, "Don't tell me you entered this contest, too."

Theodosia whipped her head around, only to find Guy Thorne standing next to her, a slightly bemused expression on his face.

"My chef, Haley, is one of the contestants," Theodosia said. She quickly introduced Thorne to Haley and added, "She's the one responsible for the scones and tea sandwiches at this morning's memorial service."

Thorne gave a curt nod. "Good stuff."

Haley flipped a hank of hair and moved away from them, her eyes completely fixated on the judges.

"I take it Trollope's has entered something as well?" Theodosia asked, mostly out of politeness.

"My pastry chef created a wedding cake,"

Thorne said. "A spectacular thing — eight layers decorated with fondant clams and strings of genuine pearls."

"It sounds lovely." Theodosia wondered if she should mention something about the ugly scene between Thorne and Carl Clewis that had occurred at the funeral luncheon. Should she? Or not? Perhaps it wasn't polite to bring that up right now.

"That was some crazy scene today, huh?" said Thorne.

Theodosia's lips twisted into a quirky smile. *On the other hand . . .*

"I'm afraid Meredith was quite upset by your ill-timed argument with Carl Clewis."

"Wasn't me who started it." Thorne waved a hand dismissively. "Besides, she'll get over it."

"Still, your dispute was quite disruptive."

"That's a good thing, right?" Thorne asked. "Isn't it important to shake up the status quo?"

"In this particular case, probably not."

Thorne rolled back on his heels and stared at her. "You don't like me much, do you?"

"I don't really know you, Mr. Thorne."

Thorne studied her. "You have a clever way about you, Miss Browning. You're polite and respectful, even gracious, one might say. But behind all those fine Southern manners, you're cautious and cagey. Your perceptive little mind is always running fancy computations. No wonder Meredith asked you, and I quote, 'to look into things.' "

"To help ease her mind. To make sure all possible suspects are nailed down and properly investigated," Theodosia said.

Thorne gave a wry smile. "I hope you don't put me in that category."

Theodosia fixed him with a level gaze. It wasn't exactly accusing, but it wasn't warm and fuzzy, either. "Gambling?" she said. Theodosia wanted *Thorne* to know that *she* knew about the missing profits.

Thorne looked shocked. "Me? Hey, you got some bad information there."

"Did I?"

Thorne practically bared his teeth at her. "When exactly did *I* become a suspect?"

Theodosia continued to stare at him. "I guess you must have blinked and missed it."

Thirty minutes later, the judging was complete. Now it was time for all the entrants and their guests to move to the ballroom's stage, where the winners would soon be announced.

"I feel like I'm going to break out in hives." Haley laughed.

"Don't do that," Theodosia said. "Just shake off your nervousness."

Haley bounced up and down on the balls of her feet. "But there were so many great entries."

"Including yours. So please don't —" Theodosia cut her words short as Bill Glass, the photographer, spotted her and headed in her direction.

"Glass," Theodosia muttered.

"I'm outa here," Haley said. And she was. Like a shot.

Glass looked moderately better this afternoon. Photojournalist jacket, three cameras slung around his neck, khaki pants. He was almost but not quite presentable.

"Tea lady," he called out. "Imagine meeting you here."

"You went home and changed," Theodosia said.

"Yeah, some guy spilled tea all over me at that funeral luncheon. Carl somebody. He was in a fight with another guy." Glass made a rude sound. "What a couple of jerks. Hey, wait until you catch next week's dynamite issue of *Shooting Star*."

"Do I have to?"

"I'm gonna put a photo of that Meredith babe right on the front cover."

"Why would you do that?"

Glass cocked his head. "To sell papers?"

"Wrong answer," Theodosia said.

"Hey, she was sobbing into her hankie like a B movie actress with that crazy horse-drawn funeral coach sitting right in the background." Glass gave a mock shudder. "Man, that thing was creepy. Like something out of a Dracula movie."

"Ladies and gentlemen," came a voice over the PA system.

"Oops, that's my cue," Glass said. "I think they're about to announce the winners." He lifted one of his cameras. "Gotta get some snaps."

Everyone crowded to the stage, where a podium and microphone sat on a raised dais. The judges were all lined up there as well as all the volunteers with sashes. Theodosia decided to stay exactly where she was.

Then the microphone crackled to life. Third, second, and first places were announced in the Wedding Cakes category, the Sculpted Cakes category, the Southern Party Treats category, and the Sculpted Confections category.

Amid all the shrieks, shouts, and bursts of applause, Theodosia hadn't heard Haley's name called out one single time.

Oh no, she's going to be so disappointed.

Theodosia thought about the fondant Earl

Grey. Absolutely adorable and perfectly sculpted, from his fine-boned muzzle to the slight curl in his tail. She decided the judges must be blind. Their taste and understanding for true art completely stunted.

And then she heard the microphone crackle to life again. They were announcing two more awards. Best of Show and Judge's Favorite.

Theodosia crossed her fingers and listened as Best of Show was awarded to Betsy Bedini for her cathedral cake. And then she couldn't believe her ears when Judge's Favorite was awarded to Haley Parker for her sugar sculpture.

Haley did win!

Two minutes later, Haley was running toward her. Pounding her way through the crowd, eyes shining, hair streaming out behind her. And she was waving a great big gold rosette ribbon.

"Did you hear?" Haley cried. "I won."

"I'm so proud of you," Theodosia said. "I never doubted you would."

Haley's smile slipped a notch. "But not in my category."

"Your award is better. Judge's Favorite." Theodosia wrapped her arms around her. "That award singles you out as being very special."

"Still."

"How many entries were there?" Theodosia asked.

Haley thought for a moment. "I guess maybe fifteen in my category?"

"And in the whole show?"

"I don't know. Something like a hundred and fifty?"

"So you beat out a hundred and forty-nine other people."

"Huh, when you put it that way, it sounds pretty good."

Theodosia smiled. "Yes, it does, Haley. It surely does."

22

Theodosia didn't have any great desire to attend the candlelight vigil in White Point Garden. But she was curious. Super curious. About who would show up and what exactly would be said. And would the bombastic Alex be in attendance?

Even with Carl Clewis and Guy Thorne running neck and neck as suspects, with Meredith, Jack Grimes, and Susan Monday a few lengths behind, Alex was still Theodosia's front-runner. Her favorite. Alex was the one who made her spider sense tingle. He was also the one who seemed the guiltiest.

As Theodosia crossed the damp grass, heading for a tight circle of folks who were all holding tiny pink candles, she saw that Alex was indeed here tonight. He was standing (fidgeting, actually) next to Meredith, while Bill Jacoby and Guy Thorne stood a few steps away. They were watching a group of women who were all wearing pink T-shirts with the words COME HOME FAWN emblazoned on the front. Arms linked, the women were doing a kind of dance as they sang a slow chorus of "Stand by Me," the song made famous by Ben E. King.

Theodosia stood and listened as the women's voices rang out clear and true.

When the night has come and the land is dark,
And the moon is the only light we'll see . . .

She imagined their notes floating out into Charleston Harbor, skimming the choppy surface, and then rising up in a shimmer of gentle prayers.

Maybe all these prayers and good wishes will work. I sure hope they do, anyway.

Pulling her jacket around her, for it was chilly tonight, Theodosia's eyes drifted from the gathering to a shadowy line of Civil War cannons. Then she scanned the inky dark sky overhead and looked out across Charleston Harbor at the shimmer of lights. These were lights and lanterns from sailboats and fishing boats, the red and green running lights of Coast Guard cutters and commercial vessels.

And somewhere out there was Fawn?

Theodosia still wasn't convinced the girl had been lost at sea. It seemed too convenient, too staged. Maybe even too tragically perfect.

Ah well.

As the singing drew to a close, the women hugged one another and broke into groups of two and three. Theodosia decided she'd better go over and greet Meredith.

Meredith saw Theodosia coming, touched a hand to her chest, and squealed, "You came. I knew you would."

"Thank you so much," said Bill Jacoby, ever the gentleman. "Your presence means so much to us."

Guy Thorne just glared at her while Alex looked perturbed and a little lost.

Theodosia hugged Meredith and whispered a few words of encouragement to her. Told her to stay strong and to keep the faith.

"Thank you," Meredith said. "And many thanks for letting us use your tea room tomorrow for the séance. I'm expecting great things."

"We can only hope," Theodosia said.

Then she turned her full attention to Alex.

"How are you holding up?" Theodosia asked him. "I apologize that I didn't get a chance to speak to you earlier today."

Alex shook his head as if he was experiencing the worst migraine in the world. "A terrible day," he moaned. "The memorial service with all that pomp and circumstance . . ." He glanced angrily in Meredith's direction, but she was busy whispering with Jacoby.

"I think the whole thing made your mom feel better," Theodosia said. "Like she was giving Reginald a final, heartfelt send-off."

"Downright embarrassing is what it was," Alex said.

"Have the police or sheriff been in touch with you?" Theodosia asked. She'd changed the subject abruptly to see how Alex would react. He didn't disappoint.

Alex scowled. "In touch with me about what?"

"Let's see," Theodosia said. "It could be regarding any new suspects that may have come to light, or possible forensic details found on your sailboat, or any messages or crank calls that you may have received."

"Nothing," Alex said. "I've heard nothing. From anyone."

"But you must have some ongoing contact with law enforcement, right? You must have shared some of your own thoughts and suspicions."

"I've tried, yes. But even *they* don't take

me seriously when I tell them that Jack Grimes murdered Reginald."

Theodosia lifted an eyebrow. "I would have thought you'd be pointing your finger at the neighbor, Carl Clewis."

Alex stared sullenly at her.

"And what about your wife's disappearance?" Theodosia continued. "Do you believe that Grimes killed Reginald, then went on to kidnap your wife? The funny thing is, Grimes never struck me as the kidnapping sort."

"Well somebody is!" Alex shouted. "Fawn didn't just disappear into thin air!"

"You're very angry."

"Actually, I'm furious that you're grilling me like a piece of raw tenderloin! Can't you see that *I'm* the one who's been wronged here? I'm the one whose wife is missing, possibly even dead!"

"I don't believe she's dead," Theodosia said softly. But Alex had already spun away from her and lurched his way into the crowd.

Five minutes later, with candles guttering in their holders and the songs and prayers all done, Delaine Dish showed up. She was clinging to the arm of Tod Slawson, an antiques dealer she'd taken to calling her paramour du jour. Delaine looked elegant and stylish in a long black coat that was belted about her tiny waist. She was also sniffling like crazy and fluttering a fancy linen hankie that seemed to serve as a fine prop.

Theodosia decided that, along with every other suspect on her list, Delaine's acting skills were honed razor-sharp.

Delaine whispered with Meredith for a few moments, then turned to greet Theodosia.

"Theo," Delaine said, dabbing at her nose. "You remember my Tody?"

"Of course," Theodosia said, turning to look at a tall man with slicked-back hair, a slight hawk nose, and darting eyes. He was wearing a blue golf jacket with a Daniel Island Club logo on it. "Nice to see you again."

Slawson gave a brief smile. "You, too." He was clearly bored out of his skull that Delaine had dragged him down here tonight and was making no effort to conceal his feelings.

Theodosia decided that perhaps the two of them were perfectly suited for each other. They both had the attention span of a gnat.

"I can only stay a few minutes," Delaine said, speaking softly and touching a hand to Theodosia's arm. "But I wanted to come and show my support for Fawn's safe return."

"Sweet of you," Theodosia said. "But Delaine . . ." She fixed her with a stern look.

"What?"

"A séance, Delaine? Really?"

"It was either that or crystals. And I've found crystals to be sadly ineffectual. Besides, it's so difficult finding good pink tourmaline these days."

"I see your point," Theodosia said. There was no arguing with Delaine. Because if you did, she would only spew nonsense.

As Delaine stared past Theodosia, she picked someone out in the crowd and her eyes narrowed. "Uh-oh, I need to leave right now before that awful Cynthia Munier comes bounding over here like a crazed puppy dog. Do you know Cynthia once bought a dress from me, tucked in the tags so she could wear it to a party, and then tried to return it?"

"Cheeky of her," Theodosia said.

"She's not like Fawn," Delaine continued. "Fawn was one of my best and most favorite customers." Delaine's eyes misted over slightly as she spoke. "She was always popping in to buy a new dress or piece of jewelry or check out our newest stash of cashmere pashminas. Now with Fawn missing . . . hopefully not dead . . . . I can only wait for news about her with bated breath."

"Uh-huh," Theodosia said.

Slawson touched a hand to Delaine's shoulder. "We really should be going, dear," he said.

But Delaine's brain had bing-bang-bonged its way onto yet another happy memory.

"I remember this one truly fabulous dress that Fawn bought," Delaine said, her mood turning brighter. "I think it was for Angela Rockler's black-tie gala during last year's Spoleto Festival. The designer, Marco Milano, called the gown jonquil yellow, but it was more a pale shimmery gold. Fawn looked just like a golden goddess in that dress. Like she was walking in moonlight."

Theodosia had a sudden thought.

"Did Alex accompany Fawn on these shopping trips?" she asked.

Delaine tilted her head from one side to the other, as if deep in thought. "Alex, the husband," she murmured to herself. Then, "No, I don't believe he ever did visit the shop with Fawn. In fact, I can't seem to recall her mentioning his name. Strange, yes?"

"You tell me," Theodosia said.

Delaine looked genuinely puzzled. "But now that you mention it, there *was* a gentleman who sometimes waited for Fawn out-side the shop in his car."

"Do you know who it was? Could it have been Alex? Or her Uber driver? Or someone else?"

Delaine blinked. "No idea."

The first thing Theodosia did when she ar-rived home was snap on Earl Grey's leash and take him for a quick walk. As they spun down Meeting Street, she said, "I should have taken you with me to White Point Garden tonight. I know it's one of your favorite spots."

Earl Grey tossed his head as if in agree-ment.

They jogged four blocks down, then four blocks back, keeping pace with each other. The chill night air and the gossamer mist that had seeped in made everything — enormous homes and gardens, the glowing globes of wrought-iron streetlamps — look almost dreamlike.

Then Theodosia said, "I almost forgot to tell you the best news of all. Haley won the Judge's Favorite award in the Sugar Arts Show today. She created the most amazing fondant sculpture." They stopped to let a car go by on Atlantic Street, crossed over, and then headed back down their own alley.

"And the sculpture was of *you,*" Theodosia exclaimed. "A sugar-sweet miniature Earl Grey."

The last of Theodosia's words were lost in an enormous roar as her neighbor, Robert Steele, screamed past them in his Porsche. Engine practically redlined, he spewed an almost lethal emission of oil and gas fumes. Halfway down the alley, tires squealed, brake lights flared, and laughter — or was that the radio? — merged with an earsplitting volley of backfires. The Porsche bucked once and shot into the three-car garage, what used to be the carriage house.

Moonlight, magnolias, and motor oil, Theodosia thought. *That's some mash-up.*

The phone was ringing as Theodosia opened the back door. She and Earl Grey both tried squeezing though the doorway at the same time and collided in a jumble of paws, knees, and legs.

Theodosia won out, grabbing for the phone and almost killing herself as she tripped over a pile of lumber that was haphazardly stacked in the middle of her kitchen.

"Yes. Hello?" She was practically breathless.

"It's me."

It was Pete Riley.

"Hey there, what's up?"

"I shouldn't be telling you this. I mean, you can't breathe a word to anyone." Riley's voice was jazzed but intense. "And you can never reveal that this came from me!"

"You haven't told me anything," Theodosia said.

"I overheard a call on my scanner."

Theodosia's ears perked up. Okay, now she was interested. Maybe this could be something.

"A call concerning what?" she asked.

There was a slight hesitation, and then Riley said, "A body just turned up in Charleston Harbor. A woman's body."

23

Theodosia squeezed her eyes shut and then opened them again. "A body floating in Charleston Harbor?" She felt dizzy. And a little sick to her stomach. Was this it? Was this the definitive answer on Fawn?

"That was the Coast Guard's initial report, yes," Riley said. "But the transmission was hurried and filled with static. And it's dark as a coal mine out there on the water, so it could be anything. Could be a turtle or large fish that got snagged in a net."

"Dear Lord," Theodosia said. "I was just down there. At White Point Garden for Fawn's vigil."

"Well, we don't know anything for sure until it's completely checked out and the Coast Guard issues an official statement."

"When would they do that?" Theodosia asked. "Wait, *where* would they do that? At the Coast Guard Station?"

"Don't go over there."

"I think I have to."

"Please don't."

"Please, yes. I really need to know. A lot of people are anxiously waiting to hear this news."

There was a long pause, and then Riley said, "It would be the Coast Guard Station just off Tradd."

"Thank you," Theodosia breathed.

When Theodosia pulled into the parking lot and stepped out of her Jeep, the night seemed even darker and a biting wind was sweeping in from the Atlantic. Where the sky had been lit with bright sprinkles of stars earlier, now there were only roiling dark clouds.

Shivering, Theodosia felt an intense sense of foreboding. Her eagerness was suddenly tamped down as damp sea air wrapped around her like an unwelcome sweater. Across the harbor, the faint drone of a foghorn sounded at Patriots Point.

The foghorn was there to warn ships. To tell them to beware. But who had been there to warn poor Fawn? Theodosia wondered.

Peering through the darkness and ever-increasing fog, Theodosia saw that a Coast Guard ship was just pulling up to its dock. It was one of their cutters, a large gray boat

292

that looked like a phantom as it emerged from the fog.

Theodosia walked out onto the dock, ignoring the official black-and-white sign that warned COAST GUARD PERSONNEL ONLY, and watched as the Coast Guardsmen tossed out their fenders. Then the cutter bumped gently against the dock, and two Coast Guardsmen jumped off to tie up their lines.

Anxious and practically quivering with nerves, unable to wait one single second more, Theodosia stepped forward.

"The body you just pulled in," Theodosia said, breathless, her words practically jumbling together. "Do you know who it is?"

The first Coast Guardsman, whose name tag read BURDICK, looked at her and said, "Ma'am, you shouldn't be here. This dock is restricted to Coast Guard personnel only."

"I understand that," Theodosia said. "And I apologize for trespassing like this. But, please, it's important. For the family's sake, I have to know. Was it Fawn Doyle? Is that whose body you found?"

"We don't know, ma'am," said the second Coast Guardsman. "We were belowdecks when it happened."

Heavy steps thudded down the gangplank as a third man joined them. This one had stripes on his sleeves. A master chief whose name tag read SCOTT.

"Is there a problem here?" Scott asked.

"This young lady is asking about a body," Burdick said.

The master chief's head snapped sideways. "What did you tell her?"

"Nothing, sir!" both men cried at once.

"It came over the police scanner," Theodosia explained. "And I . . . I have a source. A contact. So I know you pulled a body out of the water."

The master chief just stared at her.

"Again, I apologize for invading your space like this," Theodosia said in a rush. "But I have to know. I'm a friend of the family."

"This is really important to you?" Scott asked.

Theodosia nodded. "Very."

"Here then, you can take a look for yourself," the master chief said. His expression was unreadable.

Theodosia tiptoed to the edge of the dock, reached for the rail, and stepped aboard the cutter. Her heart thudded against her ribs, her breath came in short gasps, and she had a sinking feeling in the pit of her stomach. To make things worse, the howling wind flipped and whipped her hair into auburn streamers even as the Coast Guard flag with its motto of SEMPER PARATUS snapped from the top of the tall mast.

"Show her," Scott called to one of the Coast Guardsmen on deck.

The Coast Guardsman looked over at his superior officer and then to Theodosia. He said, "This way, ma'am," and led her over to what appeared to be a small pile of debris on the foredeck.

Crossing the deck slowly, very deliberately, Theodosia grimaced as the ship shifted beneath her and so did her stomach. Then she took a deep breath and stared down at a sodden blue blanket.

"You ready?" the Coast Guardsman asked. Theodosia nodded.

He slowly pulled back a corner of the blue blanket.

A cracked face stared up at her. Blue eyes, sightless, with long curling lashes. Dirty, ragged clothing clung to the small figure.

Theodosia could hardly believe what she was seeing.

"A doll!" Theodosia cried. It was an ugly, cracked plastic doll. She was so relieved that she gripped the arm of the Coast Guardsman and sagged against him.

"A waterlogged doll," the Coast Guardsman said. "One of our stranger finds."

"But nothing else was dredged up?" Theodosia asked. "So the radio transmission was inaccurate? You never found an actual *person* floating in the harbor?"

The Coast Guardsman touched a finger to his cap. "Not yet, ma'am. But we'll keep looking."

"Thank you, thank you all so much," Theodosia practically whispered. She lurched her way off the cutter and onto the dock.

"Take care now," Master Chief Scott said after her.

Theodosia nodded as she staggered away. She slowly crossed the parking lot and leaned up against the side of her car. The battering wind, the frantic worry, and the constant tension had chilled her to the bone and given her the shakes.

But thank you, dear Lord, that it wasn't Fawn. Sing hallelujah for that.

Theodosia climbed into her Jeep, turned on the heat, and waited for the tension to drain away. She'd have to call Pete Riley when she got home and tell him what strange item the Coast Guard had found floating in the harbor.

Or maybe he already knew? Maybe a more complete report had already been radioed in since that initial one?

Either way, Theodosia felt as if she'd escaped some sort of horror show. At least for the time being. Okay, so now what?

I've got to go home. Go home and get some sleep.

Putting her car in gear, Theodosia pulled out of the parking lot and turned down Bay Street. She drove carefully and methodically, like someone who feared getting stopped for a minor traffic ticket. It wasn't until she was halfway home that she began to wonder:

Was this just a stupid doll that had been bobbing around Charleston Harbor for weeks? Or could this have been a deliberate and very cruel prank?

24

Drayton bent forward over the counter, listening intently as Theodosia hastily brought him up to speed on last night's strange happenings — the vigil for Fawn at White Point Garden, the phone call from Riley, her frantic mission to the Coast Guard Station.

When she got to the part about pulling back the blanket, Drayton paused, his teacup halfway to his mouth.

"And then?" he said in a hoarse whisper. "It wasn't her, was it? I mean, you would have called me immediately, right?"

"It was a doll." Theodosia shuddered at the memory of it. "A horrible life-size doll with a chipped face, sodden clothes, and weird blue eyes."

"Have mercy!" Drayton clapped a hand to the side of his face. "You must have jumped out of your skin."

"I almost did," Theodosia said. "You know

those spooky doll movies with Chucky and Annabelle?"

Drayton shook his head. No, he didn't know. But Theodosia was on a roll and was going to tell him anyway.

"Well, that's what it was like. Like some creepy horror show doll that suddenly becomes animated." The terrible image from last night was still seared in Theodosia's brain. She'd even had nightmares about it.

"Cool," Haley said. She'd snuck in to eavesdrop on Theodosia's story.

"Not cool," Theodosia said.

"But what a blessing that it wasn't Fawn," Drayton said.

"Where do you think Fawn disappeared to?" Haley asked. "She has to be somewhere. Was she kidnapped by pirates? Did she run off to start a new life? And do you think her disappearance is somehow connected to Reginald Doyle's murder?"

"All good questions," Drayton said.

"But we don't have any good answers," Theodosia said. After all her sleuthing and snooping, she felt a terrible dread welling up inside her. What if she continued to come up empty? What if no murderer — no perpetrator — was ever caught and brought to justice? The notion chafed against Theodosia's sense of right and wrong.

"Do you think Fawn might really be dead?" Haley asked.

"Bite your tongue," Drayton said.

"I'm praying she's not," Theodosia said.

"But what do you *think*?" Haley asked. "What does your gut tell you?"

"My gut feeling is that she didn't drown," Theodosia said.

"But you were worried enough that you hurried over to the Coast Guard Station last night," Haley said.

"And then I was proved wrong," Theodosia said.

"Thank goodness for that." Drayton set his teacup into his saucer with a resounding *clink.* "And now, if you'll both allow me to get on with my morning endeavors, I need to select and brew a few wonderful, exotic teas that will enchant and warm our guests. Who will, I believe" — he flicked his wrist and glanced at his antique Patek Philippe watch — "be darkening our doorstep in less than ten minutes."

"More like five," Theodosia said, suddenly feeling the time crunch. "Since your watch always runs a tad slow."

Haley rushed back to her kitchen while Theodosia did a final check of the tea room. Small tea light candles were lit, cream and sugars set out on each table, fresh zinnias bobbed their shaggy heads in crystal vases. She'd set the tables with Pembroke by Aynsley plates and teacups, loving how the bluebirds and flowers seemed to complement what was turning into a bright sunshiny day. Even though her mood wasn't quite there yet.

Because it was Friday, the Indigo Tea Shop turned out to be extra busy this morning. A plethora of tourists had arrived in Charleston for the weekend, eager to bed down in fancy B and Bs, as well as visit the Historic District, the French Quarter, Rainbow Row, and maybe even take in some fall colors.

Theodosia welcomed and seated her guests, took orders, poured tea, and then delivered their goodies. They were offering a special cream tea this morning, which included a small pot of Earl Grey white tip tea paired with a maple scone, Devonshire cream, and a fruit cup. Haley had also baked raspberry scones and banana-chocolate muffins.

The local shopkeepers popped in, too. Leigh Carroll, the owner of the Cabbage Patch Gift Shop just down the block, was a pretty African-American woman who'd developed a taste for tea. Today, she'd brought along her own ceramic mug.

"I'm guessing you'd like me to fill that up?" Drayton said. "I've just brewed a luscious Chinese green tea from the Hunan province that I think you'd enjoy."

Leigh smiled at him with her lovely almond eyes and said in honeyed tones, "Will it keep me going all day?"

"If it doesn't, just pop back in here for a refill, dear lady."

When the morning mail arrived, Julie, their mail delivery person, handed over a thick stack of letters and magazines to Drayton who, in turn, put a takeaway cup of Darjeeling (Julie's favorite tea) into her hand.

"Many thanks," Julie said as she rushed back out the door to finish her route.

"Here you go." Drayton handed the stack of mail to Theodosia, who suddenly pinched her brows together when she noticed what was sitting on top.

"Problem?" Drayton asked. "From your expression, it looks as if you just received a nasty notice from the IRS. Which I know you didn't, since you're phobic about paying quarterly taxes."

"It's worse than that," Theodosia said. Her stomach had started to churn all over again. *Stop that flip-flopping,* she told herself. But to no avail.

"What?" Drayton was suddenly concerned. When Theodosia was feeling at odds and ends, so was he.

"Our copy of *Tea Faire* just arrived." Theodosia held up the magazine with its shiny cover featuring a silver tea set on a paisley tablecloth.

"It's only the tea magazine that . . . Oh, sweet Fanny Adams!" The teaspoon Drayton had been holding clattered to the counter. "Is that the issue with the review of our Beaux Arts Tea?"

Theodosia nodded. She tried to smile but her mouth felt numb. Actually, her whole face felt numb.

"Do you think the review might be, um, concerning?" Drayton couldn't bring himself to utter the word *terrible*.

"I don't know. I'm petrified to look."

"We must have faith." Drayton pulled his glasses from his jacket pocket and plucked the magazine from Theodosia's hands. "Let us see now . . ." He was hastily turning pages.

"This could be a disaster," Theodosia said. She knew that a bad review, or even a mediocre one, could negatively affect business.

"Of epic proportions," Drayton said, both

agreeing with her and trying to pacify her. He was still thumbing through pages like mad. "But I don't think —"

"Hurry up!" Theodosia was on pins and needles.

"Okay, here we are." Drayton opened the magazine wide and laid it on the counter. "Mmn, lovely photo of our tea shop."

"Is it?" Theodosia quavered. She was almost afraid to look.

"Now let's see what they . . . Oh. *Oh my.*"

"Bad?"

"The review kicks off, and I quote, 'On a quaint street in Charleston's famed Historic District, a lovely little tea shop occupies space in a renovated carriage house. Step through the front door of the Indigo Tea Shop and you are immediately transported to a cozy world filled with chintz and china, tea and treasures.' "

"That's good, that's good!" Theodosia squealed. "Is there more?"

"Lots more." Drayton pushed the magazine toward her. "And it's *verrry* complimentary."

Theodosia's eyes lit up as they fairly danced across the words.

"This is more of an article than a review," she said. "They go on to talk about the Beaux Arts Tea. And it's wonderful. They like us! They really do!"

Drayton was already back at work, measuring out scoops of black tea with plum and quince and dumping them into a Royal Crown Derby teapot. "I'm not the least bit surprised," he said. "Our tea and scones are beyond compare, and our themed teas are always superlative."

Theodosia gazed at him. "Don't act so blasé. A minute ago you were worried to death. You might as well admit it."

Drayton gave a small mousy smile. "Perhaps just a tiny bit."

Once Theodosia had finished reading the article, she went back to work with a happy heart, practically gliding across the tea room floor and singing out greetings to customers. She powered through the morning, then began clearing tables so she could ready the shop for lunch. Because Theodosia was good at her job — she was a huge believer in planning and preplanning — she ended up with an extra ten minutes to spare.

Perfect. I can sit in my office and skim through the rest of today's mail.

And that's exactly what she did.

Sitting at her desk, Theodosia put the bills in one stack, the junk mail in another. As she was sorting through everything, she noticed a familiar return address on one of the envelopes.

"What's this?"

Her curiosity turned to confusion as she slit open the envelope and pulled out an invoice from Huntley's Ltd.

"This can't be right. Because I prepaid for Drayton's shooting vest. Didn't I?"

Theodosia was already reaching for the phone to call the haberdashery. This invoice had to be a mistake; she was sure of it. Seconds later, when she got George Huntley on the phone, she explained her dilemma.

"Let me check on this," Huntley said. He sounded busy but professional at the same time.

Theodosia waited a minute or so, and then he came back on the line.

"Well, yes," Huntley said. "You ordered a Continental shooting vest in the classic estate style, with the suede shoulder pads and cartridge pockets."

"That's correct."

There was a rustle of paper, and Huntley said, "And our records *do* indicate that your item was paid for and delivered."

"Right," Theodosia said. "So what is *this* invoice for?"

"At the moment, I'm not sure," Huntley said. "But please do ignore it for now, because I'm positive it's a mistake on our part. What probably happened was a mix-up in our billing department."

"Okay, thank you. But let me know when you figure it out, will you?"

"Of course."

"I'm calling this our Autumn Harvest Menu," Haley said.

Theodosia was standing in their small, overheated kitchen as Haley ticked off their luncheon offerings.

"Pear and fig scones, pumpkin cream soup, pecan salad, and tea sandwiches with roast beef and cheddar," Haley said. "Plus we've still got plenty of raspberry scones, and I baked a cinnamon-apple Dobos torte."

"This is a spectacular menu, Haley," Theodosia said. "Everything sounds delicious."

"And fresh. I hit up the farmers market first thing this morning and sourced all sorts of good stuff. All the growers must have had bumper crops this year."

"What about the menu for our Lavender Lady Tea tomorrow?" Theodosia asked.

"Lavender scones, of course. And an edible flower salad. The rest I'm still noodling around, though I am tending to lean toward serving a puff baby for our entrée."

"I leave everything in your capable hands, then."

BAM. BAM. BAM.

Somebody was pounding on the back door.

"A delivery?" Haley said. "I wasn't expecting anything else."

"You want me to . . . ?"

"No, it's okay, I got it," Haley said, disappearing out the door and around the corner.

Theodosia listened as Haley ran through her office, then pulled open the back door. She returned in a flash, dwarfed by the enormous cardboard box she was carrying.

"What's in that?" Theodosia asked.

"You tell me." Haley plopped the box down on the floor and flipped open the lid. "Oh wow. It looks like Susan Monday sent us more lavender for tomorrow."

"Fantastic." The scent of lavender was suddenly wafting everywhere.

Haley gave the box a sideways kick and sent it spinning underneath her butcher block table. She dusted her hands together and said, "This place is going to look like a purple palace by the time we get done."

Back at the front counter, Drayton was grumbling about the séance that was scheduled to take place this afternoon.

"We'll have to make sure all our regular customers are finished and out the door. Otherwise this could prove to be highly embarrassing," he said.

"Were you embarrassed when we invited a psychic to our Nancy Drew Tea a couple of months ago?"

"Not really, because that was for amusement purposes only," Drayton said. "According to Delaine, this séance is intended to part the curtains on the universe." He let loose a snort. "As if that could actually happen."

"You don't think this is worthwhile even if it helps to ease Meredith's mind?"

"I don't believe gazing into the future is even remotely possible. I prefer to let future events unfold in their own time and pace."

"If it's worth anything, I agree with you," Theodosia said, just as the front door flew open and the first of their luncheon guests spilled in.

Not only were they frantically busy for lunch, but Haley's menu proved to be enormously popular. The pumpkin cream soup and raspberry scones were huge hits, followed closely by the pecan salad.

For dessert Haley had made a chai-spiced fruit compote that she served over vanilla yogurt. It was so popular that the last couple of guests who ordered it were out of luck. They had to be told there was no more compote left.

"But let me package up a few scones for you to take home," Theodosia told them. "As a kind of consolation prize."

When the last bowl of soup had been devoured, Bill Jacoby walked through the front door. Dressed in a three-piece dove gray suit, looking like he'd just come from a business meeting, he glanced around. When he saw Theodosia standing at the counter, he lifted a big hand in greeting.

She sped over to him and said, "Can I get you a table? Are you here for lunch?"

Jacoby shook his head. "I was in the neighborhood and thought I'd drop by. Had a luncheon over at the Lattice Inn."

"Are they still serving those wonderful pecan-breaded oysters?" Theodosia asked.

"They were on the menu, yes," Jacoby said. Then, "I wanted to thank you for all the help you've been giving Meredith."

"I'm not sure I've been much help at all," Theodosia said. "After all, there's still a killer walking around out there."

But Jacoby was insistent. "No, you've been a rock through all of this. You've inspired Meredith, been a shoulder for her to cry on, and lent her some of your own strength. As you probably noticed, Meredith can be flighty. And somewhat unstable. But you've managed to help keep her on a fairly even keel, and for that I am truly grateful."

"Did Meredith tell you about the séance we're having this afternoon?"

Jacoby's jaw clenched reflexively. "She did. I'm afraid the poor dear is grasping at straws. But it's very kind of you to indulge her."

"Would you like to stay and be part of it?" Drayton called from behind the counter. He was half-serious, half-kidding.

"Unfortunately, I have to get back to the office. But if you've got a take-out cup of tea . . ."

Drayton was already pouring an amber stream into one of their signature indigo blue cups.

"Assam tea good for you?" Drayton asked.

Jacoby nodded. "As long as it's hot and strong."

"Here you go," Drayton said, handing him the cup. "Nice threads, by the way."

25

Theodosia was sweeping a few errant crumbs from the floor when a red-haired woman in a dark-blue cape rushed into the tea room. It was midafternoon and all her customers had departed. So this had to be . . .

"Hello?" the woman called out in a melodic voice. With her dark, kohl-rimmed eyes, dangly gold earrings, and slightly prominent nose, she looked like central casting's answer to the perfect psychic.

"Madame Emilia?" Theodosia asked. She wanted to make sure this wasn't just an exotic visitor looking for her tea fix.

The woman nodded. "That's right. I was invited here to conduct a séance?"

"Of course you were. Welcome to the Indigo Tea Shop. I'm Theodosia, the owner."

"Hello, Theodosia, thank you for inviting me."

At that very same moment, Drayton wan-

312

dered back from the kitchen. He stopped dead in his tracks, hitched down his vest, and said, "By George, I'll bet you're the fortune-teller."

"Medium," said Madame Emilia. She let loose a warm, throaty laugh. "But that's perfectly okay. I've been called a great many things in my career."

"This is our tea sommelier, Drayton, by the way," Theodosia said. "Now. How can we help you get comfortable?"

"I'll need a table," Madame Emilia said. "And can we darken the room?"

Theodosia glanced at the pleasant afternoon sunshine that streamed through her windows, at the chintz curtains that were tied back. "I suppose."

"Excellent. And then I have to smudge the room."

"Pardon?" Drayton said.

"I'm going to burn a stick of sage and smudge the room," Madame Emilia said casually, as if it were an everyday occurrence.

Drayton brushed at his lapel. "For what purpose?"

"Burning sage is a spiritual room cleansing, if you will. A technique I use to cleanse a room's aura. Sage helps absorb conflict, deflect anger, and chase away evil."

"It wards off evil? Then smudge away to your heart's content," Drayton said. "By all means. And while you're perfuming the room with sage, do you mind if I continue brewing tea? There won't be any kind of aromatic conflict, will there?"

"Not at all," Madame Emilia said. "In fact, the two may be quite complementary."

Madame Emilia set her large velvet tote bag on the table and pulled out a small stick of sage. She touched a lighter to it and began waving it around. Then she broke into a low chanting.

"Too bad she can't use lavender instead," Drayton whispered to Theodosia. "We've got buckets."

While Madame Emilia continued her smudging and chanting ritual, Theodosia set out teacups, napkins, silverware, and plates. She had decided to sit in with Meredith and Delaine, while Drayton, who was séance averse, preferred to keep his distance.

Then, just as Theodosia brought out a tray of scones from the kitchen, Delaine came bustling in.

"What *is* that weird aroma?" Delaine demanded in her usual bossy manner. She took a sniff and twisted her nose. "It smells like there's a commune of hippies smoking weed in here. Like the second coming of

Woodstock."

"It's smudge," Drayton said with a knowing smile.

Delaine's face took on a slightly addled expression. "Fudge?"

"Madame Emilia just finished *smudging* the tea room," Theodosia explained. "She burned a stick of sage. To cleanse it."

"Oh." That explanation stopped Delaine dead in her tracks. She peered around the darkened tea room until she finally spotted Madame Emilia. "There you are!" Delaine hustled toward her table, her black pencil skirt hindering progress and forcing her to take tiny, mincing steps. "I'm Delaine. Remember me from Kitty Roper's party?"

"Of course," Madame Emilia said.

Theodosia smiled. She doubted that Madame Emilia had any residual psychic remembrance of Delaine, but she was pretty sure the good madame knew darn well which side her bread was buttered on.

Meredith arrived in a flurry some five minutes later.

"Theodosia, this is extremely kind of you to allow our séance to take place in your tea room. I'm so grateful!" Meredith burbled.

"Not a problem," Theodosia said. To be honest, she was curious about what sort of questions Meredith planned to ask. And

315

whether they might reveal something critical — such as, did Meredith know more than she was admitting to?

Meredith was introduced to Madame Emilia amid much squealing and fawning. Then, when they were finally all seated, Drayton stepped to the table with a steaming teapot.

"I brewed a special tea for this most interesting occasion. An oolong tea from Nepal. It has a lovely silky texture with sweet honey notes." He moved around the table, filling everyone's teacup. "Please do enjoy."

The ladies took a sip of tea and murmured their approval. All except Meredith. She was anxiously perched on the edge of her chair, obviously waiting for some type of supernatural manifestation.

When nothing magically appeared out of thin air, Meredith said, "I can hardly wait to get started." Her bright, inquisitive eyes were focused squarely on Madame Emilia. "How exactly does this work? Do you use a crystal ball or read the tarot cards? Or just free your mind to mentally engage with the spirit world?"

Madame Emilia nodded pleasantly. Then she reached into her velvet bag and drew out a Ouija board.

"Oh," Meredith said. She looked stunned. Delaine just looked dismayed. "Eyew," she said, making a lemon face. "I thought those silly things were only used for Halloween parties at sorority houses."

Unfazed by Delaine's negativity, Madame Emilia said, "One can learn a great deal through the Ouija board. It can help divine the truth, peer into the future, administer critical advice, find lost objects . . ."

"And lost people?" Meredith asked. "Can it help with that?"

"We can certainly make an attempt," Madame Emilia said.

"Because my daughter-in-law is missing and . . ."

Madame Emilia inclined her head toward Meredith. "Yes, Delaine told me all about your circumstances."

"And . . . and you know that my husband was murdered, too," Meredith said. Now she leaned back in her chair and dug into her pocketbook for a hankie. "Can you believe the dreadful luck I've had?" Tears clung to the tips of her false eyelashes, then dribbled down her cheeks. "It's enough to drive a person completely bonkers."

"What would you like to try first?" Madame Emilia asked in a kindly voice. "Perhaps we could attempt to connect with your missing daughter-in-law?"

"Yes . . . absolutely," Meredith said. "My son is . . ." She waved a hand. "He's beside himself with grief."

Theodosia's brows might have raised a half inch at that last statement.

"Will everyone please lean forward and touch their fingers to the planchette?" Madame Emilia asked.

"Really?" Delaine said.

"Please," Madame Emilia said.

"I suppose," Delaine huffed. "But this Ouija stuff has never worked for me." She poked an index finger at the planchette as if it were a dead rat. "I'm more of a tarot card kind of girl."

"Just give it a shot, Delaine," Theodosia urged. *The sooner we cooperate, the sooner this will be over.*

When everyone's fingertips were gently touching the planchette, Madame Emilia asked in a deep, resonant voice, "Oh, spirit guide, we ask you to please manifest and help us make contact with our dear missing Fawn. Please use your powers for good to locate our lost girl."

Theodosia glanced around the table. Madame Emilia was definitely into this, Meredith had her eyes squeezed shut, and Delaine just looked bored.

"Spirit guide?" Madame Emilia said again. "We implore your help."

Nothing happened. The planchette remained sitting stolidly in the middle of the board.

"It's not working," Meredith said in a trembling voice.

"Maybe it needs to warm up," Delaine said. "Like a sports car. I had an Alfa Romeo once that —"

"Maybe if we ask a more direct question?" Theodosia said.

"Yes!" Meredith said. "Like . . . is Fawn still alive?"

That seemed to be the impetus the planchette needed, because it suddenly spun toward the upper left corner of the board to the image of a smiling sun and the word YES.

"Oh, thank goodness!" Meredith rejoiced. "She's alive! Fawn is still alive!"

"But where is she?" Delaine asked. "I don't mean to be a buzzkill here, but we need some hard facts." She took a finger off the planchette and tapped the board insistently.

"I don't think we should be so demanding," Meredith said. "Just *knowing* Fawn is still alive is enough for me right now."

"So we should move on?" Theodosia asked.

"Absolutely," Meredith said. She stifled a little hiccup. "There's the matter of poor Reginald."

"I guess a dead husband is important, too," Delaine said.

"Kindly place your fingers on the planchette again," Madame Emilia instructed. Everyone complied, and then Madame Emilia said, "Go ahead, Meredith, ask your question."

"I want to know who murdered Reginald!" she spat out. "Who stole my beloved, my soul mate, away from me!"

"That's a fair question," Delaine murmured.

But once again, the planchette was reluctant to move.

"Please!" Meredith implored. "Not knowing is *killing* me!"

The planchette just sat there.

"Again," Madame Emilia urged.

Meredith repeated her question.

"Nothing's happening," Delaine said. "The thing's dead as a doornail."

Madame Emilia shook her head. "There's a blockage in this room. Someone is holding on to a deep, dark secret."

A look of panic suddenly swept across

Delaine's face. "I hope you're not going to reveal anything too personal, are you?"

"I feel it is . . . an old secret of the heart," Madame Emilia said in a low voice.

Now Delaine looked interested. She leaned forward and said, "What's the secret?" Her eyes roamed the table. "And who's holding on to it?"

The Ouija board planchette gave a sudden, spasmodic jerk, then began crawling steadily toward the letters in the center of the board.

"Now we're getting somewhere," Delaine said.

Meredith lifted her fingers as if she'd just touched a hot stove. "Who's doing that?" she asked. "Who's . . . who's making it move so fast like that?"

Three hands remained touching the planchette: those of Theodosia, Madame Emilia, and Delaine.

"This is scaring me!" Meredith cried out. "Make it stop!"

Meredith was making such a fuss that even Drayton came over to watch.

There was no stopping the planchette now as it lurched from the letter C to A then R.

"Car?" Delaine said.

"I think it's spelling out Carl Clewis," Theodosia said softly. The planchette was moving even faster now, gathering up speed as it tore across the board.

"That's it! That's it exactly!" Drayton said. He was suddenly spellbound by the frantic movement of the planchette, the name it was hastily spelling out.

"Carl Clewis," Madame Emilia said. "This definitely involves . . . a matter of the heart?" She lifted her head and gazed squarely at Meredith.

Meredith's eyes bulged as she practically exploded out of her chair. Then she threw her hands in the air and screamed, "Carl Clewis! So what if I used to date him! That means absolutely nothing!"

"Whoa," Drayton said.

"You used to *date* him?" Theodosia cried. She was incredulous; she couldn't believe what she was hearing.

"It was years ago!" An edge of pure hysteria had crept into Meredith's voice. "And then it was only for a few months!"

"How interesting," Delaine purred.

Holy buckets, Theodosia thought. This was a new revelation that could have given Meredith yet another reason to get rid of Reginald. Maybe Meredith had suddenly, out of the blue, decided to change partners. Yes, it might be perceived as being a little late in the game, but it could have happened that way. On the other hand, Carl Clewis could have murdered Reginald to settle an old score. Maybe Clewis had nursed his hurt and anger all these many years, only to finally explode with rage.

Meredith had backed away from the table, looking like she was on the verge of spontaneous combustion. Not knowing what to do, embarrassed by her revelation, she cast a pleading glance at Theodosia.

"Theo?" she gasped.

"I think we're probably done for today," Theodosia said in an even tone.

Delaine pushed her chair back from the table and stood up. "It's been grand, folks. This séance didn't turn out exactly the way I thought it would, but it was interesting, to say the least."

Meredith was still struggling to regain her composure. "I'm sorry everyone. I thought this would . . . help clear . . ."

Her cell phone suddenly shrilled from deep inside her purse.

Meredith gave a soft sigh, dug it out, and said, "This isn't a good time right now —" Then she stopped abruptly. "Yes, yes," she said, her body jerking as if she'd been touched by an electric wire. "You have my attention. I'm listening."

"Now what's going on?" Delaine hissed.

Meredith threw up a hand to halt any further conversation. And listened for a few more moments, her eyes growing larger and larger. Finally, she screamed, "This is unbelievable! It's like a voice from the great beyond!"

Everyone, especially Madame Emilia, looked stunned. What *was* going on? Who had called Meredith and upset her like this?

Theodosia was the first to recover. "Meredith, what's happening? Who's on the phone with you?"

Meredith looked as if she'd just seen a ghost. Or at least talked to one. "This call . . . It's about Fawn!"

Theodosia grabbed the phone from Meredith's hands, held it to her ear, and said, "Hello? Who is this?"

"Put the old lady back on," a cold, hollow voice ordered. It sounded as if it were coming from the depths of the earth. But the sound was kind of mechanical, too.

Stunned, Theodosia handed the phone back to Meredith and leaned in to listen.

"What?" Meredith quavered as she held the phone to her ear. "What do you want?" She listened for a few more moments, then her face suddenly crumpled. Her shoulders slumped, and her demeanor became that of a hundred-year-old woman who was barely hanging on by a thread.

"What's wrong?" Drayton asked. He nodded to the phone, which was still clutched in Meredith's hand. "Who is it? What do they want?"

But Meredith raised an arm and batted him away. "Shush, will you? I'm trying to *listen*!"

Meredith nodded, said, "Uh-huh, uh-huh," a couple more times, then sat down and dropped the phone in her lap.

"Who is it?" Theodosia asked. But she had a terrible, nagging feeling that she already knew.

"It's the man who-who-who kidnapped Fawn," Meredith suddenly babbled. "And he's demanding five million dollars in ransom!"

26

It was as if someone had let all the air out of the room. Nobody moved, everything remained completely still, as if in suspended animation. Then Theodosia held out her hand and said, "Let me talk to him."

Meredith practically threw the phone at Theodosia.

"Hello?" Theodosia said. "Who is this and what exactly do you want?"

"Five million dollars," the mechanical-sounding voice said. "Cash."

"Sure," Theodosia said. She tried to fight the rising tide of panic in her voice and sound halfway reasonable. "But that's an awful lot of money. How do I know this isn't a scam? You could be any random thug who's read about Meredith's trouble in the newspaper and is trying to take advantage of her."

"I assure you I'm not. I've got the old lady's daughter-in-law, and if her family wants to see her alive, they'll do exactly as I say," the cold voice commanded.

Whoever this is, they're using a voice changer, Theodosia thought. One of those gadgets that pitches your voice to a mechanized, almost monotone level.

"Are you listening?" the voice asked.

"I'm here," Theodosia said.

"Five million dollars. Cash," the voice said again. "If my terms aren't met, I put the girl in a gunnysack and drop her in a swamp."

If only I could somehow record this conversation. So Riley could hear it for himself.

"But you —" Theodosia began.

"Do not screw around, because you don't have much time," the voice interrupted.

"How much time *do* we have? And where exactly are we supposed to make this exchange?" Theodosia didn't really believe any money would change hands or that Fawn would be returned; she was stalling for time, trying to think. Trying to come up with a *plan.*

"Tell the old lady I'll call her tomorrow," the voice said.

"Wait a minute," Theodosia cried. "You can't just . . . We need more . . . ."

But she was talking to dead air. The mysterious caller had hung up.

"What's happening?" Meredith asked in a hoarse whisper. "What'd they say?" She ran a hand through her short hair, causing it to stick up straight and make her look completely unhinged.

"Whoever it was, they're gone," Theodosia said. "They hung up."

"And this caller really demanded five million dollars for the return of Fawn?" Drayton asked.

Meredith's chin quivered. "I *think* that's what they said." She stared mournfully at Theodosia. "That's what you heard, too, right?"

"I'm afraid so," Theodosia said.

"This has to be the most bizarre thing ever," Drayton sputtered. "A murder . . . a kidnapping, and now a ransom. Was all of this engineered by the same person? The same . . . mastermind?"

"I wouldn't categorize it quite that way," Theodosia said. She figured the perpetrator had to be someone close to Meredith. Which meant they were an inexperienced amateur versus a master criminal. And because they were probably driven by both rage and greed, they were bound to trip up sooner or later. She just hoped it would be sooner.

"Five million dollars," Meredith muttered.

Her eyes fluttered uncontrollably, and her body shook with worry.

Delaine, on the other hand, looked more curious than frightened. "Do you actually *have* five million dollars?" she asked.

Meredith fought to pull her thoughts and emotions together. "Not in cash, I don't." She reached down, grabbed her handbag, and opened it. As if she was expecting to find five million dollars stashed inside. "But . . . I suppose if I met with my personal banker, sold some stocks, and mortgaged Creekmore Plantation and all the land surrounding it, I could come up with that amount."

"Goodness." Delaine was clearly impressed.

Theodosia was not.

"We still don't know if this is a scam," Theodosia said. "Like I said before, this could be any random dude who knows about Reginald's murder and Fawn's disappearance. And is trying to take advantage of you."

"It sounded real to me," Meredith said. She was clearly conflicted.

"You should have demanded proof of life," Delaine said.

Now Meredith looked even more confused. "I don't know what that means."

"Like in the movies," Delaine said. "Where you get a photo of a person holding a newspaper showing the current date. So you know they're still alive and kicking."

Theodosia didn't know about proof of life. Or what Hollywood's version of a ransom demand would be. What she did know was they were in over their heads and needed serious professional help. As in, *Come right away because this is an emergency.* Which is why she snatched Meredith's phone away from her and promptly dialed 911.

Tidwell came roaring into the tea shop some ten minutes later, face flushed, his khaki trench coat flapping open over his stomach. Pete Riley followed close on his heels. No trench coat, no stomach.

Tidwell took one look around, studied everyone's faces, took careful note of Madame Emilia, and said in a sour tone, "What the Sam Hill is going on here?"

Everyone started talking at once. It sounded like a cocktail party full of grackles.

"No, no, no," Tidwell boomed. "One at a time."

When nobody ceased talking, Tidwell decided to divide and conquer. He assigned Drayton and Madame Emilia to Detective Riley, while he interviewed Theodosia and

Meredith. Delaine was the odd man out, probably because Tidwell knew her contribution would be drivel. Yup, the cheese stands alone.

"It was a ransom demand," Theodosia told Tidwell. "Five million dollars in exchange for the return of Fawn Doyle."

"That's what it was, pure and simple," Meredith said in a dry voice, nodding her head crazily like a bobblehead doll.

"And this caller did not identify himself?" Tidwell asked.

From the sidelines, Delaine said, "Duh."

"I'll thank you to keep your opinions to yourself," Tidwell shot back at her.

That buttoned Delaine up. For a while.

Tidwell turned back to Theodosia. "No identifiers that either of you could discern?"

"Not possible, since the caller used a voice changer," Theodosia said.

"Yours for thirty-nine ninety-five via the Internet," Tidwell said.

"With that horrid, mechanical voice, it could have been anyone," Meredith whispered. "Man or woman."

"Quite right," Tidwell said. "But do you think this call was legitimate? That the caller is actually holding Fawn prisoner somewhere?"

"Yes," Meredith said.

"Maybe," Theodosia said.

"What else can you recall?" Tidwell asked. "Was any timeline given?" He held up a hand. "Take your time; try to remember each and every detail. Nothing is too insignificant." Tidwell could be charming and faux courtly until . . . he wasn't.

"That horrible voice told me he'd call back tomorrow with instructions," Meredith said.

"There must be something more you can tell me," Tidwell said.

Meredith tried again, stumbling along tearfully, trying to recount her exact conversation. Theodosia interjected a few helpful notes here and there until, finally, Meredith dissolved into a puddle of tears. "I-I can't go on," she wailed.

Tidwell pursed his lips and frowned.

Theodosia stared at Tidwell. "You've pretty much heard the full story. Now what do you think she should do?"

"For now, I would advise pretending to follow the caller's instructions to the letter," Tidwell said. "Try to pacify them until we can get a plan in place." Then, seemingly immune to female hysterics, he swiveled his big head toward a tearful Meredith and said, "*Can* you get that much money together in the allotted time frame?"

"I think so." Meredith sniffled. "Probably."

"Good," Tidwell said. "Do that. But under no circumstance are you to hand over any of your money to this so-called kidnapper."

"No?" Meredith squeaked. "But what . . . ?"

"We're going to play a game of cat and mouse," Tidwell said. "For starters, we're going to tap your phones. So if and when the kidnapper calls back, we'll be privy to the conversation."

"Whatever you say," Meredith said. "What . . . what else?"

"Once you gather the funds together, you dare not sit home by yourself. It's far too dangerous."

"She's been staying at the Lady Goodwood Inn," Theodosia said.

"In their Dream Suite," Meredith said, trying to be helpful.

"Not secure enough," Tidwell said. "I'll have to put a couple men on you. And then tomorrow . . . we'll need a place where we can keep a careful watch over you."

"What if I came *here* tomorrow?" Meredith asked. "Came to Theodosia's Lavender Lady Tea."

Theodosia was about to protest — Meredith's presence would put everyone in danger, wouldn't it? — when Tidwell said, "Strangely enough, that might work. Miss Browning, I imagine you already have a list of guests who plan to attend?"

"Yes, but —"

Tidwell held up a hand. "And you're familiar with all of these people? You've basically vetted them?"

"Yes, but —"

"This tea party might be the perfect foil," Tidwell said.

"Will *you* be here? Lurking among the scones?" Theodosia asked, somewhat acerbically. She felt like she was being railroaded. Well, she was.

"I won't be present, but several of my men will," Tidwell said.

"Inside? Outside?" Theodosia didn't want her Lavender Lady Tea to be ruined by men in black nylon SWAT gear who were brandishing guns and radios.

"Details to be worked out," Tidwell said.

"Hmm," Theodosia said. His plan sounded awfully loosey-goosey to her.

Twenty minutes later, interviews concluded, Tidwell and Riley put their heads together while everyone sat waiting with bated breath.

"This was quite unreasonable," Delaine complained as the two men talked. "They didn't even want my two cents' worth."

"You should be thankful for that," Drayton said. "We were practically grilled." He pulled out a folded white hankie and wiped his brow.

Tidwell stalked over to where they were all sitting, Riley right behind him.

"All right, everyone, listen up," Tidwell said.

They sat there, alert and ready to listen.

"We'll have a plan in place shortly," Tidwell said with a small amount of bravado and flourish.

"A plan that will carefully address this ransom business," Riley said. He came across as thoughtful, and at times sardonic, to Tidwell's outright bluster.

"Now I ask for each of you to remain absolutely mum on the subject," Tidwell said. "Don't tell anyone what happened here today or what you think might happen tomorrow. Is that clear?"

Tidwell's beetle brows descended over his eyes like window shades.

Everyone noted his intensity and nodded politely.

"Good. Excellent," Tidwell said.

"It looks as if our Robbery and Homicide Division has its work cut out for it," Riley said.

Theodosia raised a hand. "If I could just —"

"No, you cannot," Tidwell cut in. "Nope, nada, no way. Now it is time for you, Miss Browning, to bow out gracefully. We — and by that I mean Detective Riley and myself, with the aid of Sheriff Burney and a number of other officers — will handle this case by ourselves. From here on out. Is that understood?"

Again, everyone gave pleasant nods and murmurs. Including Theodosia. She figured it was better to go along to get along. Detective Tidwell's words didn't sit well with her, but right now there wasn't much she could do about it. But maybe tomorrow . . .

As Tidwell and Riley turned to leave, Meredith grabbed Theodosia's arm and pulled her aside.

"I hope you don't mind my coming to your Lavender Lady Tea tomorrow. Using it as a kind of security blanket."

"It should be fine," Theodosia said. She tried to sound amiable and agreeable, even though she was screaming a little bit inside.

"And I'm praying that it's okay to bring Alex and Bill Jacoby with me, too." Still visibly shaken, Meredith licked her lips and quickly added, "I thought maybe they could serve as my guardian angel posse. Would that be a problem?"

"No, I'll just squeeze in another few chairs." *Along with the police officers that will be hiding under the tables and in the cupboards.*

Meredith's relief was palpable. "Bless you for your kindness."

Friday night and Theodosia paced inside her own home. This was usually date night for her and Riley. Take in a movie, check out a new restaurant, cozy up in front of the fireplace with a good bottle of wine. Except tonight Riley was working. Or rather, Tidwell had him on overtime, probably riding him like a rented mule.

Would Riley call her? Bring her up to speed on the plan — whatever that plan might be?

Probably not.

Rats.

Theodosia fed Earl Grey and warmed up some leftover lentil soup for herself. With time hanging heavy, she tried to read a book, lost interest in that, and turned on the TV. But found nothing that appealed to her.

Finally, at quarter to nine, Riley called.

"What?" Theodosia practically yelled into the phone. "What's going on?"

"Not much at the moment."

"No clues? Nothing?"

"Clues and forensic evidence are critical, but most breaks come when somebody talks."

"Is anybody talking?"

"No."

"But surely you people must have drawn up a suspect list by now. Somebody close to Meredith, to Reginald Doyle." Theodosia rattled on, breathless now. "Because what I'm thinking is this . . . the killer is also the kidnapper. So there have to be some distinct possibilities. And . . . and you *must* have traced that phone call."

"We tried, but the phone turned out to be a burner. The kidnapper probably bought it at the local Walmart, used it once, then dumped it in a trash can somewhere."

"Could it have been Jack Grimes, the caretaker?"

"We already checked him out. He's gone. Moved to Georgia. Some place in Clutch County."

"Clinch County," Theodosia said.

"You *know* where he relocated? Jeez, Tidwell was right. You are way too involved."

"What about Guy Thorne?"

"What about him?"

"He's a good possibility," Theodosia said.

"We know the man is financially strapped."

"Thorne has been working at his restaurant all day," Riley said. "Trollope's is jampacked with customers, plus there's some kind of prewedding event going on in their private dining room."

"But maybe . . ."

"Also, we've been watching him. We got a court order and tapped his phones."

"So he . . ."

"Didn't do it," Riley said. "Like I said, he's been honchoing a busy restaurant but hasn't, to our knowledge, called in any kind of ransom demand."

"Carl Clewis or Alex, then," Theodosia practically shouted. "Either of them could have easily made that ransom call."

"You can't just keep throwing out names," Riley said. "There has to be some supporting evidence."

"Alex, then. He and Fawn weren't getting along. Plus, he despised Reginald."

"Maybe so," Riley said. "But our plan right now is to sit tight until the ransom demand is made. Then we . . ."

"Follow the money," Theodosia said. "I know."

"Trust me, we've got this under control."

No, Theodosia thought, *nobody's got this thing under control.* Except perhaps that one shadowy figure who was out there on the fringe, jerking everyone's chain.

And come tomorrow, hopefully not mine as well.

27

On Saturday morning Theodosia's head was spinning with questions as she worked to get her tea shop decorated and ready for their Lavender Lady Tea. Was Fawn still alive? Was her kidnapping connected to Reginald's death? Who was playing evil puppeteer and creating all this havoc?

She was sipping a cup of gunpowder green tea, tapping a foot, when her cell phone burped in the pocket of her apron.

She looked at the screen. Riley.

"Hey, there!" Theodosia cried as she answered the phone. Maybe he had news?

"Do you remember when you asked me to check on Carl Clewis's whereabouts for last Sunday afternoon?" Riley asked. "Well, I finally got around to doing that."

"Where was he? What was Clewis doing?"

"Giving a guest lecture on restoring wetlands to the McClellanville Upland Grouse Club."

"Oh." Theodosia hadn't expected to hear such an ironclad alibi. "That's . . . Are you sure?"

"Yes."

"Then it looks as if Clewis is out of the equation." Theodosia felt disheartened. Clewis had seemed like such a logical suspect. For Reginald's murder as well as Fawn's kidnapping and ransom demand.

"In my book, Clewis is in the clear," Riley said. "Unless he's got a twin brother stashed somewhere."

"So what happens now? I mean, today, with Meredith?" With her prime suspects dropping like flies, Theodosia didn't feel one bit encouraged.

"We have a team that will cover Meredith Doyle while she makes a stop at her bank to collect the money. Then we'll have eyes on her constantly as she makes her way to your tea shop. A veritable tag team of officers. What time is your Lavender Lady Tea supposed to kick off?"

"Twelve sharp."

"We'll be set up there by ten thirty, then," Riley said. "Possibly even earlier."

"You'll be outside? Inside?" *Knock, knock, didn't I ask this question yesterday?*

"Our plan is to remain fluid," Riley said. "So we'll let you know."

"Well, let me know sometime *soon,* will you?"

"What dishes do you want me to put out, honey?" Miss Dimple asked. She had shown up at the Indigo Tea Shop some fifteen minutes ago and was bustling about, doing her best to assist Theodosia. They'd arranged the tables and set them with white linen place mats and crystal stemware, but that was it so far.

"Grab those lavender toile dishes out of the cupboard, will you?" Theodosia asked.

Miss Dimple stood on tippy-toes and pulled down a stack of plates. She looked at them and smiled.

"Toile," she said. "A French convention, yes?"

"That's exactly right," Theodosia said. "*Toile de jouy* was originally a pattern on French linen and canvas. But now that it's grown so much in popularity, the word *toile* pretty much refers to any repeated pattern that depicts a lovely scene."

"Such as this delicious garden scene," Miss Dimple said, studying one of the plates. She turned it over. "Who made these?"

"They're by Staffordshire, but lots of different makers do toile designs. You'll see

343

pastoral scenes, Chinese pagodas, Venetian gondolas, horses and carriages, and even picnic scenes."

"Well, I can't believe you've got the perfect lavender dishes for your Lavender Lady Tea!"

"You wouldn't believe all the sets of china Drayton and I have collected over the years. If you look hard enough, you'll find them stashed all over the place," Theodosia said. "Even upstairs in Haley's apartment."

Miss Dimple grinned. "A treasure hunt. What fun."

"While you set out the dishes, I'm going to run into my office and grab the lavender candles and sachets."

Theodosia pushed through the celadon velvet curtain that separated the front of the tea shop from the back. She glanced right, saw Haley bent over her stove, and continued into her office, where the phone started ringing.

"Hello?"

It was George Huntley from Huntley's Ltd.

"You can toss that invoice in the trash, Miss Browning. It was a mistake, pure and simple, just as I thought."

"Okay," Theodosia said. "That's great. Thanks."

She was about to hang up the phone when Huntley said, "The mix-up came about because we were also asked to custom design a concealed pistol holster."

"What?" Theodosia said. Had she heard him right?

It would seem so.

"And you see," Huntley continued, "the pistol holster that we crafted in a lovely soft Brazilian suede was delivered to the same place as your shooting vest."

Theodosia's heart started hammering inside her chest. "Excuse me, you mean delivered to Creekmore Plantation?"

"That's correct. So, obviously, you can see how a mix-up might occur."

"Yes, I can." Theodosia was so excited, so nervous, she could barely speak a word. "Thank you, Mr. Huntley, for straightening that out."

Theodosia hung up the phone and stared down at her desk.

A concealed pistol holster. Delivered to Creekmore Plantation.

Warning bells clanged inside her head. She put a hand up and massaged her forehead.

And Reginald Doyle just happened to be shot with a pistol.

Theodosia reached out and punched in

345

George Huntley's number. A minute later, she had him back on the line.

"About that pistol holster. Can you tell me who ordered it?" Theodosia asked.

"I suppose I could . . . Just let me, um, take a peek here," Huntley said.

Theodosia shifted from one foot to the other, feeling anxious and half-afraid that she was about to learn the name of Reginald Doyle's killer. She could hear Huntley riffling through papers at the other end of the line.

"That's funny," Huntley said, "but we don't seem to have a name here. Just a delivery address. Which is very strange indeed. I guess I'm going to have to do some digging if I intend to get paid."

Theodosia hung up, even more convinced that one of her prime suspects — someone dangerously close to Meredith — had murdered Reginald Doyle.

Yes, someone who carried a long gun last Sunday must have also used a concealed pistol holster. But who?

Worse yet, was this the same person who'd kidnapped Fawn?

And the big sixty-four-thousand-dollar question was — should she divulge this new information to Tidwell? Or to Riley?

Probably. Maybe.

Or should I wait and see?

Theodosia carried the box filled with lavender candles and sachets out to Miss Dimple, then walked to the front counter and crooked a finger at Drayton.

He leaned forward, a tin of tea in hand. "Yes?"

"Guess what."

"I couldn't possibly."

"I just received a call from Huntley Ltd., the company that custom designed your shooting vest. And, lo and behold, they were also tapped to design a concealed pistol holster."

"A . . . pistol holster? Did I hear you correctly?"

"The operative word being *concealed* pistol holster. George Huntley can't find the name of the person who ordered it, but he assures me the finished piece was delivered to Creekmore Plantation."

Drayton's facile mind took about two seconds to make the connection.

"You can't be serious."

"As serious as a heart attack."

"So you've been right all along! Someone in the shooting party killed Reginald Doyle," Drayton said.

"Or someone nearby."

347

"But who?"

"Take your pick," Theodosia said. "Guy Thorne. Jack Grimes. Susan Monday. Or it could have even been Meredith or Alex."

"But Fawn's disappearance . . ."

"Is part and parcel of this whole murder mystery."

Drayton thought for a moment. "You just rattled off a list of suspects. But what about Carl Clewis?"

"He has an alibi that checks out," Theodosia said.

Drayton pried the top off a tin of Assam golden tips tea. "You realize Susan Monday will be here in a couple of hours."

"And then so will Meredith and Alex," Theodosia said. "I really hate to say this, but any one of them could have pulled off that murder."

Drayton started to scoop up tea leaves and promptly spilled them. "Mother of pearl, have we unwittingly set up some kind of disaster? A weird convergence of the various players?"

Theodosia locked eyes with him. "I sincerely hope not, Drayton."

"Now I'm so rattled I don't know what I'm doing."

"Tell me about it."

"Are you going to share this information

348

about the concealed pistol holster with Detective Tidwell? Or your friend Detective Riley?"

Theodosia was quiet for a moment, then said, "I think I pretty much have to."

But before a horde of law enforcement could descend upon the Indigo Tea Shop, tables needed to be set and there was a small matter of decorating.

"Should I tie these lavender sashes on the backs of all the chairs?" Miss Dimple asked.

"Yes, just make a big floppy bow in back," Theodosia said.

"I love all these fancy touches. What else are you going to do?"

"Let's see," Theodosia said. "We need to put out the lavender bundles and sachets for favors. Tie ribbons around the long-stemmed bunches of lavender and put them in vases. Add the lavender candles to the tables. Oh, and we can't forget champagne glasses. This is also a champagne tea."

"You can't go wrong with bubbly *and* brewed tea." Miss Dimple laughed.

"I hope not," Theodosia said. But she wasn't thinking about champagne and tea at the moment. Her mind was spinning with worry about everything else.

28

Luckily, there were no worries about the food they were serving. Haley had powered through with a spectacular menu. One that Theodosia almost couldn't believe, given the size constraints of their kitchen.

"I'm blown away, Haley," Theodosia said. She stared at Haley's scribbled menu card in her hand. "This is spectacular."

Haley lifted a shoulder and grinned. "Hey, spectacular is my middle name."

"It certainly has been this week."

Haley looked serious again. "Do you think our guests will like everything I came up with?"

"Haley, they're going to be delighted."

"Because I could always —"

KNOCK! KNOCK!

"Back door!" Theodosia and Haley cried in unison.

Theodosia darted out of the kitchen, ran through her office, and pulled open the back door. Detective Pete Riley stood there flanked by two uniformed officers who carried official-looking black leather cases.

"Come in," Theodosia said as her heart did a fast blip-blip. *This is it. Now it starts.*

"Thank you, Miss Browning," Riley said. He was being formal, playing it by the book.

"Where do you intend to . . . ?"

"Set up?" Riley asked. His eyes roved about her office. "Right here, if that's okay with you."

"And there'll be . . ."

"An unmarked car parked in the alley out back as well as three more cars on Church Street," Riley said.

"But no police officers will be attending the tea," Theodosia said. She wanted to be absolutely clear on this.

"None will be in the tea room per se," Riley said. "But Officers Bowie and Smithson will be here with me."

"Guns at the ready?" Theodosia asked.

Riley shook his head. "I'm doubtful it will come to that. But if you don't mind, we're going to set up a couple of listening devices." He glanced at Officer Smithson. "Smitty? You go ahead."

Theodosia followed Officer Smithson into the tea room and watched as he pulled a couple of minuscule devices from his case.

"Where is the target sitting, ma'am?" Smithson asked.

"The target?"

"Mrs. Doyle," Smithson said.

"Oh. Of course. Right over here."

"Thank you, ma'am."

Theodosia, Drayton, and Miss Dimple watched as Officer Smithson put his tiny listening devices around the tea room.

"What are they for?" Miss Dimple asked. "Some kind of radio broadcast?"

"Something like that," Theodosia said.

Drayton made a noise in the back of his throat.

"Actually, the police are involved because there could be a spot of trouble here today," Theodosia said.

"Isn't that fascinating!" Miss Dimple exclaimed. "You people always have something exciting going on. No wonder I love working here." She did everything but clap her hands together.

Theodosia glanced at Drayton, who simply shook his head.

"Did you see Haley's menu?" Drayton asked, quickly changing the subject.

"Yes, and it's spectacular," Theodosia said. She stepped closer to the front counter. "Do you think we should tell Miss Dimple what's really going on?"

"Why worry the poor soul? Maybe nothing will happen."

"The police sure think something's going to go down. There are police officers lurking in my office and several more sitting in unmarked cars outside."

"Did you tell your friend Riley about the concealed pistol holster?"

"Not yet. Do you think I should?"

"Probably."

"Then he's really going to —"

There was a sudden loud noise out on the street.

"What was that?" Drayton cried.

Theodosia ran to the front door and peered out. Church Street was as busy as ever. Cars whizzed by, a horse-drawn jitney clip-clopped along slowly. There was also what looked like a walking tour ambling down the sidewalk, a dozen interested folks hitting some of the Historic District's high spots. But nothing looked out of place. No exploding bombs. No gunfight going on. No SWAT team tossing flash bangs.

Theodosia had just taken her hand off the doorknob and stepped back, when the door flew open, just missing her by inches. "Oh!" she cried out.

As Susan Monday peered in.

"Susan!" Theodosia said, trying to recover

but sounding a little rattled.

"I'm sorry, am I too early?" Susan asked.

"No, you're perfect. It's just that . . . well, nothing."

Susan looked suddenly curious. "Problems?" she asked.

"Not at all," Theodosia said. "We just had an, uh, electrical issue."

"I hope not in your kitchen."

"No, it's actually in the upstairs apartment. Where my chef, Haley, lives."

"Okay then," Susan said. "Where would you like me to hang out?"

"At the main table. Of course."

Theodosia did a last-minute perusal of the tea room, swept in to do a final menu check with Haley, then ran back into the tea room and grabbed her clipboard.

Good thing. Because two minutes later, a stream of guests began to arrive. Excited women wearing autumn coats, suits, and suede jackets, with the occasional jaunty hat. Theodosia was immediately engulfed in a whirlwind of greetings and warm hellos, accepting more than a few air-kisses as she checked off names and seated everyone at their assigned table.

There was a short lull during which Theodosia was able to catch her breath, and then

Brooke Carter Crocker, proprietor of Hearts Desire, arrived with her friend Marlys. Then Jennie, Helen, Dawn, and Diane (all regulars) came pouring in, along with Bonnie, Becky, and Jan.

Delaine Dish arrived in a fashionable flurry, clinging to the arm of Tod Slawson, with her niece Bettina in tow.

"I hope you don't mind that I brought Tod along," Delaine whispered to Theodosia.

"Not a problem," Theodosia whispered back. She knew that Delaine needed a man to feed her a steady stream of compliments, otherwise she grew twitchy. And a twitchy Delaine was a cranky Delaine.

When every table had filled except for the main table, where Susan Monday was seated, Meredith finally arrived with Alex and Bill Jacoby.

Theodosia put her arm around Meredith's thin shoulders and said, "Meredith, how are you doing?"

Even though Meredith looked quite stunning in a powder-blue Dior suit, she pulled her mouth into a tight grimace and said, "I'm a nervous wreck. I've been waiting on pins and needles for that second ransom call, and it simply hasn't come."

Maybe that's a good thing? Theodosia thought.

"No matter what happens, we're happy to have you with us today," Theodosia said as she led Meredith, Alex, and Bill to their table. "You'll be among friends and hopefully well protected."

Meredith raised her penciled brows. "Will I really be? Protected, I mean?"

"I'd say it's as tightly guarded as a fortress in here," Theodosia said. She was joking to keep from worrying.

"Why do I not feel reassured?" Meredith said as Alex pulled out her chair.

There was always a hushed moment before a special event kicked off. Before Theodosia made her way to the center of the crowded tea room and, with every pair of eyes focused on her, bid everyone welcome. Today that moment felt endless to Theodosia, but she recovered quickly and practically fizzed with excitement as she addressed her guests.

"Welcome, my dear friends, to our first-ever Lavender Lady Tea. Which, by the way, is also a champagne tea."

There was a round of enthusiastic applause and then Theodosia continued.

"As you know, lavender is both an herb and a flower that is well-known for inducing calm and relaxation. To that end, and to add a note of tranquility and serenity to your day, we've prepared a spectacular lavender-infused menu for you, as well as a house-blended lavender tea. We also have a special guest with us today. Miss Susan Monday, proprietor of Blue Moon Lavender Farm, will give a short talk on the unique properties and uses for her locally grown lavender."

This time the applause was even heartier.

"But first things first. Drayton, will you kindly bring our guests up to date on your special tea blend?"

Drayton stepped to the center of the tea room and clicked his well-polished heels together. With his tweed jacket, bow tie, and rigid posture, he looked like a cross between a dapper Southern gent and a fencing master.

"The Lavender Lady Tea we're about to serve you is my own special house blend. I started with Chinese black tea as a base, added a hint of bergamot, a generous amount of fresh, organic lavender buds, and finished it off with bits of vanilla and orange peel. One relaxing sip, and I guarantee you peace of mind and the feeling of being whisked away to romantic Provence!"

"And now for our menu," Theodosia said, coming forward again to join Drayton.

"First course will be a lavender scone with Devonshire cream. This will be followed by a citrus salad sprinkled with candied edible flowers."

There was some oohing and aahing at that announcement.

"For our main entrée, we'll be serving our famous Parmesan and prosciutto puff baby. And for dessert, lemon-lavender shortbread with lavender gelato."

As Theodosia finished with a flourish, Miss Dimple began pouring the champagne, Drayton began serving tea, and Haley emerged from the kitchen carrying a silver tray stacked with lavender scones. Theodosia immediately began helping Haley serve the scones while encouraging her guests to help themselves to the heaping bowls of Devonshire cream.

When everyone was happily drinking tea (or champagne or both) and munching scones, Theodosia gave the high sign to Susan Monday.

Susan stood up, did a quick introduction, and much to Theodosia's delight, gave a wonderfully entertaining and enlightening presentation. She talked about how lavender was an herb that could help reduce anxiety. That lavender was often used in balms, salves, and perfumes. She explained that lavender's dried buds could be used in cooking and how lavender flowers yielded abundant nectar from which bees made high-quality honey. Theodosia was even surprised to learn that there were two hundred varieties of lavender in the world, with colors that ranged from white to pink, to all shades of blue.

Clearly, the tea was off to a rousing start. Susan received thanks and praise while Theodosia and Drayton also enjoyed a multitude of compliments. It was only after Theodosia had served the citrus salads that she remembered Detective Riley and his merry band of men were hanging out in her office.

That brought her back down to earth with a thud.

Theodosia made sure everything was running smoothly, then surreptitiously ducked behind the curtain.

"Riley," Theodosia said. He was sitting at her desk, fiddling with his phone. Officer Smithson was sprawled on the tuffet, wearing a set of headphones. Officer Bowie was lounging near the back door.

"What?" Riley looked up at her and smiled.

"I forgot to tell you something," Theodosia said.

Riley made a rolling hand motion, an *Okay, tell me now* gesture.

"I found out that Huntley's Ltd., the same people who delivered Drayton's hunting vest to Creekmore Plantation, also delivered a concealed pistol holster."

29

"A what!" Riley bolted from his chair so fast it almost flipped over backward. He stared at Theodosia with blazing eyes.

"A custom-designed —"

Riley's palm shot in her direction. "Stop. I heard you the first time." He stared at her, trying to process this new information. "And you waited until *now* to tell me?"

"I just found out this morning," Theodosia said. "Like, five minutes before my guests arrived." She knew she was fudging on the time, but whatever. She was telling him now, bringing him into the loop. Surely, that had to count for something.

"And who exactly was this concealed pistol holster delivered to?"

"Huntley's Ltd. doesn't seem to know. They just had instructions to deliver it to Creekmore Plantation."

"When?"

"The day of the hunt? Last Sunday?"

Theodosia said.

"Are you asking me or telling me?"

"Telling."

"Well . . . holy crap," Riley said. He clapped a hand on top of his head and scrubbed at his hair. "So somebody . . ."

". . . in the shooting party had to have shot Reginald Doyle," Theodosia said. So there, she'd told him about the concealed pistol holster and helped him make the connection. She felt slightly . . . unburdened.

"You sure you didn't know about this sooner?" Riley asked.

"No." Theodosia waited to see if Riley would say anything more. Or how he'd react. Would he call Tidwell? Would he go charging over to Huntley's Ltd.? When nothing happened, she said, "So what are you going to do with this information?"

Riley stood there for a moment looking perplexed. Then he said, "Theo, I have no idea."

Back in the tea room, Theodosia helped Miss Dimple serve the Parmesan and prosciutto puff babies. This was Haley's special concoction of cheese and prosciutto wrapped in layers of puff pastry and baked to a golden brown in a hot oven. Luckily, the individual entrées remained gorgeously inflated as they were served.

That taken care of, Theodosia grabbed two more bottles of champagne and began working her way around the tables, refilling glasses.

"Bless you," Bill Jacoby said when she got to him. "I don't mind if I do have a second glass. I was afraid this affair would be as dry as a church supper."

"And you're enjoying everything?" Theodosia asked.

"I thought a tea party meant dinky little cucumber sandwiches, but this couldn't be better."

Which was exactly what Theodosia said to Drayton when she went up to the counter.

"This tea couldn't have turned out better," she said. "Even with the police lurking in the back office and outside."

"It is going smashingly well," Drayton agreed. "Even though Alex hasn't been off his phone for a single moment and Jacoby won't lay off the scones and Devonshire cream."

"Those are the least of our worries."

"And *nothing* has happened with Meredith."

Theodosia nodded. "Her phone hasn't rung, hasn't even vibrated. There've been no calls, texts, or e-mails."

"Thank goodness for that," Drayton said, just as the front door opened and Guy Thorne walked in. Thorne took three steps into the tea shop, then stopped in his tracks and frowned.

Theodosia hurried over to greet him. And to halt any more forward progress. "Mr. Thorne, how can I help you?" *Maybe he's come for takeout?*

But no.

"I need to speak with Meredith," Thorne said. He wasn't exactly confrontational, but he wasn't super friendly, either.

"That's fine, but we're right in the middle of our Lavender Lady Tea right now," Theodosia said.

Thorne raised his brows in a dismissive manner. "This is important."

"I'm sure it is. Maybe if you could . . ."

"Explain my problem?"

"I was going to say come back," Theodosia said.

But Thorne wasn't about to budge.

"Here's the thing: Meredith called me last night, crying hysterically and pleading with me to buy her share of Trollope's Restaurant. She's trying to raise money for —"

Thorne stopped suddenly and gave Theodosia a condescending look.

"You're the town busybody, so you probably know *exactly* what's going on."

"I imagine you're referring to the ransom demand?" Theodosia kept an even tone. No way was she going to let this bully push her around.

"Bingo," Thorne said. "So Meredith is begging me to buy her out — like, instantly."

"Can you do that? Will you do that?" Theodosia asked. *Time to apply a little judicious pressure.*

This time Thorne wouldn't meet her eyes. "Truth be told, I'm a little short on cash right now. Interest rates are still in the toilet, the stock market's been yo-yoing like mad, and business is . . . well, I'm up against an awful lot of competition."

"Uh-huh," Theodosia said.

Maybe Thorne should engage the financial prognostication services of Madame Emilia? Or maybe he could just stop gambling away the profits?

"Anyway," Thorne said, "I gotta talk to her."

"All right," Theodosia said. In the back of her brain, she still worried that Thorne could, in fact, be a killer and a kidnapper. Two nasty criminal acts rolled into one.

Theodosia let Thorne into the shop while she kept an eagle eye on him, but still, nothing awful happened. He had a whispered conversation with Meredith and then left. More tea was served along with the lemon-lavender shortbread and gelato. A few guests got gently tipsy from the champagne, but nobody was overly raucous. As conversations dwindled and the afternoon wore on, guests gathered up their lavender sachets and soaps and made ready to leave.

More air-kisses were exchanged and heart-felt thank-yous were said. Everyone, it seemed, had thoroughly enjoyed the tea party.

"Thank you," Theodosia said to Susan Monday as she walked her to the front door. "You were a huge hit."

"Your *tea* was the hit," Susan said, eyes twinkling. "Everything was just wonderful."

Finally, when Meredith and her gang of two left, so did the police. Quietly and unobtrusively, without a by-your-leave. Ten minutes later, all that was left were candles guttering in their silver holders and a few stray bundles of lavender.

Drayton dropped his shoulders and exhaled loudly. He was none the worse for wear except for a smudge of lipstick on his shirt collar.

"Absolutely nothing happened to disrupt our tea," Drayton said. "No mysterious ransom demands, no hysterics, no police rushing in to slam some miscreant to the floor and handcuff them."

"We lucked out," Theodosia said.

Drayton's mouth twitched. "I imagine you're right. But . . . what about Fawn? What about the ransom demand? We've heard nothing so far."

"Maybe the kidnapper will call Meredith tonight. I mean, the police will still be protecting her, listening in . . ."

"Probably be all over her like bees to honey," Drayton said. "So it looks as if we're out of the picture now." He dusted his hands together. "Just like that."

"You sound a little disappointed," Theodosia said.

"I have to admit, this isn't how I thought our event would end," Drayton said. "I imagined fireworks, screaming, maybe even a few shots fired."

"A Bruce Willis Hollywood movie–type ending." Theodosia laughed.

Theodosia, Drayton, and Miss Dimple continued to work, picking up dishes, straightening tables, sweeping the floor.

"That's it," Theodosia said. "We're done and it's getting late. Time to go home."

"You said a mouthful," Miss Dimple said. "I am seriously tuckered out."

An earsplitting ROWR-ROWR-ROWR

suddenly exploded in the back alley. It rose to a crashing crescendo then subsided to a low rumble.

"What *is* that horrible racket?" Drayton cried.

Haley rushed out of the kitchen, looking a little frantic. She'd changed out of her chef's white coat and mushroom-shaped hat into a black leather jacket, jeans, and boots.

"Don't anybody worry, that's just my date," Haley called out.

"Driving a Sherman tank?" Drayton asked.

"It's a motorcycle," Haley said.

"A Saturday night date? On a motorcycle?" Drayton asked.

"Chill, Drayton," Haley said. "We're going to a concert."

"Well —" Drayton was about to say more when he checked himself and stopped abruptly. He waggled his fingers in a good-bye gesture and said, "Kindly wear a helmet, will you?"

"Very good," Miss Dimple whispered to Theodosia. "Drayton is making excellent forward progress."

"He's certainly trying," Theodosia said.

"And he's got lipstick on his collar," Miss Dimple said.

Drayton glanced at her and sighed.

"Merely an overenthusiastic kiss from a happy customer."

"That woman Adelle something? The one who wears so much makeup?" Theodosia asked.

"Right," Drayton said, rolling his R.

"Hmm," Miss Dimple said.

When Miss Dimple had finished thanking *them* for letting *her* work today, she toddled out the door, toting a bag of leftover scones.

"A long day," Drayton observed. He was almost but not quite yawning.

"Where's Honey Bee?" Theodosia asked.

"My next-door neighbor lady has her. The one with the adorable little shih tzu named Clover."

"I have an idea. Why don't we finish up here and then you come home with me for dinner tonight? Nothing fancy, not a four-course dinner or anything like that. More like soup and popovers. What do you say?"

Drayton smiled. "I'd say it's a fine reason to pop over."

30

"This is so relaxing and nice." Drayton was sprawled on the living room sofa while Theodosia stood at the antique British campaign chest she used as a makeshift bar and poured them each a glass of wine. Earl Grey was curled up on his cushy dog bed next to the fireplace.

"Chilly in here." Theodosia handed Drayton his drink and checked the thermostat.

"I could build a fire."

Earl Grey thumped his tail. He loved the warmth of a good fire.

"*I* could build a fire," Theodosia said as she sat down in the chair across from Drayton. "Of course, then I'd have to schlep outside and grab some kindling and a few logs."

"What you really mean is you'd have to mountain-goat it over that pile of lumber and cabinet parts that's spread out in the middle of your kitchen. It truly is a construction zone in there."

"It's terrible. But I keep telling myself this mess will be worth it in the end."

"Eventually, it will pay off, yes," Drayton said. "I remember when the workmen were refinishing my pine countertops and installing my copper sink. It drove me crackers and seemed to go on for eons." He took a sip of wine and said, "Delicious. This is the French Malbec you told me about?"

"Yup. You're supposed to be able to taste blackberries and a hint of violets."

"And I do."

They chatted about the Lavender Lady Tea, and Theodosia began to relax as she felt the wine starting to warm her. Then, as if an alarm had gone off, her mind buzzed into action again. "Do you think Meredith got her ransom call yet?"

"Search me," Drayton said.

"Maybe this has all been a ruse."

"Meredith seemed to think it was legitimate," Drayton said. "The police are taking it seriously."

"No, what I meant was, what if Fawn really wasn't kidnapped? What if she's in collusion with someone?"

Drayton was taken aback. "With who?"

"I'm not sure," Theodosia said.

"You've certainly done an about-face. You

don't even believe that Fawn is dead."

"Not anymore, I don't. No."

"What changed your mind?"

Theodosia thought for a few moments. "I guess . . . maybe it's all been too much of a coincidence?"

"You mean Reginald getting shot and then Fawn pretty much dropping off the face of the earth?" Drayton asked.

"Exactly."

"Well, it's not ours to worry about anymore. I'm assuming the Charleston Police have everything under control. If that awful kidnapper person calls Meredith with instructions about delivering the ransom money, the police will probably pounce on him like a duck on a June bug." Drayton took another sip of wine. "I hope they will, anyway."

"They've probably dressed a female SWAT officer up to look like Meredith."

"That would be a clever thing to do," Drayton said.

Theodosia stood up. "I'm going to heat some wild rice soup and slip the popovers in the oven."

"Need my help?"

"You stay right where you are. There's barely enough room for me in that kitchen."

Theodosia set her drink on the sideboard

as she walked through the dining room, keenly aware of the *click click click* of toenails following directly behind her.

"I'm afraid there isn't room for you in the kitchen, either," she told Earl Grey.

The dog favored her with a baleful gaze.

"Oh, all right. But please be careful. Watch your paws and don't go tripping over anything."

Then, as Theodosia stepped into her kitchen, that's exactly what *she* did.

"Uh . . . ouch!" she cried as her foot smacked hard against a stack of two-by-fours. A split second later, she'd lost her balance and was starting to fall. "No!" she cried, a flash of anger ripping through her. Theodosia flailed her arms and, at the last moment, caught herself and managed to right herself.

"Are you all right?" Drayton's voice floated back to her.

"Perfectly fine," she said, though her heart was still doing flip-flops.

Theodosia stood there trying to shake it off. Finally, she blew out a glut of air, leaned down, and hastily gathered up the stack of boards. "This is *not* how I'm going to spend the rest of the weekend." She ground her teeth together for emphasis. "This ends *now.*"

Juggling her armful of wood, struggling to get the back door open, practically kicking her way outside, Theodosia carried the offending boards out and dumped them on her back patio.

"There," she said, the boards clattering horribly as they hit the patio stones. "This stuff can sit right here until Monday morning when my cabinet guy is supposed to come back."

Theodosia was still muttering to herself and to Earl Grey, who'd followed her outside. But she was rudely interrupted when her neighbor suddenly roared up his driveway, shattering a quiet — well, relatively quiet — evening.

Is that Steele's Porsche making all that noise? Again?

Miffed by the racket, thinking she might do the neighbors a great favor by saying something to him, Theodosia took a few steps forward and peered through the dense boxwood hedge that separated her side yard from his driveway. The sun had dropped below the horizon, but she could still make out his car.

Look at that, tonight he's driving his big, honkin' BMW.

Robert Steele drove his black BMW 740i as if he were a NASCAR driver at Daytona

International Speedway. Fast and furious, often taking chances. Someday, Theodosia thought, Steele was going to hit something. Cripple a person or smash another car. And then where would he be?

Probably not in court, seeing as how he's been slipping in and out of lawsuits his entire career.

Two voices, Steele's deep tones and those of a higher-pitched female, both raised in laughter, could be heard over the slam of car doors.

Is this another of his Saturday night special girlfriends?

Theodosia was about to turn and go inside when her curiosity reared up and got the best of her. She moved quietly along the hedge, following the sound of voices, until she came to a spot where she could peek through the leaves.

I suppose I shouldn't be doing this . . .

She looked anyway and could hardly believe her eyes.

What?

With a startled intake of breath, Theodosia whirled about and sprinted for her house.

It couldn't be, it couldn't be, her brain hammered out frantically.

She was moving so fast, not watching where she was going, that she practically smacked into Drayton, who was standing just inside her kitchen door.

"Whoa there." Drayton grabbed Theodosia by the shoulders to steady her and keep her from tumbling head over teakettle. "I wondered where you'd run off to." He was smiling, but concern shone in his gray eyes.

"I . . . saw something that weirded me out," Theodosia said. Her frenzied brain tried to make sense of the image she'd seen as sparks twirled before her eyes.

"Actually, you look like you saw a ghost."

"I think I did." Theodosia was flustered, unsure how to explain herself. Could she trust her own eyes? She'd only seen that split-second flash . . .

Drayton started to chuckle, then quit abruptly when Theodosia didn't join in. "What?" he asked. "A ghost in a shroud?"

Theodosia shook her head. "This ghost was all gold and shimmery." She tried to put her words together and said, "Do you remember . . . ?" Then stopped.

"Go on. What were you about to say?" Drayton urged.

"A couple of days ago Delaine was rambling on about a dress Fawn bought at her shop."

"Okay."

"Anyway, Delaine was rhapsodizing over this fabulous gold dress that Fawn bought at her shop. Said it made her look like she was walking in moonlight or something."

"Wait one minute. Is *that* what you think you saw?"

Theodosia lifted a shoulder. "Maybe."

"It had to be a figment of your imagination," Drayton said. "Maybe a leftover impression sparked by that awful séance yesterday."

"You're right. It was probably nothing," Theodosia said.

She tried to dismiss it, banish the fleeting image of the golden girl from her mind, but she couldn't. It was stuck there like a visual earworm that wouldn't go away, no matter what.

"Or maybe it *was* something. Maybe I really did see . . . Fawn," Theodosia said haltingly.

Drayton frowned at the mention of Fawn's name.

An ember of uncertainty burned in Theodosia's brain. "I have to know. And there's only one way to find out for sure."

Now Drayton's brows shot up. "What are you saying?"

Theodosia touched a hand to his arm. "Come with me. I have to get a second opinion on this, or I'll go crazy." She turned and grabbed her keys, then darted out the back door, and ran lightly across the patio.

"Are you quite mad?" Drayton asked, but he lurched after her anyway, closing the door on Earl Grey.

"Come on." Theodosia had already wedged herself into the boxwood hedge. She figured if she wiggled and squiggled she could push all the way through to her neighbor's yard.

"You want me to sneak over there with you? In the dark?" Drayton's voice was a low whisper. He was keenly aware of voices coming from the other side of the hedge.

"Yes, right now in the dark."

"This is preposterous," Drayton said, holding up both hands to caution her. "Like kids sneaking into a graveyard on a dare."

"Don't be so dramatic, Drayton. I just . . . Ouch . . ." Theodosia flinched. She was firmly wedged inside the hedge, unable to go any farther, a dozen sharp branches poking her ribs like dull knives. "I think I might need some help here." She was hopelessly trapped among the unyielding branches.

"Good grief. Give me your hand, and I'll try to . . ."

Theodosia held out her hand for Drayton to grasp. He pulled, tugged, tried to maneuver her sideways.

"Nothing's working," he said, looking perplexed.

"Pull harder."

Drayton finally rammed his entire arm in and shoved back several sharp branches. Then he gently eased Theodosia back out.

"Now that you've been extricated, I suggest we take a civilized walk *around* this hedge. That's if you're still bound and determined to investigate," Drayton said.

"I am," Theodosia said. She had to settle her burning curiosity, one way or the other.

They crept down the stone walkway that ran alongside Theodosia's house, reached the end of the hedge, then turned and tiptoed up Robert Steele's cobblestone driveway.

"This is crazy," Drayton muttered. He kept tripping on the uneven cobblestones.

Theodosia put a finger to her mouth as they crept past hydrangeas and late-blooming dahlias. "Shhh."

Steele's mansion loomed up before them in the dark. It was an enormous Gilded Age mansion that had been built just after the Civil War. Columns and triangular pediments graced the front of the house, and a fanciful cupola sat on top. Inside were crystal chandeliers, hand-carved marble fireplaces, and Tiffany stained glass. Theodosia knew this because she'd been inside.

Voices floated in and out of range, like a radio with a faulty signal.

"I think they're still out back," Theodosia said. No light escaped from around the edges of the heavy draperies, so she figured that Steele and his lady friend hadn't gone inside yet.

Drayton nodded as he gamely made his way along.

And lo and behold, as they reached the corner of the mansion, the voices floating back to them grew louder and more recognizable.

They peeked around the corner at the back patio, where a gas firepit lit up the night. It was showy and modern, built in a perfect square with jets of flame hissing upward. Two people sat in wicker chairs drawn up next to the firepit.

"That's Robert Steele, but it's difficult to make out who the other person is," Theodosia said.

Drayton shook his head. "I'm not sure, either." As the night cooled, fog from the nearby harbor slowly crept in, giving everything a soft-focus appearance.

"We need to get closer."

They shuffled dangerously close, staying

hidden in the shadows, trying to get a better look. And then . . .

There, on the back patio, curled up in a lounge chair and silhouetted against flickering orange and yellow flames, was Fawn Doyle.

"It *is* her!" Theodosia said in a shocked-bordering-on-triumphant whisper. She finally had a positive ID!

Drayton was completely stunned. "My stars! Fawn's come back from the dead!"

"No, she's come back from wherever she's been hiding out," Theodosia whispered. She felt angry and betrayed. And could only imagine how awful Meredith and Alex would feel when they found out that Fawn was alive and well. And that this selfish, conniving girl had put them through an ocean of worry.

"It's shocking to see her looking so . . . happy," Drayton said.

Theodosia didn't give a crap about Fawn's state of mind. She was suddenly furious with the girl, furious they'd all been duped. "Fawn's been working some kind of con," Theodosia said. "Maybe a kidnapping scheme that . . ." She held up a hand to stop herself. "Wait, let's try to listen in."

They leaned forward, straining hard to hear the conversation. And were stunned when they realized that Steele and Fawn were sniping at each other, having a sort of argument.

"Come on, I thought we were going to the Charleston Grill for dinner," Steele said in a petulant tone. "You're all dressed up and I made reservations. Now you're backing out on me?" He made a rude sound with his mouth. "Plus, you want to borrow my car again?" He was obviously a man who was used to getting his way and didn't much tolerate being trifled with.

Fawn reached out and took Steele's hand. Her voice was soft and wheedling, but it was almost impossible to make out her exact words.

"Where are you running off to now?" Steele asked. "Dang, woman, you're the most mysterious person I've ever met."

"Holy cats," Theodosia whispered.

"Something very important has come up," Fawn said. "Something that simply can't wait. But I don't want you to worry, because I promise to bring your car back safe and sound." She laughed, a high, tinkling laugh, as if she were privy to some private joke. "I won't be long, so let's just plan for a fashionably late dinner."

They couldn't make out the rest of Steele and Fawn's exchange, but they did hear a jingle of keys and then the sound of a car door opening and closing. Seconds later, there was a throaty roar from the BMW.

Theodosia and Drayton streaked back down the driveway and dived behind a clump of palmetto trees that sat in the elegantly landscaped front yard.

They watched in awe as Steele's black BMW shot past them, Fawn at the wheel looking grim and determined. Then Theodosia said, "Come on, we have to follow her!" They were thirty yards from where her Jeep was parked on the street.

"You mean chase after her?" Drayton was seriously reluctant. "That's a terrible idea!"

But Theodosia was already running, pounding across the lawn in the dark, leaping over a flower bed, dodging a clipped topiary. She had a good head start on Drayton as she reached her Jeep, jumped in, cranked the ignition, and flipped on the headlights. There was no stopping her now, no pulling her back. She revved her engine in a high, trembling whine.

And then . . .

Drayton hesitated for a moment more, then he bolted for the passenger door. "Wait for me!"

31

Theodosia drove one-handed as she grappled for her cell phone in the bottom of her bag. When she found it, she thumbed through her CONTACTS list, hit a button, and prayed that Riley would answer.

He did. On the very first ring.

"This is Riley. What's up?"

"Riley, this is super important," Theodosia said with as much urgency as she could muster. "I need to know . . . did the ransom call come through to Meredith? Did someone call and tell her where to drop the money?"

"I'm not supposed to talk to you about that. I've been warned."

"Duly noted. But here's the thing, I'm following Fawn Doyle right now as she's blasting through town. And I'm wondering if maybe —"

"You're *what*?"

Theodosia frowned, tapped the phone

against her steering wheel, then put it back to her ear. "Do we have a bad connection or something? I just said that I'm following —"

"Pull over! Stop right this instant!" Riley shouted at the top of his lungs.

Theodosia gunned her engine as she shot through a red light. "That's not going to happen."

"You're chasing Fawn Doyle? You mean she's actually *alive*?"

"She's not only alive, she's actually a pretty reckless driver. I'm having a heck of a time . . ."

"You can't get involved in this," Riley pleaded.

"I already am," Theodosia said. "Because I suspect something very important is going down with Fawn."

Theodosia glanced over at Drayton, who was jammed into the passenger seat. His heels were wedged against the front floorboard; his hands gripped the dashboard.

"Yellow light!" Drayton yelped.

Theodosia blew right through it.

"The ransom call came through, didn't it?" Theodosia said to Riley.

"Okay, yes, it did. I'll level with you. But you've got to forget any silly notion of . . ."

"And Meredith delivered her bag of

money?"

"It was a female officer dressed up to look like Meredith, but . . ."

"But what? Where did your officer drop the ransom money?"

There were a few moments of dead air, and then Riley said in an anguished voice, "What does it matter? We lost the guy."

"The guy? What guy?" Theodosia asked.

"Whoever picked up the duffel bag of ransom money."

"How could you people be so careless?" Theodosia was practically shouting now.

"We had a team on it, but whoever picked up the ransom took this twisty detour down Longitude Lane."

"That can't happen," Theodosia said. "Longitude Lane dead-ends. There is no exit."

"Our boy created one. Rammed into a wooden fence and plowed through someone's prized rose garden. Toppled some expensive statuary, too."

"Then what?" Theodosia asked.

"And then I don't know what happened exactly. We think he drove down Tradd and hit East Bay Street. But it's horribly foggy over there by the river, and there's a possibility the guy pulled a fast one. Maybe changed cars in the Prioleau Street Garage . . . whatever. The point is, he's gone. Disappeared like a thief in the night."

"That's all the more reason for me to follow Fawn!" Theodosia cried. "Don't you see the connection? Come on, Riley, think hard and put the pieces together. Fawn has to be involved!"

"No! Do *not* follow Fawn. Give up this chase. It's a terrible idea," Riley said.

Theodosia glanced over at Drayton again. "Riley says this chase is a terrible idea."

Drayton clenched his teeth together and gave a tight nod. "He's right."

"I'm sorry," Theodosia said to Riley, "but I'm going to stay on Fawn's tail. Stick to her like glue. Try to figure where she's going . . . where she'll lead us." Her eyes followed the black BMW as it sped along ahead of her, weaving its way down Meeting Street.

"Now, Theodosia, I want you to tell me exactly where you are," Riley said. He'd suddenly switched to his nicey-nice voice. The voice cops generally use when they really want to get their way. "Tell me exactly what street you're on and what intersection you're approaching."

"Sorry. What?" Theodosia handed the phone to Drayton.

"Hello?" Drayton warbled. He had one

eye glued to the speedometer, one eye on the road ahead.

"Drayton! Talk some sense into her!" Riley cried.

Drayton listened to Riley's pleas for a few moments, then dropped the phone to his chest. "He wants me to talk some sense into you."

"Good luck with that," Theodosia said. She'd just seen Fawn hang a hard right onto Atlantic, so she moved into the right lane and put on her blinker. Never mind that a semi tractor trailer was in the way.

"Careful!" Drayton shrilled. Then he waggled the phone at her. "What am I supposed to tell . . . ?"

"Just hang up. Turn off the phone."

Theodosia followed Fawn through a warren of narrow streets and then onto the more traffic-heavy East Bay Street.

"This is the same route the ransom guy took," she said softly.

"Hmm?" Drayton said.

As they passed Rainbow Row, Theodosia said, "How much do you bet Fawn's heading out of the city?" A couple more blocks and she said, "Yes, here we go. She's taking the entrance ramp to the Ravenel Bridge."

"Stay back! Don't let her see you," Drayton warned.

Theodosia stayed two cars back as they hummed across the impressive Ravenel Bridge. The intricate network of guy wires strummed overhead; the Cooper River flowed dark and silent below them.

Once across the bridge, they were in Mt. Pleasant, moving at a fairly good clip. Fawn was a strong, aggressive driver who was unafraid to dodge in and out of traffic.

"You're being very sneaky, keeping a couple of cars for cover between you and Fawn," Drayton remarked.

"I saw this in a Vin Diesel movie once." Theodosia tapped the side of her head. "I always figured the technique might come in handy someday."

"Indeed," Drayton said. Though he looked like he might lose his cookies at any moment.

"So why was Fawn in hiding?" Theodosia wondered aloud. "What exactly is her game?"

"Do you think Fawn was the one who murdered Reginald? Could she have shot him?"

"Maybe."

"And you're quite convinced that Fawn is linked to the ransom demand as well?" Drayton asked.

"I'd say she has to be."

"Do you think Fawn hired someone to grab the ransom for her?"

"If the kidnapping has all been faked — and that certainly seems to be the case — then my best guess is that Fawn has a partner."

"A compadre in crime," Drayton murmured. "Someone to pick up the ransom money for her."

"So maybe it was her partner who killed Reginald," Theodosia speculated.

"No matter who committed the murder, it looks as if Fawn is a nasty schemer." Drayton pursed his lips together. "And here I thought she was such a sweet girl."

"Let that be a lesson to you," Theodosia said. She was half-serious, half-joking.

Traffic had thinned out somewhat as they followed Highway 41 into a slightly more rural area.

"Be careful now," Drayton warned. "We don't want Fawn to figure out she's being followed."

Theodosia lifted her foot from the accelerator and fell back another hundred yards. They passed a strip mall, barbecue joint, market with pumpkins and squash piled up outside, used-car lot, and several small office complexes.

"Good thing Fawn's driving that big BMW. It's a recognizable car, easy to follow," she said.

When they were well out into the countryside, gliding past the occasional seafood joint, gun range, and mom-and-pop store, Fawn slowed, then turned down Rutledge Road.

"Now what?" Drayton asked.

As if to answer his question, Theodosia turned off her lights.

"Good thing there's a hint of moonlight out here," Drayton said as they ghosted along behind Fawn.

"Let's just hope some hotshot in a pickup truck doesn't come roaring up behind us, only to see us at the last minute," Theodosia said.

The road dipped slightly, and off to their right, moonlight glistened like oil on a pond of brackish water. Tupelo and white pine trees stood like sentinels.

"If I can rightly recall that map you printed out, doesn't the Lavender Lady live out this way?"

"Blue Moon Lavender Farm is just down the road a piece, yes." Theodosia was starting to feel sick at heart that Susan Monday might be involved in this murder-kidnapping scheme after all.

391

But when Fawn reached the turnoff for Blue Moon Lavender Farm, she sailed right past it. Didn't hesitate, didn't pass go, didn't collect two hundred dollars.

"She didn't turn in," Theodosia whispered. Maybe she could breathe easy about Susan Monday's innocence now?

"So where are we going?" Drayton asked.

"No idea."

"What if Fawn just keeps driving? All the way to the Florida-Georgia line?"

"Then we'll wave goodbye to her and buy a crate of oranges for our trouble."

"Or peaches," Drayton said.

But they didn't have to go quite that far.

Some eight miles later, Fawn passed a small white church with a soaring steeple — what Southerners often call a praise house — and then turned down a narrow dirt road.

"Here we go. Something's happening now," Drayton said.

Theodosia slowed, made the turn, and bumped along. Now Fawn was easy to follow — she was jouncing along ahead of them, kicking up a hellacious cloud of dust.

"She's surely got a meet-up with someone," Theodosia said as the road narrowed to a faint dirt track.

"Who can it be?" Drayton asked.

"I don't know," Theodosia said. "We know it's not Susan Monday, Clewis has already been cleared, and I don't think Guy Thorne has the guts or the smarts for this type of intrigue."

"Not Meredith?" Drayton asked.

"Meredith and Alex were the ones who got the ransom money together and entrusted it to the police. So who's left?"

"Jack Grimes?"

"You think he came sneaking back from his brother's place? That he was able to arrange all this?"

"Grimes did not strike me as a smart, methodical planner," Drayton said.

"That's putting it kindly."

Theodosia felt like she was driving into a maelstrom as trees began to close in on her, blotting out the night sky and making everything seem darker. The road was turning to sticky mud beneath her wheels. Low-hanging branches swatted her windshield. Every once in a while, when she topped a slight rise, she could see the red taillights of the BMW still ahead of her.

Drayton gazed out the side window. "Spooky out here."

Theodosia squinted through the haze, trying to make out the squishy dirt track that seemed to be getting more and more difficult to follow. Now and then, her head-lights caught a pair of shining eyes.

"What was that?" Drayton asked as a pair of bright eyes stared at them, then disappeared into the ditch.

"Raccoon. Or maybe an opossum."

"Are there alligators out here?"

"Yes, but probably not on this road."

Suddenly, the BMW's brake lights flared red.

"Something's happening," Theodosia said.

Drayton leaned forward expectantly. "Is Fawn stopping?"

"I think there's some sort of —" Theodosia hit the brakes and slowed her Jeep to a crawl. "There's, like, a barn up ahead."

"Out here in the middle of nowhere?"

"Maybe it wasn't the middle of nowhere when the barn was built," Theodosia said. She knew this land had once been occupied by dozens of rice and indigo plantations.

"Please be careful," Drayton said as they coasted in closer.

They rolled to a stop in the shelter of a gnarled oak tree and watched as Fawn jumped out of her car and walked toward a small, dilapidated one-story barn. Almost instantly, a light flared inside the barn, as if a lantern had been lit or a flashlight turned on.

"Come on." Theodosia grabbed a flashlight from her glove box, opened her door slowly, and eased her way out. Drayton followed suit.

They tiptoed slowly through tall, dry grass that made a soft whoosh-whooshing sound. There was the hoot of an owl off to their left, accompanied by a small, die-hard chorus of crickets. Dampness hung heavy in the air. They were in boggy territory now, probably close to one of the many creeks that honeycombed this area. Back in the eighteen hundreds, rice had been the cash crop here. Carolina Gold. Many of the old rice dikes and ditches, canals and ponds, still remained, dotting the landscape.

Theodosia and Drayton moved ever closer, wondering what Fawn's secret meeting was all about. They could make out faint voices. But who on earth was she talking to in there?

They snuck up to a dusty, grimy window, hesitated, and then surreptitiously peered in.

There, in the dim light, was Fawn Doyle, resplendent in her lovely gold dress. She looked strangely out of place in the dingy surroundings. Yet there she was, holding out a green leather satchel as if she were asking someone to fill it with spun gold.

Who was supposed to fill it? Theodosia wondered. And with what? The ransom money? Okay, so just who was Fawn's mysterious accomplice?

Off in the darkness of the barn, a shadow moved, then lengthened, as a man stepped into the light.

Theodosia blinked, barely able to believe her eyes.

It was Bill Jacoby! Reginald Doyle's business partner!

Jacoby was talking to Fawn, speaking urgently. But this wasn't the hail-hearty Bill Jacoby that Theodosia had seen before. This Bill Jacoby wore a nasty, tight smile on his face.

Killer was the first word that streaked like lightning through Theodosia's brain. *This man is a stone-cold killer.*

"Have you got it?" Fawn demanded in a loud, authoritative voice. "Did the old lady drop off the money like you asked?" Fawn's personality had also done an about-face. Where her voice had been soft and almost whispery before, her demeanor diffident, she'd suddenly assumed an aggressive stance and spoke in a harsh, abrasive manner.

"I got it," Jacoby said. "Boy, did I get it."

He let loose the nervous cackle of a psychopath.

"Nobody followed you?"

"Not a chance," Jacoby said. "Not the route I drove." He puffed up his chest, just this side of bragging.

"You're positive?" Fawn pressed. "You're not exactly the brightest bulb in the box."

They're fighting, Theodosia thought. *They're not together on this at all. Which could be . . . a good thing?*

Jacoby's mouth pulled into a snarl. "Don't be such a witch. Maybe *you* were followed."

Fawn gave a snort and lifted her chin. "Nobody knows where I am, remember?" She sounded almost contemptuous. "For all they know, I'm fish food at the bottom of Charleston Harbor."

She fooled us all, Theodosia told herself as she watched this bizarre tableau play out.

"Good thing I own a boat or you couldn't have pulled that off," Jacoby said.

"Good thing I intercepted your package from Huntley Ltd.," Fawn shot back at him. "I wondered what you were going to do with that concealed pistol holster. Then I realized you were probably up to no good, and all I had to do was lie back in the weeds and follow you. See what poor schmuck was on your personal hit list. And lo and behold,

397

there you were, slinking away from Reginald Doyle with the proverbial smoking gun clutched in your hand." She uttered a sharp laugh. "It was textbook perfect."

"That's enough out of you," Jacoby barked. "Shut up!"

"You shut up." Fawn tossed her leather satchel at Jacoby, where it landed at his feet. "I want my cut. Half. Just like we agreed."

Jacoby reached back and grabbed a brown duffel bag. It was fat and obviously stuffed with money. He reached in and grabbed a packet of hundred-dollar bills, stared at it, then handed it to Fawn.

"That's it," Jacoby said. "There's your cut."

"Not on your life!" Fawn shouted as the money fluttered in her hand. "This doesn't even come close to what we agreed to. I want half. I *deserve* half."

Jacoby stared at her for a long, hard moment. When he finally spoke, his voice was slippery as grease.

"I'm thinking we need to renegotiate our terms."

"Are you out of your freaking mind?" Fawn yelled. "We had a deal. I not only kept my mouth shut about your cold-blooded murder, I helped you figure out an even better scheme — my own kidnapping and ransom demand." She bared her teeth in an ugly snarl. "So I get half. Because I earned every single penny of it!"

"Little girl, I'm not sure you're worth two and a half million dollars."

"You incompetent fool. Don't you realize I can make a call just like that to law enforcement?" The threat was imminent in Fawn's voice. "All I have to do is accuse you of murder and kidnapping. Of holding me for ransom. Then where would you be?"

"Aren't you the clever girl," Jacoby said with a menacing sneer.

"So don't *dare* try to cheat me." Fawn's face pulled into a nasty mask, her voice dropped to a grating, guttural rasp.

She sounded, Theodosia thought, just like the possessed child from *The Exorcist.*

"Or what?" Jacoby demanded.

"Or you can spend the next thirty years twiddling your fat fingers in an eight-by-ten-foot cell at Lee Correctional? How would you like that?"

"I know a better way to settle this argument." With a superior smile, Jacoby reached into his jacket, pulled out a pistol, and aimed it directly at Fawn.

Good grief, Theodosia thought. He had that pistol stuck in his jacket. *There's your concealed weapon. The murder weapon.*

"You see, my dear Fawn," Jacoby said in a low, menacing tone, "you do *not* have the upper hand. You never did. It was all . . . an illusion."

"You're a ridiculous fool," Fawn snarled. "How dare you."

"Better to shut your mouth and whisper a final prayer," Jacoby said as he lifted his pistol and aimed it directly at Fawn's heart.

"You'll never get away . . ." Fawn sputtered. All of a sudden, realizing her dire situation, she could barely speak. Her face, her body, betrayed it all. Fawn was stunned by the sudden turn of events, the hasty reversal of fortune. Blood drained from her face as she stared at Jacoby and whimpered, "Don't. Please, don't do it."

Theodosia couldn't bear it any longer. She knew she had to act fast, she had to do *something* to keep Fawn from being shot to death! She watched in horror as Jacoby's finger, as if moving in slow motion, curled around the trigger.

Theodosia lifted her flashlight high above her head and swung it with all her might, as if she were hitting the winning home run in the final game of the World Series. As the flashlight crashed into the dusty window, the old glass shattered like skim ice on a pond. Shards of brittle glass flew like a hail of bullets. Theodosia felt a sting hit her forehead, watched as hundreds more sharp pieces blew into the old barn.

"Stop!" Theodosia screamed with all the sound and fury she could muster. "Drop the gun, Jacoby!"

Caught off guard by the sudden noise and slivers of glass that had come blasting out of nowhere, Jacoby's hand wavered slightly as he squeezed the trigger.

32

BOOM!

Standing as close as she was, Theodosia was rocked by the sudden explosion. This was no tidy POP like she'd heard in the woods last week. From barely six feet away, the noise from Jacoby's pistol rattled her brain and made her ears scream with pain. Then . . .

"Owwww!" came a high-pitched howl.

Fawn had been hit. Jacoby's wayward bullet had caught Fawn in her right shoulder and spun her around like an unsuspecting prairie dog that had just been popped.

"Drop it!" Theodosia shouted again. She doubted that Jacoby would stop to heed her warning, but she had to try.

"Police!" Drayton yelled, in a deeper, more authoritative rumble. "You're surrounded!"

It was a game deception they were trying to sell, but Jacoby wasn't buying it. They

402

watched in stunned horror through a window frame that gaped like an empty eye socket as Jacoby bent down and scooped up the duffel bag full of money. With nary a look over his shoulder at the wounded Fawn, he rushed out a side door and disappeared.

Theodosia and Drayton scrambled into the barn to help Fawn, but she was already struggling to her feet, screaming and practically gnashing her teeth.

"He shot me!" Bleary-eyed with anger, stunned by the sudden pain, Fawn writhed and hissed like a crazed banshee.

"Calm down, it's a shoulder wound," Theodosia said. "I know it hurts like the devil, but you'll live." She dug in her purse for a clean hankie to cover the wound even as she heard a car start up outside. Jacoby's car must have been parked on the far side of the barn. Now he was getting away!

Fawn suddenly stopped sputtering and jerked her head around frantically. "The money!" she cried. "Where's my money?"

"Jacoby took it," Theodosia told her. "Your trusted accomplice." She leaned in until she was barely an inch from Fawn's face. "And by the way, missy, it wasn't your money."

Fawn's anger and craziness ratcheted to

greater heights. "We have to go after him!" she screamed. "We've got to get that money back!"

"You've been shot," Drayton said. He was trying his best to calm Fawn down as they led her outside to Theodosia's Jeep. "You're in shock. We have to get you to a hospital."

Fawn shook her head back and forth so fast it was practically a blur. "No. Got to get . . . money."

"No, no, no," Drayton said, still trying to be reasonable. He opened the back door and half lifted a slowly weakening Fawn into the vehicle. Then he climbed in after her and closed the door.

"Buckle those seat belts," Theodosia shouted as she scrambled behind the wheel and cranked the ignition. Her tires spun for a split second, and then they were off and running like a scalded cat.

"Where are we going?" Drayton yelped. "That isn't the way to . . . Wait, what do you think you're doing?"

"I'm following the money," Theodosia yelled back at him. "This is called hot pursuit!" She pointed her Jeep in the direction she figured Jacoby had taken off in, which was essentially cross-country.

"He can't go far. There's nothing out here but woods and creeks and swamps!" Drayton cried. "Best to turn around."

Theodosia ignored him. "Hang on," she said as they jounced along. "And keep Fawn still." She was trying to follow the trail of flattened grass that Jacoby's car had made. "I've got this."

"I don't think you do!" Drayton shouted back.

Theodosia half turned. "You really want Jacoby to escape with all that money?"

"No, but I don't relish getting shot, either," Drayton said.

"Well then, just . . . stay low."

"Lord have mercy," Drayton muttered.

Theodosia couldn't see Jacoby's taillights in front of her as she goosed her Jeep from thirty to forty, then edged up toward fifty, but she could follow his trail. She just had to . . .

CLUNK.

. . . be mindful of all the old stumps and humps she was flying over. Make one wrong move, take her eyes off the trail for one second, and she could rip the undercarriage out of her car.

"This is so not a good idea," Drayton said. "It's like the dark side of the moon out here."

And it *was* dark. Trees loomed up to

startle Theodosia, then the land rose, dipped, and turned suddenly muddy again. Right now, they appeared to be running parallel to a creek. Theodosia knew she should phone Riley, or maybe Sheriff Burney — he was probably closer — but she needed to keep both hands on the wheel. She was practically outdriving her headlights as the rutted earth grabbed and tugged her vehicle from side to side.

"How's Fawn doing?" Theodosia dared to take a quick peek in her rearview mirror.

"She needs medical attention," Drayton said. "What do you think?"

"Fawn?" Theodosia said.

"Hurts some, but please keep going," Fawn pleaded. "Run that bonehead down."

Theodosia wanted to remind Fawn that she was just as much of a bonehead as Jacoby, but she held her tongue. For the time being anyway.

A spark of red up ahead caught Theodosia's eye.

There he is.

She tromped down on the accelerator, and her engine roared in response. She intended to run him to ground, like a wily fox after a skittering hare.

Theodosia was starting to close the gap between her and Jacoby. If she could get close enough, she could ram him hard with her reinforced front bumper and send him careening into a tree. Or drive him into a creek.

Creek! There's one just ahead of me!

A dark stream of free-flowing water suddenly appeared in Theodosia's headlights. A shallow creek, maybe six or seven inches deep. There were cuts in both banks, so this was clearly the spot where Jacoby had crossed. Without hesitating, she plunged down the bank.

SPLASH!

"What's happening?" Drayton cried.

"Creek," Theodosia called out. Her voice was level and calm, as if she were a Charleston trolley driver calling out stops along Church Street or King Street.

Theodosia flipped on her windshield wipers as her Jeep bucked and shimmied its way up the opposite bank. It wasn't a steep climb, maybe a thirty-degree pitch. But when Theodosia was back on terra firma, tearing through a small woodlot, Jacoby seemed to have vanished. There were no taillights, no tire tracks, no clues to be found anywhere.

Where are you? Where did you go?

"This is terrifying," Drayton complained. "I feel like I'm in a pivotal scene right out of *Thelma and Louise.*"

But Theodosia remained quiet and on guard as she drove along. Though she was pulsing with adrenaline, she was also trying to puzzle out where Jacoby had disappeared to. Was there a road she hadn't seen? Some obscure trail that Jacoby had snuck down?

She tried to recall the Google map she'd printed out some six days ago. Tried to conjure up the roads and terrain markers in her mind so she could figure out which road she'd initially turned down and where she was right now. Had this chase after Jacoby taken her in a long, lazy loop? If so, which way? Deeper into the woods and swamps? Back toward Creekmore Plantation? Theodosia wasn't sure where she was. The night was so dark and the surroundings so wild. Even worse, she could be a sitting duck.

"Drayton, do you remember if —" Theodosia began.

BOOM! CRASH!

The rear window of Theodosia's Jeep suddenly exploded in a barrage of glass!

"Merde!" Drayton shouted.

"Watch out, watch out!" Theodosia cried as all three of them ducked low and covered their heads with their hands to protect themselves from flying shards. Then, "Are you hurt, Drayton? Fawn?" Theodosia called out urgently. She couldn't believe what'd just happened. That rat Jacoby had hidden in the weeds and snuck up behind her.

And shot at us!

"Anybody hurt?" Theodosia called again.

"No, we're . . ." Drayton was trying to brush small pieces of glass from their shoulders. "We're still in one piece."

"That's it!" Theodosia cried. "That's enough!" She grasped her steering wheel and juked it hard. The engine screamed as she spun her vehicle in a tight circle, her tires digging in and throwing up huge chunks of sod.

"Don't," Drayton cried.

"Get him," Fawn shouted.

The chase was back on. Theodosia bumped over humps and hillocks, following after Jacoby's car, trying desperately to catch him. This was war. Now she knew what she had to do — she had to run him down and ram him. Crawl up on one side of his car and give him a hard push so he'd slam-bam into a tree.

But at the same time, Theodosia worried. Was she following the rabbit down the rabbit hole only to come to a foolish conclusion? Theodosia wasn't sure. Right now she was angry as a hornet at Jacoby. Everything

409

else — all logic — had been stripped away to bare naked emotion. But could she really cause the man serious harm?

Time to find out.

They screamed up a hillside, Jacoby weaving back and forth wildly, trying frantically to lose her. Her Jeep bucked like a bronco, but Theodosia remained doggedly on his tail.

But where am I? Theodosia wondered. *It would help enormously if I knew . . .*

In her headlights, the hill looked as if it were topped with gentle clouds . . . clouds that slowly materialized into a faint blur of purple.

Yes!

They were roaring past one of Susan Monday's lavender fields. These little lavender beacons weren't bright like the navigation buoys in Charleston Harbor, but they still signified a safe harbor and told her where she was. Which meant that Axson Creek was probably nearby.

But which way? Left or right, right or left?

The land leveled out, and Theodosia roared up alongside Jacoby. Gritting her teeth, she made a wild move and swung the nose of her Jeep into his rear bumper. There was a horrific screech of metal as the two vehicles collided. They roared along that way, sparks flying, bumping hard, metal grinding against metal, until Theodosia gave her wheel a final, hard jerk and drove Jacoby down, down, down a hill and into . . .

Yes, there it is!

. . . Axson Creek.

As Jacoby's car plunged into the creek, Theodosia hit her brakes hard. Her car fishtailed badly, shuddered, jounced, and finally came to a molar-jarring stop a precipitous four inches from the bank of the fast-moving creek.

Nobody spoke until Drayton asked, "Are we dead yet?"

But Theodosia knew this chase was only half-over.

"Stay here," she ordered. "Stay safe."

"Wait," Drayton said. "Where do you think *you're* going?"

But Theodosia still had her flashlight and was already out of her Jeep and running toward Jacoby's car. She was panting hard, practically out of breath, as she slid down the muddy embankment. Knee-deep in water now, shivering from the cold and the sudden burst of adrenaline, she sloshed her way toward Jacoby's car.

It was upside down, nose half-submerged in the creek. All the windows were shattered.

Is Jacoby still alive?

Theodosia turned on her flashlight and shone it into the car. The thin beam of light barely penetrated the darkness and tendrils of ground fog that had quickly seeped in. But it was enough to pinpoint Bill Jacoby.

He was hanging upside down, seat belt still pulled tight across his broad chest.

"Help me," Jacoby croaked. Blood dribbled from his nose; one eye was badly swollen and starting to close.

"Where's your pistol?" Theodosia asked. She wasn't about to venture any closer until she knew the exact whereabouts of his weapon.

"I don't know."

Theodosia probed the darkness with her flashlight, searching for that pistol. It was strange to peer into a car that was upside down. Like being in some weird, netherworld fun house that wasn't the least bit fun. Stranger still to be confronting a man she'd come to think of as a friend.

A glint of black metal winked at her.

There it is.

Theodosia stuck a hand through the shattered side window and grabbed Jacoby's pistol. Pulled it out. It was a Sig Sauer P938, compact and dangerous-looking, with a black hard-coated anodized frame and rubber grip. It looked, Theodosia thought, like a black mamba poised to strike.

Flipping on the safety, then checking the safety a second time to make sure, Theodosia tucked the Sig Sauer in her jacket pocket and pulled out her cell phone.

Jacoby let loose a low moan. "Help me. I think my arm is broken. My ribs are on fire."

"I'm sorry you're injured," Theodosia said. "But you did shoot at me. You did try to kill me."

"I didn't mean to," Jacoby sobbed.

"Like you didn't mean to kill Reginald Doyle?"

"I didn't . . ."

"Why?" Theodosia asked, moving closer to him. "Why would you do it? Why *did* you do it?"

Jacoby shook his head as tears oozed from his swollen eyes. "Reginald had so much, and I . . . I wanted more."

"Okay," Theodosia said. She was trying to sound agreeable, hoping this might prompt Jacoby to talk. She moved her phone close to Jacoby and thumbed on the recorder. "I can understand that. You wanted more."

"First there was the lure of key partner insurance," Jacoby said with a moan. "One million dollars." For a moment, his expression turned slightly beatific. "Do you know

413

what you can buy for one million dollars?"

"A lot, I suppose."

"But then that little weasel of a girl jumped out at me. Moments after I shot him. She threatened to rat me out if I didn't pay her." Jacoby coughed hard, grimacing from the pain. "So I thought and I thought. What could I do? How could I stop her? I mean, I couldn't risk *another* shooting . . ."

The answer hit Theodosia like a ton of bricks. "You tried to kill her when you set fire to the house."

"Yes, but she escaped from the house."

Theodosia could hardly believe what she was hearing.

"So then I thought, what else?" Jacoby whimpered.

"The phony kidnapping?"

"She was the one who proposed it!" Jacoby said, pouncing on Theodosia's words. "Fawn with her twisted, devious mind."

"You kept digging yourself into a hole that got deeper and deeper," Theodosia said.

"I didn't think so. At the time, I thought I was quite brilliant."

Theodosia shook her head. "Greed. You know it's one of the seven deadly sins, don't you?"

"Seven . . . what?"

"Did you drop that doll in the harbor for the Coast Guard to find?" Theodosia asked.

"Doll?" Jacoby's face was a blank.

"Never mind." Theodosia turned her back on Jacoby and climbed back up the muddy creek bank. She sat down on a nearby log and studied her phone. She still had two bars left. Plenty of juice to call Riley.

"What's going on out there?" Drayton called from the car.

"Jacoby just confessed," Theodosia called back.

"You mean to the murder?"

"And the fake kidnapping."

"Two birds with one stone." Drayton sounded impressed. "Imagine that." Then he turned sober. "People are injured here, Theo. We need to get help."

"I'm going to call Riley right now, let him deal with the logistics."

Not sure what to expect, Theodosia drew a deep breath and called.

Once again, Riley answered on the first ring.

"Theodosia! Where are you? What are you up to? Why aren't you answering your phone? I've been pulling my hair out!" Riley sounded frantic. And angry, really angry.

"Sorry, but I've been kind of busy."

"That sounds suspiciously like a pre-apology. Where have you been? What happened?"

Theodosia drew a deep breath. "There was a chase . . ."

"You mean after Fawn?"

"Actually, there was *another* chase. Which ended with a car wreck."

"Wha . . . ?" Riley blurted.

"But I've managed to capture your killer and your fake kidnapper. Even managed to get a confession on tape."

Pete Riley was momentarily stunned. All he could manage was, "No."

"Yes." Theodosia sounded tired but confident.

"Who?"

"Bill Jacoby."

"The business partner?" Now Riley was incredulous. "He wasn't even on our radar."

"And Fawn. It would appear that Fawn was in cahoots with Jacoby all along. Well, not exactly *all* along. Fawn's the one who saw Jacoby shoot Reginald Doyle. Then, sweetheart that she is, she pretty much blackmailed Jacoby into helping her stage a phony kidnapping."

"And demand a real-life ransom," Riley said.

"Five million dollars' worth. I guess Fawn really wanted to get away from that husband

416

of hers."

"So that's it?"

"There are a few other wrinkles and permutations," Theodosia said. "But that's pretty much the gist of it."

"Dear Lord."

"Oh, and we could use an ambulance and some law enforcement out here ASAP, so I'll text you a map and try to pinpoint where I think . . ." Theodosia paused. "Riley?" When he didn't respond, she said, "Are you there?" Nothing. No answer back. An icicle of dread touched her heart. "Riley, are you still . . . are you mad at me?"

There was a hiss of dead air, and Theodosia felt her heart slowly sinking. Riley was mad at her for ignoring his direct order and tearing off on her own. He was probably so furious that he'd never speak to her again for as long as she lived. Theodosia wanted to sob. No more Riley in her life. No more movies curled up on the couch together. No more tea and croissants while they read the Sunday paper. No more picnics with Earl Grey or hikes in Francis Marion National Forest.

Then his voice came back and he said, "I'm sending help now. Holy Christmas, Theodosia, you really did figure it out."

"Riley!" Theodosia cried as tears stung

her eyes. Tears of joy. "You're not mad?"

"Mad? More like overwhelmed by it all. Now about that map . . ."

33

Lights blazing, a half-dozen vehicles came
bumping toward them out of the night. Two
ambulances, two sheriff's cars, a police
cruiser, and an older Crown Victoria.

"Tidwell," Theodosia murmured to herself
when she saw the Crown Vic. "He's still
driving that old heap." Something about the
familiarity of the car made her smile.

The EMTs arrived first and scrambled out
of the ambulances to tend to Fawn and
Jacoby. Pete Riley made a beeline for Theodosia.

"I was so worried about you," he said,
wrapping her up in a warm embrace.

"I was worried about me," Theodosia said.
It felt good to finally be nestled in Riley's
arms. Safe. She savored the moment and
then said, "Am I in trouble? With Tidwell?
Are you in trouble?"

"You're all in trouble," Tidwell barked as
he stalked his way toward them. In his

baggy khaki slacks and rumpled USC sweat-shirt, he looked burly and unkempt. An object of amusement, if he hadn't been so terrifyingly growly and grumpy.

"I'm sorry," Theodosia said. She hoped an apology might appease him.

It didn't.

"You were told in no uncertain terms *not* to interfere in police business," Tidwell said as Sheriff Burney stood beside him, taking it all in. "To stay away from this particular *case.*"

"Things got tricky real fast," Theodosia responded. "When Fawn Doyle suddenly turned up next door at my neighbor's house, I knew she was privy to something. Had to be."

"So you figured Fawn was in on the kidnapping," Tidwell said.

"The phony kidnapping," Riley added.

Theodosia nodded. "That's right."

"Is your neighbor also involved?" Tidwell asked. "What's his name . . . Steele?"

"Robert Steele," Theodosia said.

"I remember him," Tidwell said. "The Angel Oak hedge fund guy. A real piece of work. Do you think he was in on the deception with Fawn?"

"Doubtful," Theodosia said. "Steele seemed genuinely puzzled that Fawn wanted to borrow his car and dash off somewhere instead of sticking around to enjoy his charming company."

"*Is* he charming?" Riley asked suddenly.

"On a scale of one to ten, imagine a rattlesnake at ten. Then go down from there," Theodosia said.

"Ouch," Riley said. But he seemed amused by Theodosia's characterization.

"We still have to talk to him," Tidwell said. They all stood there and watched as Jacoby was extricated from his car and put on a backboard. The duffel bag of money was pulled out and tossed aside.

"Oh," Theodosia said. She dug into her jacket pocket. "And this was his pistol."

"I'll take that if you don't mind." Tidwell reached a big hand out and grabbed the Sig Sauer. He frowned, held it up to his nose, and said, "It's been fired recently."

"Jacoby wounded Fawn," Theodosia said. "And he shot out the back window of my Jeep."

"He shot at you!" Riley cried.

"How on earth did he manage that?" Tidwell asked. "If you were chasing after him."

"Jacoby hid in the weeds, circled back around, and got the drop on me," Theodosia said.

"If Mr. Jacoby is such a wily driver, why is his vehicle upside down in the creek while yours isn't?" Tidwell asked.

"Oh, that?" Theodosia shrugged. "Just some tricky maneuvering on my part, I guess." She paused. "And it helps to know the lay of the land."

Tidwell gave a noncommittal grunt, then wandered off to make a few phone calls. Finally, he got Meredith on the line and gave a quick explanation of the evening's strange chain of events.

"May I talk to her?" Theodosia asked.

Tidwell handed over his phone.

"I guess Detective Tidwell told you that we got your money back?" Theodosia said.

Meredith was practically giddy with delight. "Thank goodness, yes. And the detective was quite complimentary about you. Said you were a hero, the woman of the hour."

"I don't know about that. But, um, you know we also managed to apprehend Fawn."

"I can hardly believe she was in on it. The kidnapping and the ransom," Meredith said. "Just so . . . bizarre."

"I'm sure this is very difficult for you to digest."

"And poor Alex, when he learns how Fawn betrayed him — betrayed all of us —

he's going to be utterly heartbroken."

"If you say so," Theodosia said. She bid goodbye to Meredith and then handed the phone back to Tidwell.

As Tidwell mumbled something more to Meredith, Theodosia walked over to where Jacoby's car remained upended, searched around in the nearby bushes, and picked up the bag of ransom money. She discovered it was not only heavy, but cumbersome.

So this is what five million dollars feels like.

When Tidwell saw her advancing toward him, struggling with the money, he held up a hand to stop her.

"Hold everything. *You're* taking the money? For your information, that's key evidence."

"I made a promise to Meredith," Theodosia said. "To help find her husband's killer."

"At which you certainly succeeded."

"But to make everything proper and right, I have to go one more step." Theodosia locked eyes with Tidwell.

"Ah. You want to return the money," Tidwell said.

"Tonight, if possible."

Tidwell's face was unreadable as he considered her words. Then he turned to Riley and said, "Detective Riley, would you trust

Theodosia with five million dollars?"

Pete Riley turned his gaze on Theodosia. She was streaked with mud, her clothing was soaked, and tendrils of auburn hair swirled wildly about her head in a Medusa-like halo. Still, she appeared fiercely capable, and her eyes shone with a luminous energy. Riley didn't think he'd ever seen her looking lovelier.

Giving a quick nod in Tidwell's direction, Riley said, "Sir, I'd trust Theodosia with my life."

FAVORITE RECIPES FROM
THE INDIGO TEA SHOP

Haley's Hawaiian Tea Sandwiches
1/2 cup crushed pineapple, drained
4 maraschino cherries, chopped
1 pkg. (3 oz.) cream cheese, softened
6 slices bread (date-nut bread works best)
3 slices ham
3 lettuce leaves

Combine pineapple, maraschino cherries, and cream cheese. Spread mixture on all 6 bread slices. Top 3 of the bread slices with ham and lettuce. Then add the top slice, trim crusts, and cut into quarters. Yields 12 tea sandwiches.

Pear Butter
1/2 cup butter, softened
2 Tbsp. pear preserves
1/2 tsp. rosemary, finely chopped

Mix together all ingredients, then place in a

small glass dish or roll into a log using wax paper. Chill, but serve at room temperature. Yields 1/2 cup.

Drayton's Ham and Sun-Dried Tomato Pasta

8 oz. uncooked linguine
1 Tbsp. butter
1/4 cup sun-dried tomatoes, oil-packed and chopped
1 cup heavy cream
1/2 cup Parmesan cheese, grated
1 cup ham, fully cooked and cubed

Cook linguine according to package directions. Melt butter in large skillet and sauté sun-dried tomatoes for 1 minute. Reduce heat and stir in cream and Parmesan cheese. Bring to a gentle boil over medium heat. Simmer, uncovered, for 5 to 6 minutes or until sauce thickens. Drain linguine and stir into sauce mixture. Add ham and heat gently. Yields 4 servings.

Ginger-Cardamom Tea Cookies

1 cup butter, softened
1/2 cup sugar
1/2 tsp. salt
1 tsp. vanilla extract
2 cups flour

1 Tbsp. cinnamon
1 tsp. ground ginger
1/2 tsp. ground cardamom
Leaves from 1 English breakfast tea bag
1 cup white chocolate chips

Preheat oven to 350 degrees. In mixer, beat together butter, sugar, salt, and vanilla until smooth. In a separate bowl, stir together flour, cinnamon, ginger, cardamom, and tea. Add dry mixture to butter mixture and beat on low speed until blended. Stir in white chocolate chips. Drop tablespoon-sized balls of dough 1 inch apart, using 2 greased cookie sheets. Flatten balls slightly with a floured glass. Bake for 15 to 18 minutes, switching cookie sheets around halfway through baking. Cool and enjoy. Yields 36 to 40 cookies.

Chicken Breasts with Lemon Caper Sauce
4 chicken breast halves
3 Tbsp. butter
2 Tbsp. shallots, minced
1/4 cup dry white wine
1/2 cup chicken broth
1/2 cup heavy cream
Grated peel and juice of 1 lemon
1 Tbsp. capers

Sauté chicken breasts in butter for 4 minutes. Turn chicken and sauté for 3 minutes. Set aside and keep warm. Add shallots to skillet and cook until transparent. Stir in wine. Add chicken broth and bring to a boil, cooking until it's reduced by half. Slowly stir in cream. Cook over medium heat, stirring, until cream begins to boil. Turn off heat, stir in lemon peel, lemon juice, and capers. Serve sauce over chicken. Yields 4 servings.

Cream Cheese and Green Olive Tea Sandwiches

1 pkg. (8 oz.) cream cheese, softened
2 Tbsp. almonds, finely chopped
2 Tbsp. sunflower seeds, finely chopped
3 Tbsp. green olives, finely chopped
1 Tbsp. cream
Butter
10 slices wheat bread

Combine cream cheese, almonds, sunflower seeds, green olives, and cream. Butter bread, then spread an even amount of mixture on 5 slices of bread. Cover with the remaining slices. Trim off crusts and cut each piece into 4 triangles. Yields 20 small tea sandwiches.

Poogan's Porch Buttermilk Biscuits
Taken from a May 2008 edition of the *Pittsburgh Post-Gazette*

5 cups self-rising flour
1/4 cup sugar
2 Tbsp. baking powder
1/4 lb. shortening
2 cups buttermilk

Combine first 3 ingredients and mix well. Add shortening and mix with hands until shortening is broken up into quarter-sized pieces. Add buttermilk and mix until all is incorporated. Roll out to 3/4-inch thickness and cut with biscuit cutter. Place on parchment-covered sheet pans 1/2-inch apart. Bake at 350 degrees until golden brown, about 10 to 15 minutes. Yields about 3 dozen biscuits.

Parsley and Bacon Tea Rounds
6 slices white bread
Butter
1 lb. bacon, fried crisp and crumbled
2 bunches parsley, finely chopped
1/2 tsp. Worcestershire sauce
1/4 cup mayonnaise

Remove crusts from fresh bread and flatten with rolling pin. Butter flattened bread. Mix together bacon, parsley, Worcestershire, and mayonnaise, adding a bit more mayonnaise if needed. Spread parsley-bacon mixture on bread. Roll up each piece of bread and freeze in airtight container. When ready to serve, take out rolls and slice into rounds while still frozen. (Rounds will thaw quickly.) Yields approximately 18 rounds.

Drayton's London Fog Latte

1 cup brewed Earl Grey tea
1/2 cup milk
1/2 tsp. vanilla extract
Sweetener (optional)

While Earl Grey tea is steeping, place milk in small saucepan and warm over medium heat. Whisk the milk as it's heating (about 4 to 5 minutes) until it's nice and frothy — but do not boil. Pour tea into teacup or tall glass and add frothed milk. Swirl vanilla extract on top of the foam, then stir in. Add sweetener if desired.

Chai-Spiced Fruit Compote

1 3/4 cups water
2 chai tea bags
4 Tbsp. honey
1/2 cup dried apricots, chopped
1/2 cup prunes, pitted and chopped

1/2 cup golden raisins

In a 2-quart saucepan, bring water to a boil. Turn off heat and add tea bags. Steep for 5 minutes, then discard tea bags. Add honey, apricots, prunes, and raisins to the saucepan. Bring to a boil over high heat, then reduce heat to medium-low. Simmer for 18 to 20 minutes, stirring occasionally until liquid thickens to a light syrup. Transfer to a bowl, cover, and chill for 4 hours. Use as a topping for yogurt or ice cream. Yields 4 servings.

Parmesan and Prosciutto Puff Baby

1/2 cup flour
1/2 cup whole milk
2 eggs
1/2 tsp. salt
1/2 cup prosciutto, diced
1/2 cup Parmesan cheese
1/4 cup parsley, finely chopped
2 Tbsp. fresh thyme, chopped
2 Tbsp. butter

Place flour, milk, eggs, and salt in blender and process for 30 seconds. Pour batter into bowl and let set for 20 to 30 minutes. Put a 10-inch skillet in the oven and preheat the oven to 450 degrees. Stir diced prosciutto, Parmesan, parsley, and thyme into the batter. Remove skillet from oven, add the butter, and swirl around until skillet is coated. Pour the batter into the skillet and bake for 15 to 20 minutes. Puff baby should rise and be lightly browned on top. When ready, slide puff baby onto a platter, cut in pieces, and serve immediately. Yields 2 to 4 pieces.

Candied Edible Flowers

2 cups edible flowers
1/4 cup egg whites, beaten
3/4 cup superfine sugar

Clean and dry your flowers or petals. Use a brush to paint a thin layer of egg white on each side of the petals or blossoms. Gently place them in a shallow bowl of superfine sugar and sprinkle more sugar over them. Remove from bowl and place on waxed paper. Sprinkle a little more sugar over them. Allow flower to dry until stiff, about 8 hours. Store at room temperature in an airtight container. Sprinkle flowers on your tea tray or onto your salads.

NOTE: Buy your edible flowers at the grocery store or use carnations, hibiscus, hollyhocks, orange blossoms, rose petals, pansies, and violets from your garden. If you are concerned about using raw egg whites, use pasteurized egg whites, which are usually found in the dairy section.

TEA TIME TIPS FROM
LAURA CHILDS

Lavender Lady Tea

Just like the Indigo Tea Shop, you, too, can host a Lavender Lady Tea. Blue, purple, or lavender china will set the tone perfectly, then add bunches of lavender in clay pots, lavender candles, and lavender soaps or sachets as party favors. Begin your tea with lavender scones (buy culinary lavender buds at the co-op or health food store), then serve a variety of chicken salad, crab salad, and cream cheese and cucumber tea sandwiches. Dessert might be lemon-lavender short bread. If you're having a Drayton moment, blend some of those lavender buds into your favorite black tea.

Queen's Tea

Pull out your best china and crystal, then decorate your table with British-themed teapots, tea tins, Toby mugs, or sparkling crowns and "crown jewels" from your local party store. Serve cream scones with traditional Devonshire cream and marmalade, as well as the Queen's favorite jam pennies (tiny raspberry jam sandwiches cut into circles). Your main entrée might be grilled chicken breast with a citrus salad, and your dessert a honey and cream sponge cake. Williams-Sonoma, the Republic of Tea, and Twinings all offer a special Queen's blend tea.

Music Tea

Music really does soothe the soul — whether you play recorded music or invite a budding musician to give an afternoon recital or musical performance. Set your tea table with your best china and crystal, then add floral centerpieces interspersed with stacks of records, CDs, sheet music, or whatever you have. Serve ginger scones, a cheddar cheese quiche, and sherbet. Champagne wouldn't be one bit out of line here, along with a Tung Ting oolong tea with floral notes.

Paint and Sip Tea

If you've got crafty friends, invite them in for a Paint and Sip Tea. Use a painter's drop cloth instead of a tablecloth, add some fun art pottery, then arrange your table with small canvases, paints, and brushes. Every guest should also have a cup and saucer and small plate. For ease of serving, arrange your scones, tea sandwiches, and desserts on a three-tiered serving tray so everyone can help themselves while they're painting. For brewed tea, consider serving something creative such as Indian spice or gunpowder green with citrus.

Color Me Pink Tea

Who doesn't love to think pink, especially when it comes to your tea table? Gather up all your pink floral plates and teacups, add a pink tablecloth, pink candles, and bouquets of pink flowers. Your tea luncheon might start with maraschino cherry scones drizzled with pink frosting or a chilled raspberry soup. Shrimp cocktail in avocado halves or a lovely shrimp quiche would make a perfect entrée. For dessert, think pomegranate sherbet and cranberry bars. A rich black tea flavored with rosebuds is the perfect accompaniment.

Flowering Tea Party

Once reserved for Chinese emperors and dignitaries, flowering teas are not only delicious to drink, they make a fascinating centerpiece. Round up two or three clear glass teapots, buy several bundles of dried flowering tea leaves at your local tea shop, and you're in business. Place bundles in glass teapots, pour in hot water, and watch them magically bloom. A wonderful accompaniment to this delightful tea might be cranberry-orange scones, tea sandwiches of curried egg salad and deviled ham, and madeleines for dessert. And, yes, you do drink the flowering tea!

TEA RESOURCES

Tea Magazines and Publications

TeaTime — A luscious magazine profiling tea and tea lore. Filled with glossy photos and wonderful recipes. (teatimemagazine .com)

Southern Lady — From the publishers of *TeaTime,* with a focus on people and places in the South as well as wonderful teatime recipes. (southernladymagazine .com)

The Tea House Times — Go to theteahouse times.com for subscription information and dozens of links to tea shops, purveyors of tea, gift shops, and tea events. Visit the Laura Childs guest blog!

Victoria — Articles and pictorials on homes, home design, gardens, and tea. (victoria mag.com)

Fresh Cup Magazine — For tea and coffee professionals. (freshcup.com)

Tea & Coffee — Trade journal for the tea

and coffee industry. (teaandcoffee.net)

Bruce Richardson — This author has written several definitive books on tea. (store.elmwoodinn.com)

Jane Pettigrew — This author has written seventeen books on the varied aspects of tea and its history and culture. (jane pettigrew.com/books)

A Tea Reader — by Katrina Avila Munichiello, an anthology of tea stories and reflections.

American Tea Plantations

Charleston Tea Plantation — The oldest and largest tea plantation in the United States. Order their fine black tea or schedule a visit at bigelowtea.com.

Table Rock Tea Company — This Pickens, South Carolina, plantation is growing premium whole-leaf tea. (tablerocktea .com)

The Great Mississippi Tea Company — Up-and-coming Mississippi tea farm. (greatms teacompany.com)

Sakuma Brothers Farm — This tea garden just outside Burlington, Washington, has been growing white and green tea for almost twenty years. (sakumabros.com/ sakumabroswp/)

Big Island Tea — Organic artisan tea from

440

Hawaii. (bigislandtea.com)

Mauna Kea Tea — Organic green and oolong tea from Hawaii's Big Island. (mauna keatea.com)

Onomea Tea Company — Nine-acre tea estate near Hilo, Hawaii. (onotea.com)

Tea Websites and Interesting Blogs

Destinationtea.com — State-by-state directory of afternoon tea venues.

Teamap.com — Directory of hundreds of tea shops in the U.S. and Canada.

Afternoontea.co.uk — Guide to tea rooms in the U.K.

Teacottagemysteries.com — Wonderful website with tea lore, mystery reviews, recipes, and home and garden.

Cookingwithideas.typepad.com — Recipes and book reviews for the Bibliochef.

Seedrack.com — Order *Camellia sinensis* seeds and grow your own tea!

Jennybakes.com — Fabulous recipes from a real make-it-from-scratch baker.

Cozyupwithkathy.blogspot.com — Cozy mystery reviews.

Southernwritersmagazine.com — Inspiration, writing advice, and author interviews of Southern writers.

Thedailytea.com — Formerly *Tea Magazine,* this online publication is filled with tea news, recipes, inspiration, and tea travel.

Allteapots.com — Teapots from around the world.

Fireflyspirits.com — South Carolina purveyors of Sweet Tea Vodka.

Teasquared.blogspot.com — Fun, well-written blog about tea, tea shops, and tea musings.

Relevanttealeaf.blogspot.com — All about tea.

Stephcupoftea.blogspot.com — Blog on tea, food, and inspiration.

Teawithfriends.blogspot.com — Lovely blog on tea, friendship, and tea accoutrements.

Bellaonline.com/site/tea — Features and forums on tea.

Napkinfoldingguide.com — Photo illustrations of 27 different (and sometimes elaborate) napkin folds.

Worldteaexpo.com — This premier business-to-business trade show features more than 300 tea suppliers, vendors, and tea innovators.

Fatcatscones.com — Frozen ready-to-bake scones.

Kingarthurflour.com — One of the best flours for baking. This is what many professional pastry chefs use.

Californiateahouse.com — Order Machu's Blend, a special herbal tea for dogs that promotes healthy skin, lowers stress, and aids digestion.

Vintageteaworks.com — This company offers six unique wine-flavored tea blends that celebrate wine and respect the tea.

Downtonabbeycooks.com — A *Downton Abbey* blog with news and recipes.

Auntannie.com — Crafting site that will teach you how to make your own petal envelopes, pillow boxes, gift bags, etc.

Victorianhousescones.com — Scone, biscuit, and cookie mixes for both retail and wholesale orders. Plus baking and scone-making tips.

Englishteastore.com — Buy a jar of English Double Devon Cream here as well as British foods and candies.

Stickyfingersbakeries.com — Scone mixes and English curds.

TeaSippersSociety.com — Join this international tea community of tea sippers, growers, and educators. A terrific newsletter!

Melhadtea.com — Adventures of a traveling tea sommelier.

Purveyors of Fine Tea
Plumdeluxe.com
Globalteamart.com
Adagio.com
Elmwoodinn.com

Capitalteas.com
Harney.com
Stashtea.com
Serendipitea.com
Marktwendell.com
Republicoftea.com
Teazaanti.com
Bigelowtea.com
Celestialseasonings.com
Goldenmoontea.com
Uptontea.com
Svtea.com (Simpson & Vail)
Gracetea.com
Davidstea.com

Visiting Charleston

Charleston.com — Travel and hotel guide.

Charlestoncvb.com — The official Charleston convention and visitor bureau.

Charlestontour.wordpress.com — Private tours of homes and gardens, some including lunch or tea.

Charlestonplace.com — Charleston Place Hotel serves an excellent afternoon tea, Thursday through Saturday, 1 to 3.

Culinarytoursofcharleston.com — Sample specialties from Charleston's local eateries, markets, and bakeries.

Poogansporch.com — This restored Victorian house serves traditional low-country cuisine. Be sure to ask about Poogan!

Preservationsociety.org — Hosts Charleston's annual Fall Candlelight Tour.

Palmettocarriage.com — Horse-drawn carriage rides.

Charlestonharbortours.com — Boat tours and harbor cruises.

Ghostwalk.net — Stroll into Charleston's haunted history. Ask them about the "original" Theodosia!

Charlestontours.net — Ghost tours plus tours of plantations and historic homes.

Follybeach.com — Official guide to Folly Beach activities, hotels, rentals, restaurants, and events.

ABOUT THE AUTHOR

Laura Childs is the *New York Times* best-selling author of the Tea Shop Mysteries, the Scrapbooking Mysteries, and the Cackleberry Club Mysteries. In her previous life she was CEO of her own marketing firm, authored several screenplays, and produced a reality TV show. She is married to Dr. Bob, a professor of Chinese art history, enjoys travel, and has two Shar-Peis.